PRAISE FOR M. K. HALE

"Full of charm, wit, and utterly loveable characters. Each year, it seems Adam and Evie's tumultuous summer romance is destined to repeat itself in a doomed cycle of 'almosts,' like a sexually frustrating version of Groundhog Day. M. K. Hale is a romance writer on the rise."

— LEISA RAYVEN, INTERNATIONAL BESTSELLING AUTHOR OF BAD ROMEO

"Banter on point! Seriously, I'm still in a bit of stunned disbelief!"

— RACHEL VAN DYKEN, NY TIMES BESTSELLING AUTHOR

"She is the best. I love her. Even though she writes sex scenes."

— MOM

ALSO FROM M. K. HALE

NEW ADULT ROMANCE

Hating Him
Disobeying Him
Timeshare Boyfriend

ADULT ROMANCE

Costumer Misconduct (Novella)

MIDDLE GRADE PARANORMAL ROMANCE

Shatter: Boys are Demons

TIMESHARE BOYFRIEND

M. K. HALE

This is a work of fiction. Names, characters, places, and incidents are products of the author's imagination or are used fictitiously and are not to be construed as real. Any resemblance to actual events, locales, organizations, or persons, living or dead, is entirely coincidental.

TIMESHARE BOYFRIEND. Copyright © 2022 by M. K. Hale.

All rights reserved.

No part of this book may be used or reproduced in any manner whatsoever or by any electronic or mechanical means, including information storage and retrieval systems, without written permission from the author, except for the use of brief quotations embodied in critical articles and reviews.

Publication Date: June 3, 2022

FIRST EDITION

Designed by M. K. Hale

Cover graphic illustrations © Sketchify/Canva, Inc.

M. K. Hale - http://www.mkhale.com

Ebook ASIN: B09XKGXKDW

Ebook ISBN: 979-8-2017106-6-8

Paperback ISBN: 979-8-9861402-0-9

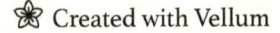

❦ Created with Vellum

To my parents, who bought a Myrtle Beach timeshare

And to my younger self, who thought boys (and good grades) were everything and that summer was for romance and sunburns

Content Warning:
Though this book begins in young adulthood, it transitions with summer time-jumps until the characters are new adults in college. As a new adult romance novel, the story contains mature situations and sexual scenes. It is recommended that readers be over the age of 18.

Timeshare Boyfriend

A NEW ADULT ROMANTIC COMEDY

M. K. HALE

THE FIRST SUMMER

"We go home tomorrow," Adam said in a low voice as he stared out at the water.

The moonlight blanketed the waves, a shimmering silver film. Yet, the ocean had never looked so dark. So dangerous. So sad. Like every salty drop mourned over the end of summer.

My mood shifted with the sand under my feet. I had only known him for two sun-kissed weeks, but imagining a day without him and the smell of chlorine in his hair caused a tightness in my chest. "We do." What else was there to say?

At ten years old, my parents still did not allow me to have a cellphone. I had no way to contact him. *Should I offer to write him letters? No, Evie, think of the trees.* A summer love was just that. One summer.

I wanted every summer. Luckily, our parents had bought a "timeshare," an apartment for two weeks every year in the same place at the same time. This particular timeshare was in Myrtle Beach, South Carolina, and Adam's family had purchased the same two July weeks in the unit next to mine.

This is far from the end.

He bent down and picked up several rocks in the dark sand. "I'm going to miss you."

My stomach warmed. "Me too."

"If I throw this rock and it bounces three times, we'll see each other again," he stated.

My eyes were glued to the rock in his hand. He leaned back and whipped out his arm. The rock skipped over the waves. Once. Twice. Thrice.

The nervous knot inside me unraveled, only to tie itself up again when he said, "If I throw this rock and it bounces three times, it means you like me."

One. Two. Three. Four.

He smiled. "I like you too."

My heart melted. Turned into honest to God goo.

"If I throw this rock and it bounces three times, the next time I see you, I'm going to kiss you."

Heart attacks were uncommon at ten years old, right? Because I was currently having one.

He threw. The rock bounced. One. Two.

It plopped through the water and sank to the bottom.

We stared at the ocean as if it would cough the rock back up for another round.

After a minute, Adam picked up a new rock and

threw that one. One. Two. Three. He then turned and grinned. "That was close."

I smiled back and reached out my hand. He took it. Squeezed it. Held it.

"I don't want to leave. I can't wait a whole year to see you again," he said.

"It's only fifty more weeks."

He barked out a short laugh. "Always positive."

I leaned into him, and his arms tightened around me. When he pulled back, he fiddled with the plastic turtle ring on my finger. He had won the ring for me at the arcade a few hours earlier. I had won him a ring as well. Because, feminism. "Next time we see each other, we'll wear these, and it'll be like no time has passed," he said.

"Okay," I agreed. He could have said anything, and I would have agreed.

"This..." He entwined his fingers with mine. "This is forever."

And at that point, it felt like it would be forever.

1

THERE IS NO LOVE LIKE THE FIRST LOVE...OR THE FIRST HATE

The Next Summer, Five Years Later

PENNY: *It's been five years, are you sure he'll remember you?*

I stared at my best friend's text message in the backseat of the car on the drive down to South Carolina. Since the first summer of the timeshare, Adam and I had not seen each other. His family either became too busy and had to rent the two weeks out to someone else while my family was there or vice versa. Now, five years later, we were going to be at the beach together for two weeks.

Me: *I mean, he did swear his love to me.*
Penny: *He was eleven...*

Me: *What happened to a summer of positivity and optimism?*

I knew it seemed like a stretch that sixteen-year-old Adam would feel as strongly for me as his eleven-year-old self did, but after seeing what high school freshman boys considered romantic, I couldn't help thinking about the boy who had said, *"This is forever."* The boy who skipped rocks and promised to kiss me. And gosh, was I ready for that first kiss. *Fifteen and never been kissed.* I had packed extra mints, mouthwash, and mint gum.

My fingers twisted the too-small-for-my-normal-fingers-so-now-it's-on-my-pinky turtle ring. I had saved it, waiting for a summer when we would both be back at the Myrtle Beach timeshare at the same time.

Penny: *Realism happened. You've been fantasizing about this guy forever. What if he's horrific-looking?*

Me: *He won't be.*

Penny: *But what if he is? What if, within five years, he turned into the Hunchback of Notre Dame?*

I began typing back a response, but Penny beat me to it.

Penny: *And don't say you'll love him anyway. No one is that nice.*

Me: *He's not going to be ugly. He was a cute kid.*

Penny: *Cute kids either turn ugly or hot. Sixty/forty.*

I shook my head at my phone.

The truth was, I was not at all worried about whether or not Adam would be attractive. I knew he would be. I worried most about what he would think of me.

Me: *What if he's out of my league? What if he takes one look at me and decides I'm the Hunchback of Notre Dame?*

Penny: *Hush your entirely wrong and stupid mouth. If he dares to not think you are the most beautiful girl he has ever seen, I will personally drive down there and strangle him with his own pool noodle.*

Me: *1. You are fifteen and do not have a driver's license. 2. Was the "pool noodle" an innuendo or do you think he'll actually be using one?*

Penny: *If he is sixteen and still doesn't know how to swim without a noodle, then he doesn't deserve you.*

Me: *Thanks.*

She realized her mistake.

Penny: *Damn, I forgot you still don't know how to swim.*

Deep bodies of water terrified me from a young age. During my summer with Adam, he had entertained me in the shallow end among kids half our age just so I felt less alone. *Swoon.*

Me: *It's okay. Maybe this is the year I'll learn.*

I fantasized about Adam teaching me how to swim: his warm hand on my back as he showed me how to float. Him diving after me if I started to drown. Maybe a minute or two or seven of mouth-to-mouth...

My heart beat faster in my chest as our car passed the "Welcome to South Carolina" sign.

I felt it deep in my bones. This would be a summer I would never forget.

My dad knocked on my bathroom door. "Evie, we're leaving in five minutes to meet the Pierces for dinner. Make sure you're ready."

Since arriving at the timeshare building, the past two hours had been spent selecting the perfect outfit, as well as attempting to put on makeup for the third time in my life.

With the limited extent of my makeup knowledge, I had attempted an eye shadow look that turned out more like a black eye than a smoky one.

"Two more minutes, Evie," my dad yelled through the door. He knew I was never late, so I assumed his yell to me was more for the benefit of my mother who was probably still figuring out what dress to wear to see her old college friend, Maryam Pierce.

All I could remember about Adam's mother was that her manicured fingers always gripped a wine cooler and she was self-employed as a matchmaker.

My thoughts traveled back in time.

"Adam and Eve. Sounds like a match made in heaven," she had said when I met Adam for the first time at the beach.

I stared at him. He stared back. At a couple of months older than me, he stood about an inch shorter—thank you, early female maturity—and wore the expression of someone who had brushed his teeth and mistakenly sipped from a glass of orange juice.

I spoke first, like the ten-year-old social butterfly I was most definitely not. "Hi."

He tilted his head and frowned. "Your mouth is red."

My tongue pressed against my teeth as I remembered the cherry Popsicle I had devoured half an hour earlier.

My mother laughed and responded for me, "Her mouth is always red. She'll eat anything if it's cherry-flavored." She turned to where my father and Mr. Pierce sat, watching us with light smiles. "It's saved us from having to force medicine down her throat when she has a fever. Once, she snuck into the cabinet and drank half a bottle of cherry Tylenol just because she was thirsty."

"That's gross," Adam told me.

"You're gross," I thought but kept my red, cherry mouth closed.

"It looks like you drink blood," he added for good measure.

"Keep insulting me and I'll drink yours." *None of those words came out.*

He stared at me some more. A sliver of silence passed before, "Can she not say anything other than 'hi?'" he asked my mother.

"Eve is just a bit shy." My mom twirled a piece of my brown hair and pulled on it like a puppeteer. "Say something, sweetie."

"Something."

My mom loved Maryam, but she spent large

amounts of time trying to impress and outshine her. My father didn't care what he looked like for dinner. He just wanted to eat.

I did the finishing touches on my wild, dark and curly hair, which acted more moldable today as if it knew it had someone to impress. Adam.

A sigh escaped me before my dad knocked again on the bathroom door.

I laughed and walked into the medium-sized living room of the unit to join him on the couch in waiting for my mother. I again twisted the small turtle ring on my pinky, an anxious habit I'd developed.

"Are you excited to see the Pierces again?" Dad asked me, and I shifted on the cushion.

"Yes."

"Especially Adam?"

I lifted my right shoulder and broke eye contact. "I enjoy all the Pierces equally."

He chuckled before my mother opened her door and came out to join us. Her straight hair reached her shoulders, and her eyelashes reached her eyebrows. "Let's go."

My stomach flipped.

Ready.

My mother parked in front of the fancy restaurant the Pierces' chose for dinner. "I hope they don't blast the air conditioning; I forgot my shawl in the unit," she said as she took her time getting out of the car, careful not to cause any wrinkles in her outfit.

Once she was out, my father bumped her hip with his. "You could always cuddle up with me for warmth," he flirted with her.

A small smile stretched my lips at the way my mom's cold exterior melted for him. Would Adam cuddle me for warmth if I said I forgot my jacket? I left it in the car just in case.

My mother walked up to the hostess stand. "Hello, the reservation should be under the name Pierce. There are seven of us."

Adam now had a five-year-old brother who had been born shortly after our first summer together. I had seen pictures of him, but we'd never met.

"Hannah!" Maryam's high-pitched voice broke through the mellow chatter of the other restaurant customers. I turned around to see her rushing over with the classic suburban mom speed-walker pace to hug my mother.

My eyes scanned the room until I saw him.

His gaze was on Maryam, but it moved to the left and found me within seconds. We stared at each other.

And it was like getting hit with a knockout wave.

Saltwater straight to the eyes.

Legs taken out from under me.

The boy was hot.

He stood at a height finally taller than me and still

had long black hair. He must have gotten into sports because his broad chest and arms were muscular. My first thought was that I bet he could pick me up. We could perform one of those lover reunions like in the movies where I run at him and he grabs my waist, and suddenly I'm in the air being twirled around as he looks at me like I'm his soulmate.

But he wasn't looking at me like I was his soulmate at all.

I grinned. He frowned. Not the reaction I had waited for. And certainly not the reaction I had put a layer of makeup on for either.

Why was he frowning? Was he trying to remember exactly what heartfelt thing he had been planning to say to me the moment he saw me again after those five years apart? Was there something in his eye affecting his vision of my beauty? I knew the last one was a stretch, but I wanted to stay confident.

He broke eye contact with me and sat back down at the table next to his little brother, James. James at least smiled at us as we joined them at the table.

"Eve, sit across from Adam," Maryam instructed me.

I gratefully followed the instruction, sitting in front of him. He still did not look at me. Was I the Hunchback of Notre Dame in this situation? No, wait. Maybe he was holding back his passion for me. Maybe looking at me filled him with the desire to embrace me.

I really needed to stop reading so many romance novels.

My foot knocked against his under the table, causing me to jump in my seat a bit at the small contact. He met my gaze again only to glare at me. "Sorry," I said.

"I'm James," the little five-year-old sitting next to him informed me with a smile.

I turned my attention to the only Pierce who had smiled at me today. "I'm Eve."

"Eve. That's Adam." He paused as if remembering something. Had his brother told him about me? "Adam and Eve. That's like in the Bible."

I nodded, disappointment flooding my chest. Had he never heard my name before now? "It sure is. James is in the Bible too."

He blinked at me, a wave of pure amazement washing over his face. "It is?"

"Yeah, but I prefer other James characters." I glanced over at Adam, but he wasn't paying any attention to us. In fact, he studied the menu as if he would be tested on it later.

James leaned in to hear me better. "Like who?"

"Have you ever heard of James Bond?"

"No."

I leaned in too and whispered as if it was a cool secret, "He's a spy who wears suits and likes things shaken, not stirred."

His eyes widened with wonder. "He sounds cool."

"Probably a little bit less cool than you."

He nodded, accepting the compliment with no hesitation. "Probably."

"So, Eve, what are you doing now?" Maryam asked me the same way someone might ask a college graduate ready to start life.

What was I doing? I was a high schooler on summer vacation, hoping I would finally experience the kind of love story I read about.

"She just finished her first year of high school with all A's," my dad answered for me.

"Really?" Maryam looked at Adam. "How impressive."

"I—" I began answering for myself when my mom took over the task.

"That's right. She's very smart. Always was more mature than her age group."

Adam made a small scoffing noise at the word "mature" and stared down at the turtle ring on my finger. Was it childish of me to wear it? I thought he would have seen it as cute and endearing.

My eyes prickled. My chest hurt. I moved my hand under the table and worked the small ring off my pinky finger, the ring which represented our first summer together. Swallowing hard, I placed it into one of my pockets.

When my hand went above the table without the ring, Adam's eyes darkened for such a flash second, I thought I had imagined it.

The rest of dinner was as disappointing as it was painful. I mostly helped James color a picture of a wolf in his drawing book. It made me wonder how long it had taken Adam to throw away the wolf arcade ring I had won him. A year? Two? A day?

I sipped my sweet cherry lemonade, but it soured in my mouth as Adam continued to look anywhere but at me. And when he did meet my gaze, it was only to glare.

What had I done wrong?

I hadn't done anything wrong.

Why did it hurt so much? It was two weeks, five years ago. Had I built it up in my head to be more? *He was the one who had said, "This is forever."* I wasn't delusional enough to make that up.

When we went to leave the restaurant, I pulled on Adam's arm before he escaped and stopped him in front of me. "Why are you acting like you hate me?"

He blinked, letting the silence toy with my emotions as much as his attitude did. "I'm sorry, were you expecting me to wear that plastic childhood ring and swear my undying love?" Dormant anger lingered just below the surface of his voice like he barely held back some kind of contempt for me. Why? His blue eyes, once light, were so *dark*. "Am I not living up to your expectations?"

"I—"

His gaze flicked over me, indifferent and unimpressed. "Because the feeling is mutual," he said.

My mouth fell open.

My heart dropped to the tiled floor of the restaurant, seeming to have an audible ping.

"What are you saying?" I barely stuttered the words out through my shock and pain.

"I'm saying, I think we should stay out of each other's way this summer. I'm not about to waste my vacation babysitting you again."

Babysitting me? He was only a couple of months older! Who the heck did he think he was? I was about to turn sixteen. I was not a child. *At least he doesn't know you still can't swim.*

As Adam turned on his heel to follow our families out of the restaurant, I stood there, frozen. Ice chilled the blood in my veins. There was no way he had been "babysitting" me or entertaining me that first summer. He had promised to kiss me; only politicians went around kissing babies.

What had happened to him within the past five years to change the boy I knew to this... I didn't even know what to think of him. Who cared what had happened to alter him? Not me. Well, a little bit me.

He said I didn't live up to his expectations.

The realization triggered as much hurt as it did anger.

If it was my boyish sense of style, whatever. If it was that I had never really meant that much to him, whatever. If it was because he looked at me and didn't like what he saw, what-the-heck-ever.

Call me the Hunchback of Notre Dame. No wait—call me an Australian man who had just chugged four pitchers of beer. Because I was pissed.

2

ABSENCE MAKES THE HEART GROW FONDER...AND STUPIDER

It was the summer of Mad-dam. Mad Adam and mad at Adam. Every day after that first dinner with the Pierces, he had avoided me or acted like I was some sticky sand stuck on the bottom of his expensive sandals.

One night at dinner, my mother asked his mom if she had any "tanning lotion" for me because I was insecure about my "pale hue"—the truth, but an embarrassing one that Adam had not needed to overhear. After she said it, Adam glared at me for the rest of the night—nothing new there. As if my wanting to have artificially sun-kissed skin was a personal affront to him. The next day, when Maryam said she couldn't find her tanning lotion, Adam smiled. He freaking grinned like a British villain in a high-stakes spy movie. Had he hidden it? Thrown it away? Just so I couldn't have it?

And he called *me* immature?

Even as my family hung around the Pierces, I did not see as much of Adam as I had our past summer together. Apparently, he had made friends over the couple of years he had been at the timeshare while we skipped and rented it out. He went out to the beach and the pool with them, leaving me to entertain his younger brother, James.

Adam was the one who said he didn't want to be my "babysitter;" yet, there I was spending most of my time with his five-year-old brother. But being around James was fine with me. He was adorable and hilarious for a little kid. *Nicer than his jerk of an older brother.*

"Evie, you can't just add another bedroom to the castle. It's unrealistic."

I laughed as James rearranged my sand pile.

An old memory tugged at me.

While I created a masterpiece out of sand, Adam circled my castle, narrowing his eyes on it. "Your castle needs a mote."

"The kingdom is peaceful. No need to keep anyone out."

He watched me pat on more sand, glancing over to his parents where they sat in their beach chairs. Adam said softly, "There's always a need to keep someone out."

James patted on more sand and pulled me from the memory by saying, "I wonder why Adam doesn't like you." Oh, the mouths of babes. Forever open and spewing truth, unwanted or not. "I like you. You're cool for a girl."

I smiled. "Why thank you, kind sir."

He snorted. "You are a little weird."

"Again, I repeat, thank you."

A wave crashed near us, and water lapped at the side of the sandcastle before retreating to the ocean.

"He doesn't like Mom and Dad, and they like you," James said.

Adam had never admitted to me how he felt about his parents, but it was easy to tell. Whenever they were near, his demeanor went from cold to frozen.

I lifted one tense shoulder in a half shrug. "He doesn't have to like me if he doesn't want to."

"But you like him?"

Was James a secret mind-reading genius? "Why would you think that?"

His eyes narrowed on me as if he knew I avoided the question. Maybe he *could* read minds. "You look at him a lot," he said.

"People look at other people all the time, it doesn't mean they like them—"

"Head's up!" a young male voice yelled behind me before a force pushed my face into the sand. A sharp pain throbbed in the back of my head as I removed my face from our now ruined sandcastle. A beach volleyball laid beside me, the evident weapon. "Yikes, talk about a face dive," the shirtless guy said. He looked around my age. A group of high school boys approached us behind him. I then noticed one of the specific high school boys. Adam.

"No need to apologize, it's just Eve," Adam told them. "The sand is probably an improvement."

The boys laughed behind him, one yelling, "Daaaaaaaaamn!"

I touched my face and felt the sand sticking to my sunscreen-slathered skin. I tried to rub some off, but the gritty texture clung to my pores like a face mask from Hell.

James pouted at him. "Don't be mean. Eve is my friend."

Adam frowned and lost a bit of his confident demeanor as he watched James's disappointed expression. "She was my friend once too. Things change."

My face went red and so did my vision as I stood and poked a finger at his hard, muscular chest. *Evie, stop feeling tingles from simply poking him. It's embarrassing.* "What the heck did I ever do to you?"

"Heck?" he mocked. "Can't even say 'Hell,' can you?" He took a step closer to me, and my feet instantly took a step back at the challenge. My ankle twisted in the sand, and he caught me quick enough to make my inner traitor swoon. I pushed his hands off me and gained my balance back without too much embarrassment. "You're still the same little girl you were five years ago," he said.

"Not so little anymore," a random guy remarked.

"She's not your type." Adam twisted to glare at him, meeting the eyes of all his friends before he said, "She's not anyone's type."

Timeshare Boyfriend

His words might as well have stapled themselves in the corner of my skull, haunting my thoughts forever after.

Tears prickled my eyes again. Rage and hurt battled within me. I wanted to slap him. *No, stay cool, Evie. Be a cool, indifferent cucumber.* Crossing my shaky arms, I shot back, "As if I care what you think of me."

His eyes held the same heat I had fantasized about before coming back to the timeshare just to discover he was a jerk. "Yeah, you don't care about anything, do you? You never did," he said confusing me.

"What?"

Something flashed in his expression before he masked the vulnerable emotion and waved to his friends. "Let's go, the girls are waiting."

Blocking his path, I couldn't stop my stupid mouth from asking, "What girls?"

But it was clear where the group of shirtless, attractive, high school boys were headed.

A short distance up the beach stood four perfectly tan, thin, and perfectly *not me* girls, waving at them. While wearing bikinis. Without modesty shorts—like mine. With skin even the sun couldn't help but kiss. The perfect tans. And they waved at Adam.

So, this is rage.

"*Now* you want to hang out with those girls?" one of Adam's friends asked, sounding surprised. "But you'd said—"

"Shut up, Ryan." Stepping around me in the sand, Adam dismissed me with an "Enjoy your sandcastles."

But considering I would never allow him the power of having the last word again, I yelled to his back as he walked away, "Oh, we will. Sand has never built more attractive real estate. We're two hours away from a beach HGTV show discovering our talent!"

His posse of boys chuckled at my words as they followed him, striding away.

But Adam never turned back around to look at me.

I'll give him something to look at by the end of this summer.

I sat there, steaming like the batch of crabs our families shared for dinner the prior night. Rubbing more of the sandcastle sand off my face, I commented, "I kind of hate your brother."

James didn't say anything, but he nodded as we watched the group of boys disappear down the beach. His response was clear without him having to say it. "Right now, I kind of hate him too."

<hr>

PENNY: *I'll kill him. Let me kill him.*

Reading the text from Penny caused me to smile for the first time in several days.

Penny: *I can't believe he's acting like such an asshole.*
Me: *Penny!*
Penny: *What? Say it. It's what he is being. 'Jerk' is not*

good enough. Asshole. The hole of an ass. What are you going to do?

<u>Me</u>: *What can I do?*

Avoid him? Impossible, considering our families were together more often than peanut butter and jelly on bread. Try to talk to him? Haha, that was a "No" from me. Act like a jerk back to him and give him a taste of his own medicine? I would need about four more backbones and whatever the Wizard gave the cowardly lion at the end of *The Wizard of Oz*.

<u>Penny</u>: *Whatever, you don't need him to have a summer romance. Go find some boy with less issues. Better yet, flirt with one of his friends! Make him see what he's missing.*

<u>Me</u>: *Did we enter an alternate universe where you think there is a version of me who has the guts to do that?*

<u>Penny</u>: *You don't even have to actually flirt to make him jealous. Just pretend to. Talk to one of the guys about something normal but make it look to Adam like you're flirting. Touch his arm, chest... You know the drill. We read the same books.*

<u>Me</u>: *You want me to touch some random guy's chest?*

<u>Penny</u>: *A random, 'Adam's friend' guy. Yes.*

The more I thought it over, the less crazy it sounded. I could fake flirt.

I got an A in sex-ed. Granted, most of the class was about general health and the horrible not-fun side effects of illegal drugs. I had also blushed so hard during the one actual "sex" day that I fainted, and the bulky gym teacher Mr. Curtis had to carry me to the nurse's office, which just made my embarrassed, blushing-self blush even harder.

Funny how a person could read a million raunchy romance novels but put her in a situation with judge-y high school boys and throw the word "penis" around, and suddenly the world is ending.

You can do this, I told myself. I could flirt.

The desire to see Adam's reaction to it fueled my confidence.

He thought of me as a little girl. Said I had not met his "expectations."

Time to make him regret it.

Was I over him romantically? Yes. Did I still want him to want me? Also, yes. I wanted him to want me, so *I* could be the one to turn my back on him and say no. And I would say no... I would most likely say no.

3

IF HE IS HOT, HE CAN BURN YOU

I sat on the beach, wearing a pair of my mother's sunglasses that my father had once told her made her look like "Jackie O." Did I know who Jackie O was? Just that she was some president's wife, but—most importantly—his comment made her blush. So, from context clues, I assumed the sunglasses would make me look good as well.

Holding up one of my mom's fashion magazines as a decoy, I waited to spot one of Adam's summer friends.

A tan chest caught my eye. It belonged to Adam's friend who at least had the decency to yell, "*Head's up*," when the volleyball attacked the back of my head a couple of days earlier. He separated himself from the "Pierce posse," or so I had started calling them, to head over to the ocean waves. He dipped his feet in and proceeded to wash some of the sand from his smooth golden skin. He wasn't bad-looking. Long blond hair and blue eyes. Very hippie-like.

Still, it didn't matter whether he was attractive, I wasn't really flirting. Just fake flirting.

Time to get in the zone.

A few things society, books, and movies have taught me about flirting:

1. Start with a good joke. If you're not funny, maybe skip this. It can be worse to throw off the whole conversation by opening with a not punny pun or a dark joke involving the last well-known tragedy. Definitely do not use the line "You're hotter than Joan of Arc before the match was thrown." It's not tasteful or funny, and it never works, no matter the setting. No, I have not tried that one before. Yes, I am lying.

2. Maintain strong eye contact and smile as much as possible. Unless your teeth are not as white as the toothpaste commercials say they need to be, then smile a bit less. Closed-mouth smiles still go a long way. Anyway, eye contact is key. Confidence. But also not all confidence. Bite your lip to appear nervous and shy, yet sexy and alluring. And not too much eye contact; that freaks guys out. Use enough to show interest, but mix it up with some fluttering of your eyelashes and long gazes away from him. <u>Try not to think about how many contradictions there are in what is expected of you.</u>

3. Ask questions about his interests. What are your hobbies? What's your favorite movie? Try not to get into a lengthy debate over how *The Princess Bride* is the best

movie ever created and to compare it to *Top Gun* is ludicrous.

4. Laugh. A lot. Make it seem like he is as hilarious as the idea that *Top Gun* could ever be better than *The Princess Bride*.

5. Touch him. Just a small touch on the arm, or playfully nudge him, or knock your foot lightly against his. Be careful not to accidentally kick him. That is a move not easy to walk away from successfully.

I strutted up to Adam's blond friend and opened with, "Beach sand sure gets everywhere, huh?" Not a funny joke—then again, female comedians never get much credit anyway.

He blinked at me with those neon blue eyes. "You're the girl who had sand all over her face."

Deep internal sigh. "Yup, that's me."

"Sorry about that by the way. Adam was kind of rude."

Suddenly, liking him much more. "Yes, Adam *was* kind of rude."

He shook his long blond hair when the wind blew it in front of his face. "I guess family teases family, huh?"

I nodded, not really listening, then paused. "Huh?"

"You're his cousin, right?"

Cousin? He said I was his *cousin*? First, the babysitting comment, and now he was cousin-zoning me?

"Well, we certainly haven't kissed." I laughed, and he chuckled awkwardly as well. My eyes darted over to where Adam continued playing beach football with the rest of the Pierce posse. "What's your favorite movie?"

Blond boy blinked again. Was I moving too quickly through topics? Shoot, I had yet to ask his name. "Hmm, that's a tough one..." Was it? I'd had the same favorite movie since seven years old. "I love the movie *Top Gun.*" Oh, God. *Stay strong, Evie.* "Actually, I think it's probably the best movie ever made."

Do not fight with him. My mouth was about to utter, "Incorrect," when I noticed Adam finally gazing over at us. Game time. "Wow, great movie choice, I totally agree." This boy needed a lesson in what made a great film great, but this was neither the time, nor the place. I needed to make Adam see how desirable I was so he boiled over in regret. Commence the flirting. I touched his arm. "You know you kind of look like the actor from *Top Gun,* Tom Cruise."

He scoffed but his smile gave him away. "No way."

Correct. There was no way. "For real. Although, you're right." My fingers trailed down his arm before letting go. *Wow, check out the professional flirter over here!* My body leaned closer to his. "I think you're taller than him."

Blond boy blushed. I made a boy *blush*. I didn't know boys *could* blush. Could I make Adam blush? I pushed the distracting thought aside and shot another glance toward the Pierce posse. Adam was not with them. Where did he go—

"Liam, what are you doing over here?" Adam asked

him, landing beside me. Close enough for my arm hair to almost touch his arm hair.

"Just talking to your cousin. She likes *Top Gun* too."

"Does she?" Adam did not appear convinced. A part of me took pride in that. I didn't need someone else on this earth thinking I believed *Top Gun* was a great movie. "Do you mind giving Eve and me a minute to talk?"

"Eve and I," I corrected him.

He narrowed his eyes on me. "Are you sure?"

I wasn't. I was a professional flirter, not a professional grammar-er. *Pretty sure anyone with grammar skills would never use the word grammar-er.*

"Sure thing, I'll head back over to the guys," Liam said. "It was nice meeting you, Eve. I hope we can—"

"Bye, Liam," Adam said in a stern voice. A sexy stern voice. So, this was jealous Adam Pierce... I liked him. *Not thinking of me as a baby in need of sitting now, are you?* I just barely held back the temptation to stick my tongue out at him.

Liam nodded and left us.

Adam cocked his head and took a step closer to me. "Are you trying to make me jealous, Evie Turner?"

I was the essence of confidence as my chin rose and I asked coyly, "Can't a girl have a conversation about *Top Gun* without raising suspicion?"

"Any other girl, yes. You, no."

I shrugged and looked out at the beautiful ocean. Eye contact was too good for him.

"You're really not over me, are you?" he asked with an expression dipped in smugness.

A dark laugh choked me. "Why would you think that?"

"Maybe because on the first day of vacation this summer, you were wearing that obnoxious twenty-five cent ring. Now, you're trying to make me jealous."

I rolled my eyes. "Please, I'm over you more than maple syrup over pancakes."

"Another example of how sweet and innocent you are." I did not miss the way his gaze dropped to my lips before jumping back up the next second. "The thing five years ago, we were kids—"

"I know that—"

"I'm over it. You should be too."

"I am."

"It's pathetic," he said. "To still not be over a childhood crush."

Boom. He had to have been descended from Medusa because, just like that, everything in me was stone. Cold, hard stone. *Pathetic. Immature. Silly.* That was what he thought of me. "You know what, Adam? I'm less than zero percent interested in you. I have too much self-respect to—"

"Are you wearing sunscreen right now?" he asked, interrupting my *you-blew-your-chance-at-the-best-girl-in-the-world* speech.

Frustrated and confused as to the drastic change of subject I asked, "What?"

"Are you wearing sunscreen?"

My arms shot up in the air, my hands aching to strangle the perplexing boy. "What does it matter?"

"You've been out here for over an hour; you're going to get burned."

What can the sun do to me that you haven't already? "I'm working on my tan," I shot back.

"What's up with your obsession with being tan this summer?"

"I'm not obsessed with being tan."

"You practically begged my mom for tanning lotion. You know it'd just make you orange?"

"Is it a crime to want to resemble something other than a ghost?" I asked. Whenever my skin hit direct sunlight, I felt like I gave people the sensation of snow blindness.

Were Adam Pierce and I now having a...*conversation?*

"So, you'd rather look like a carrot than Casper?" he asked.

"Maybe I want to have a nice summer glow like the rest of the girls on the beach," I said, crossing my arms. "I can't do that while wearing sunscreen."

"So, now you're shallow *and* you want skin cancer?"

Frustrated groan. "No."

"Then what do you want?" he asked, sounding as frustrated at me as I was at him, which made no sense. "What do you want?"

I want you to act like time with me was not so forget-

table. *I want you to see me as a woman and not a girl.* "Maybe I don't want to be the 'pale girl' at the beach anymore. Why are you acting so angry right now?" I asked.

"Because the idea of you burning your beautiful fucking skin just to look like other girls on this beach enrages me."

My heart and mind were overboiling, trying to keep up with him. First, he found me "pathetic." Now he was worried about my skin? Couldn't he just push me into the sand and scream, "*I hate you,*" like a normal person, and I would know exactly where I stood with him instead of this hazy utter confusion?

"*Enrages* you?" I was dumbfounded. Dumb. Founded. He thought my skin was beautiful? I had never even heard a teenage boy use the word beautiful. Maybe the word "hot" or "sexy." But not beautiful. Beautiful made me feel...beautiful. Why was Adam so darn confusing?

"If you don't go inside in the next five minutes, you're going to turn into a pink crisp."

"That's my choice," I said, still not knowing whether I should point to the fact that he glossed over having used the word beautiful to refer to me. Me. Evie Turner. "Why does it matter to you?"

"It doesn't."

Was I gaining confidence all of a sudden? "It clearly does."

He glared even harder. For the first time, I saw that

expression for what it was. Anger at himself. Not me. But why?

"Whatever. Burn. See if I care," he grated and stomped away from me.

For the next half an hour, he stole glances at me from where he threw a ball with his friends. Each minute that ticked by where I lounged on my towel, soaking up the pure summer sun, Adam's scowl darkened. An hour later, his teeth were practically bared, resembling a growling dog. His throws of the football were harsh and lacked any kind of aim another twenty minutes later.

Even after my skin turned pink, I stayed there, watching him watch me. Watching him seem to...hurt. For some reason, it made me feel good. Powerful. Like I knew a chink in his icy armor.

I felt a lot less powerful when I woke up the next day, my skin sweaty and stinging from my fresh, ruby sunburn.

I felt even smaller and more confused when I walked outside to my unit's living room and saw a large bottle of aloe perched on the table with a note reading, "*For Evie.*"

4
LOVE STINGS LIKE A MOTHERFLUFFER

I glanced over to where Adam laid on a beach towel close to me. James separated us as we played tic-tac-toe in the sand.

I had not seen much of Adam after the flirting fiasco and sunburn. James took me everywhere he wanted to go, but Adam disappeared like a ghost whenever he knew I'd be around, which worked for me considering I was done with him. *I was done with him, right*? However, he could not avoid "family beach day," dubbed by his mother to be one full day when our families hung out together on the beach. We even shared umbrellas.

I'm not interested in sharing even a shadow with Adam Pierce.

But, also: *If he hates me so much, why did he buy me aloe?*

And why did my fickle mind imagine him massaging it into my hot skin?

"Any interest in fishing, Eve?" Adam's father asked me, and my dad laughed before being elbowed by my mother. "My boys are too lazy, but I'd love to have someone else come along tomorrow morning with your father and me."

"I'd go fishing with you, Dad," James said.

Mr. Pierce ignored him. "Adam?"

Adam's expression sent a chill through me even though the temperature was in the high eighties. Every muscle in his body seemed to freeze over. He remained silent.

I sat up from my towel. "If James wants to go, I'll go—"

"James is too young to go fishing." Mr. Pierce did not move his gaze from Adam. "Adam?"

Adam closed his eyes and stretched back on his towel.

His father continued, "You need to learn how to fish. Or do you intend to spend the whole vacation lying around like you do at home?"

"Henry..." Maryam started but was cut off.

"Laying around sounds good to me."

"I'll go fishing," James repeated, but no one paid attention to him. No one but me.

"James, why don't you and I go for a walk?" I asked and stood on the sand. He nodded and joined me. Anything to get away from the sudden icy tension between the two elder Pierce men.

"Not going to walk with them, Adam?" Mr. Pierce questioned behind us.

"You know me, Dad. Just a lazy piece of—"

"Adam!" Maryam shouted, hers the last voice we heard as I quickly led James away from them and toward the ocean.

We stood with our feet in the water, the waves lapping at us, washing us then retreating.

James kicked a bit of wet sand. "I could fish."

"I know you could," I said. He smiled at me, and I smiled back. "Want to see if we can find any fish?"

We played in the water a bit before Adam came over to join us. His icy exterior melted after he saw a smile on his brother's face. "Can I join you on your walk?" he asked us.

Did he want a tip for "babysitting" us?

Once I moved past the initial shock of Adam wanting to spend time with me, I asked him, "Depends, are you going to act like a jerk who has no respect for others?"

He tensed at my statement. I expected him to deny his attitude, but his guilty expression gave him away. "No."

When we started the walk, James ran in front of us and scanned the sea for any wildlife. Adam and I trailed behind him. My feet sank into the wet sand with each step, and I waited for him to start up some kind of conversation. Instead, we walked in silence. Close enough to hear each other's breathing but emotionally distant enough not to know what to say. I shivered when his arm brushed mine. He noticed and smirked. Jerk.

"I didn't know I needed to bring a chisel to the beach," I said.

He raised an eyebrow. "To cut through the sexual tension?"

"I—I meant to cut through the icy atmosphere. Between you and your dad. What sexual tension?" He rolled his eyes, and I glared at him. "You could have defended James more," I said. "He could go fishing. Sure, he's not old enough to put a worm on a hook, but that sounds gross and inhumane anyway."

"Worms don't have feelings," Adam said. I waited for him to elaborate. He just continued watching James run ahead of us and pick up underwater seashells. "Saw it in a documentary."

"Worms have feelings. They're living creatures."

He shrugged. "Humans are living creatures."

I again waited for him to say more but he remained silent. "Yes. That's a well-known fact. No debate here."

"So, you think all humans have feelings then?"

I frowned. "Of course. Though with how you've acted these past two weeks, it seems debatable."

He turned his face back to where our parents sat and grew smaller and smaller from the distance.

When the silence again became awkward, I said, "You are the living and breathing embodiment of 'issues,' Adam Pierce."

Instead of becoming insulted again, he laughed. A small chuckle that lit up his eyes. Lit sparks in the air. The sound echoed in my ears as my face warmed in a blush. I wanted his laugh not to affect me. I wanted not to think of him as the most attractive boy I'd ever seen. I wanted to feel as indifferent to him as he seemed to me.

But his *laugh*.

Even the seagulls in the sky seemed to pause just at the miraculous sound of it.

"A well-known fact. No debate here," Adam quoted me.

"Are your parents the reason why you're so jaded now?" I asked. His smile faded, and I regretted prying further. "I—I mean, you're just so different from how you were that first summer."

"Just because I'm not panting after you with hearts in my eyes doesn't mean I'm jaded."

I planted myself still in the sand, and he stopped too. "Just because you don't like me anymore doesn't mean you have to be rude and mean to me. You act like a kid."

"*I* act like a kid?" He took a step closer, narrowing his eyes on me. Mayday, mayday. "You walk around like life is some fairytale. Like no time has passed—"

"I do not. You're the one always acting immature. And the whole 'boys being mean to girls they secretly like' thing? That's BS. It gives guys an excuse to act however they want at the expense of girls, and it's wrong—"

"I'm not mean to you because I *like* you—"

"You called my skin beautiful."

"I clearly had heat stroke and was dehydrated."

"You bought me aloe."

"A common side effect of heat stroke and dehydration."

James's loud shriek stole our attention. He laid on the sand, crying and holding his foot. I didn't even register that I ran toward him until I stood an inch away and dropped to my knees in front of him. Adam joined me, dropping down only a second later.

Adam pulled James's hands away from his foot and analyzed it. "What's wrong? What happened?"

"I thought it was a fish."

I wiped some of his tears away, but he continued to cry.

"It's a jellyfish sting." Adam looked around for where the creature went but turned back to James. "We have to get you back to the room, buddy."

"It hurts." James continued to cry, pulling my heartstrings. "It hurts."

"We've got to pee on it," I said, and both Pierce boys looked up at me with horror.

Adam positioned James further away from me. "No."

I inched closer, surveying the wound. "It's supposed to help with the pain and sterilize it, I swear."

"In no universe are you peeing on my brother."

"Well, yeah. You should be the one to do it. You'll

have better aim, plus I don't think I drank enough water today—"

"Evie, you are not peeing on my brother."

A sick spark ran through me as I realized he had called me *Evie* and not Eve. "Don't act like I'm trying to live out some kind of fetish. It's a real thing," I defended myself. "I saw it on TV."

"Did you see it on a TV show or a real documentary?"

I threw my hands up in the air. "Only crazy people our age watch documentaries."

"I watch documentaries."

"I rest my case."

"It HURTS!" James shouted.

We got back to business. Adam picked James up and carried him toward the timeshare building. I tried not to distract myself with his bulging muscles.

"Shouldn't we tell your parents? Or the lifeguard? Or a doctor?"

"No time." Adam carried him up the wooden steps that led off the sand and onto the cement.

"I could go grab them—"

"No, Evie." Adam cradled James closer to him as he rushed to the elevator. "My parents wouldn't help, trust me."

"What do you mean they wouldn't help? What if he needs to go to the hospital? What if—"

"Evie," he said as I started hyperventilating. The

elevator doors closed, and he used his elbow to hit our floor button. "Look at me. You're freaking out."

"Thank you, Mr. Obvious, do you want me to go crack you open a can of 'the sky is blue' and whip you up a plate of 'grass is green?'"

"Stop being weird and listen," Adam demanded in a stern voice that matched the one in my fantasies. "You're going to help me."

"I already told you, I didn't drink enough water today. I don't think I could pee if I wanted to—"

"Stop with the pee thing. It's not happening."

"Adam," James cried as the elevator doors opened and we hurried to their unit.

"I know, buddy. I know." Adam tried to support James with one arm long enough to grab his room key, but he couldn't. "Eve, I need you to reach into my pocket and take my key out, okay?"

Put my hand...where his... *Shut up, naughty self. Do this for James.* I shoved my hand into his right pocket with more force than I intended. He jumped at the contact, and I dug into the mesh, feeling the outline of certain body parts. *Adam's* body parts. Parts of Adam.

"Not the key!" Adam announced when my fingers wrapped around something. "Wrong pocket. My key is in my left pocket."

I pulled the object out of his pocket and stared at it. Shock. Awe. Every emotion ever. It was the wolf arcade ring I had won him as a kid. The ring itself was too small to fit on either of our young adult fingers but...he had kept it.

"Evie..." My gaze jumped back up to meet his. "I—"

"It stings!" James yelled at us, and I shook my head. My hand dove into his other pocket and pulled out the key card. Once the door was unlocked, Adam ran James to the bathtub.

TWENTY MINUTES LATER, James still sat with his feet in the tub of water, and Adam came out of the bathroom to join me in their living room.

"I looked it up; the pee thing isn't proven. You were right," I told him as he fell back on the couch next to me, exhausted. "How did you know to do all that? The vinegar and everything?"

He stared up at the ceiling from where he laid on the couch. "I was stung once."

I shifted, one of my hands holding the wolf ring I pulled from his pocket earlier. "I didn't know."

"It was a summer you didn't come here. I guess you had bigger and better places to be."

"I always wanted to come back here. To see you." I admitted, hoping this calmer side of Adam wouldn't turn evil again and use my words against me. "Every summer after that first one, I thought I would, but my parents always had something else planned. I was so excited to come back and see you again and..."

"A lot can change in five years."

A moment of silence hung between us before I broke it with an anvil. "You kept the ring."

He ran a hand through his hair. "Don't do this."

"You kept it, Adam. You kept it. You had it in your pocket."

"It doesn't mean anything."

"It means everything." I stood up from my chair and moved over to him. "I know you want to downplay it—"

"Evie." He got up and took the small piece of our childhood from me. "This ring means absolutely nothing to me. Do you understand?"

Breathe. "You can say that, but it was in your pocket." I moved closer, and he took a step away from me.

"After everything I've said to you these past few days, how can you still want me?" he asked, his voice strained. "Are you a masochist?"

"I hate the stuff you said, and I get that something must have happened to make you this way. I understand that you've grown up and changed, but a person doesn't change this much. This isn't you."

"It *is* me. But you wouldn't know that. You don't *know* me." The anger, the sheer pain in his voice gave me pause. "We were *kids*, Evie. What could you possibly like about me now? What could you possibly remember about me? Be honest, you came here and liked how I looked."

"That's not true." *Though you are very hot.* "Adam, I

liked you. I was prepared to like you no matter what you looked like."

He scoffed.

"Remember when our parents went to that seafood shack restaurant and hated it? Your mom complained the whole time about the waitress and how long it took to get our food. We saw how busy the place was, how stressed the server was. And when your mom chose not to leave a tip, what did you do?"

Adam stared at me, his expression too guarded for me to read him.

"You left the thirty dollars your parents gave you for her as a tip. For the whole week, you had no money for snacks or arcade games because you wanted to make someone's day better," I said. "That's who you are. Not this cold person."

Adam ran a hand over his jaw before he said, "That was a long time ago. Things *have* changed. Things you have absolutely no idea about." He shook his head, his lips curving down. "Every time I look at you now, I see everything that's gone wrong in my life since that first summer. Everything started falling apart, and each July I thought I'd see you and we'd get through it together, and you never came. You don't get to come back and act like..." He let out a frustrated noise. "You weren't *here*, Evie."

"I'm here now."

"Doesn't matter. We were kids."

"Stop saying that," I yelled at him, feeling like a

surfer being consumed by a rogue wave. Drowning. "It was more than just a childhood crush. You know it was. You said it was forever."

"Nothing lasts forever. Time to grow up." He moved and opened the sliding glass door. Warm wind wafted into the air-conditioned room as he stepped out onto the balcony. Before I could shout, "*No*," he threw the small ring out onto the beach seven floors below us. It landed close to where the sand met the waves and disappeared from sight.

The one piece of hope that Adam would ever care about me was gone.

My heart broke all over again.

5

BEAUTY IS IN THE EYE OF THE BEHOLDER, AND YOU MUST BE DAMN BLIND

*T*he Next Summer, One Year Later

PENNY: *So, what's the plan this summer?*

Me: *Find a short summer romance, have my first kiss before I turn seventeen, possibly learn how to swim, and ignore Adam Pierce with every fiber of my being.*

My birthday was a few weeks after the last week of the timeshare, so technically Adam always managed to be older than me when he saw me. A part of me hated that. It served as just another reason for him to see me as smaller than him, like the "little girl" he remembered.

I was no longer that little girl.

I also no longer looked like that little girl. I'd let my hair grow long, hit puberty, and finally learned how to correctly apply eyeliner. After becoming obsessed with dance, my legs and arms were—somewhat—made of toned muscle. As for confidence and height, I had also grown.

My every step in my polka dot flip-flops screamed, "*I'm ready for this summer. Are you?*" My toes in the flip-flops also screamed because, God, who came up with the idea to separate toes with a thick piece of plastic that scraped my toe valley raw? They were toes, not star-crossed lovers meant to forever be close but never quite touch each other.

Penny: *Make sure that first kiss doesn't get awarded to Mr. We-Never-Say-His-Full-Name-Out-Loud-Like-With-Lord-Voldemort Pierce.*

Me: *I wouldn't kiss him if it was the zombie apocalypse, I'd just been bitten, and the cure to zombie-ism was touching his lips against mine.*

His pained words from the previous summer still caused my heart to wring itself. "*You weren't here, Evie.*" Then, I remembered him throwing his arcade ring off the balcony and out into the ocean just to hurt me.

Penny: *You're becoming very dramatic with age. I like it. And if he dares to say anything negative to you, let it bounce off. You were the winner of the Wenway High talent show. You are amazing.*

I sent her a heart emoji before finishing my unpacking. Most of my clothes were red, as it was my favorite color and flavor.

One piece of clothing, however, stood out among

the others. A pink bikini with small cherries all over it. I purchased it with Adam in the back of my mind. Though I hated to admit I planned to wear something just to see a boy's reaction to it—cause of girl power and everything—I smiled at the thought of his eyes widening when he saw me in it.

I didn't want him to like me anymore. I was no longer pining for him.

But a deep, dark, vengeful part of me wanted him on his knees, begging me to forgive his cold, cruel behavior from last summer.

I wanted him to wear the wolf ring I'd won him and cry about how much he had missed me. Did I think that would ever happen? No. I wasn't crazy. I was just three-quarters delusional. My obsession with romance novels had put that idea in my head. And many more ideas... Let's just say I wanted to get this first kiss over with already. Heck, I was going to turn seventeen in less than a month. Some of my friends had sex already. Was a kiss too much to ask for?

Is it too much to ask for a boy to finally want me?

"Eve." My dad knocked on my door and gave me a heart attack since I had just been thinking about my virginity with him in the next room. "The Pierces ran into traffic, so they won't be here until later tonight. I'll make dinner for us at home."

Great.

I texted Penny to inform her of the change of plans.

I wore my *seeing-Adam-for-the-first-time-in-a-year* dress for nothing.

<u>Me</u>: *Now Adam isn't coming to dinner.*

<u>Penny</u>: *You would have blinded him with your beauty anyway.*

<u>Me</u>: *I think we might meet them at the pool later.*

<u>Penny</u>: *That's even better. Wear that cherry bikini and send him into cardiac arrest.*

<u>Me</u>: *Cardiac arrest sounds painful.*

<u>Penny</u>: *He deserves it.*

"You should really wait to swim until the Pierces get here," Mom tsked at me.

"I didn't know swimming etiquette was like eating before dinner guests arrived," I said and did several backstrokes across the shallow end of the pool. The water was the perfect temperature, warm enough to be comfortable, yet not so warm that my brain struggled to do the math of how many kids must have peed in it. "They're already half an hour later than they said they would be. I want to swim before I get gray hair."

My mother sighed. "So dramatic."

I grinned and continued to dog paddle around, avoiding the deep end. Did I realize most sixteen-year-olds had no problem swimming in the deep end of hotel pools? Yes. But most sixteen-year-olds did not have a terrifying fear of drowning. Maybe it stemmed from the scene in *Titanic* where Jack sank to the bottom, cold and lifeless and with no hope of living. Maybe it was something else.

But the idea of not being able to touch my feet to the bottom of a surface freaked me out.

Another thing for Adam to mock me about.

My dad shifted toward the pool but inched back from it after receiving a cold glare from Mom. "How much longer do you think they'll be?"

I closed my eyes and took a deep breath before going underwater to wet my hair and test my ability to become a professional mermaid. After around fifty seconds without forming gills, my head bobbed back up, out of the water. Then "Hannah!" pierced my ears, shouted by a squealing Maryam, who rushed over to Mom with open arms.

The Pierces were here.

Showtime.

I swam over to the pool ladder steps and made direct eye contact with Adam.

He looked *good*. Broad shoulders. The kind of moody jawline that made actors famous. His dark hair hung shorter than the summer before, and he appeared older, wiser, and damn hotter. Did he swallow a sexy pill? Geezus. But this wasn't the time for me to fan myself over him. It was time for him to go into cardiac arrest from seeing me. But not real cardiac arrest, because ouch.

I pulled myself up the silver poles and slowly rose from the delightful chlorine. The pool water tried to pull me back in but my new muscles, from joining the school dance club, fought the wet force of gravity with ease. The water lapped at me, droplets clinging for seconds before trailing down my body like little tongues.

Adam's dark blue eyes traced every water droplet's race down my stomach, down my legs, to my painted red toenails. His expression didn't scream cardiac arrest, but it did scream heart attack, and that was good enough for me.

Electricity sparked the air as I kept his gaze while stepping out of the pool. The beginning of Shania Twain's song *"Man I Feel Like A Woman"* blared inside my head as I imagined I was in a scene from a movie. The classic scene where the girl comes back after time away and is hot and irresistible, like *Sabrina* but with a bikini. And then, in the scene, the camera zooms in on all the guys with their mouths open.

Adam didn't have his mouth open. His hand rubbed over his jaw though, as if reminding himself not to let it drop. His eyes were everywhere but on mine as I walked toward him, finally understanding the feeling of female power. Even though I had grown taller, so had he, standing several inches above me. Still, at that moment, it felt like I wore ten-inch heels.

I bet you wish you were babysitting me, Pierce.

"Evie, you're all grown up," Maryam said, careful

not to hug me and get her outfit wet. Why did she not wear a swimsuit if she knew we were meeting them at the pool? Adam wore a sleeveless shirt and swim trunks. He got the memo.

"I'm almost seventeen," I said, half to remind her and half to remind Adam I was not some innocent kid anymore. Well, I wasn't a kid anymore. The "innocent" part was debatable.

Adam grunted, eyes still not meeting mine. The way he looked at me... *Knees, you better stop shaking.* Just because he was inhumanly attractive did not mean my body had to react to him like he was the only warm-blooded male on earth. *If anything, he's cold-blooded.*

I deserved better than Adam Pierce. It only took six years to realize it.

Adam cleared his throat as if realizing his ogling of me. "Almost," he repeated. "Almost seventeen."

Pulling my thick wet hair to the side of my shoulder, I twisted my hands to wring water from the strands. He seemed to pay special attention to the squeezing of my fingers. "So, Adam, how have you been?" That was what mature people asked each other, right?

To emphasize my new evident womanhood—cleavage—I leaned down to pick off a nonexistent piece of lint from my suit, giving him a front-row seat to how "mature" I was now.

He watched me with enough heat to burn the sun. I did the same when he whipped off his shirt, preparing for a swim. *Hey, tongue? Think you could get back inside my mouth where you belong and not outside, drooling for the world to see?* His chest had abs. Actual abs. My fingers itched to trace them, but I employed all my self-restraint.

He grinned at my obvious struggle to not look at his chest. I shook the dirty thoughts from my head just in time to hear, "I'm doing just fine. And you?"

"Absolutely dandy," I replied. *And a bit randy.* But he didn't need to know that.

"I see you're still obsessed with cherries," he said in a sweet but heavy voice. He strode closer to me, leaning in and whispering to my ear, "What a perfect metaphor." He then jumped into the deep end of the pool and began swimming laps.

Perfect metaphor? Was that a joke on my virginity?

Gosh darn, even his back had muscles. If only his swim trunks would lower and answer the ever-present question in the back of my mind—

"Eve," my mom yelled, and I tore my gaze away from him, with a "*hmm?*" expression. "James just asked you a question."

I turned to the boy who had long, shaggy hair but the same pure smile as a year ago. "Sorry, buddy. I couldn't hear you over your brother's splash. What did you ask me?"

"Do you wanna swim with me?"

An excuse to not go in the deep end while hanging out with this little cutie? "Yes, please."

He reached for my hand, and I gave it to him. He

held it while walking me over to the pool steps.

***

PENNY: *He jumped in the pool to get away from you? Damn girl, you really got to him. I bet he jumped in the pool so no one noticed the tent in his trunks.*

Me: *Penny!*

I blushed at her message even in the privacy of my own room.

I had not seen much of Adam after the first night at the pool. Between the two Pierce brothers, James was my favorite to be around. We did everything together, and I loved it. However, it did decrease my chance of finding a boy for my first kiss. Six-year-olds were lip-lock blockers.

James went to the beach with his mom, so I decided to do another pool day and put my cherry bikini to the test in helping me score a beach date and effectively stamp *"finished"* on my search for my first kiss.

I tightened the thin pink strings behind my back and looked in the mirror. My not-as-flat-as-people-once-believed-the-earth-to-be stomach hung out just enough for me to feel insecure. Maybe I'd work out in the timeshare building's gym later. Maybe I'd eat another cherry Popsicle.

I began with the hot tub instead of the pool, in the hopes that the hot water would somehow make me appear hotter in return. The indoor pool connected to the outdoor one through a narrow channel only two people could swim through at a time. The lifeguard sat on a tall orange chair in the sun outside where the majority of people swam.

I never understood why indoor pools weren't more popular. A person could swim for hours with no worry of getting a sunburn. The Jacuzzi hot tub was also indoors and less crowded than normal, probably because most people were out enjoying the beach. I was more of a swimming-in-chlorine than a swimming-in-saltwater girl, myself. Fewer sharks and less pollution. Probably the same amount of pee.

After thirty minutes of soaking in the steaming vat of water, I decided all the boys my age who were worthy of kissing were at the beach as well.

Two girls with full makeup stepped down into the hot tub as I stood to get out. Their eyeliner was done so expertly, I tipped an invisible hat to them.

As I took my first step out of the water, the girls giggled behind me. I turned around to see them grinning at me. Did I zone out and miss their joke? Was this my chance to make girl friends at the timeshare? "Sorry, what did you say?"

The redhead tossed a curl from out of her face and addressed me. "I said you might want to invest in a one-piece because no one wants to see that." Her blonde friend laughed again.

You've dealt with this before. Don't let it get to you. Or, at least, don't let it show that it got to you. "Oh, body shaming. How hip of you." *The word "hip" is the opposite of hip, Evie.*

The redhead scoffed. "I'm not body shaming you, I'm giving you advice. Certain body types should stay away from certain clothing pieces."

"Her mom is a fashion designer," the blonde commented as if that made her friend's statement any less offensive.

"I'm sure she'd be so proud of you," I said.

"How are you so pale by the way? Are you from Alaska or something?"

Remain calm. "Yes. I live in an igloo."

But they were no longer listening to me. Redhead nudged Blondie's arm and nodded toward something behind me. I sighed and turned around only to see the object of their affection and attention was Adam. These girls were probably his typical type. Curvy, gorgeous, and tan.

He stumbled when he saw me.

I guess he had finally failed in avoiding me.

His eyes widened before narrowing when he saw that I yet again wore the pink cherry bikini. He moved closer, standing in front of me, next to the hot tub. In perfect hearing range of the two girls. "I thought you were at the beach with James," he said.

I tried not to eavesdrop on the whispering going on between the redhead and Blondie. "So, you decided to come to the pool to avoid me? Should we work out a schedule like a divorced couple?" My feet shuffled me away from the hot tub. Dealing with hurtful comments from strangers was one thing, but Adam hearing them and using it as more ammo against me? No, thank you. "I wanted some time alone."

"Wait." Adam followed me and grabbed my elbow. Pinpricks of heat ran through me, sharp and tingly and hot before I moved out of his grip. My skin needed to get the memo that Adam was off-limits. "Sorry, I just—I wanted to say thank you for hanging out with my brother. He really appreciates it."

A kind statement? From Adam Pierce? "It's not a job I need to be thanked for. I appreciate him. *He* knows how to be nice to a friend."

"Not many girls your age would want to spend their vacation looking after a six-year-old."

"I guess you don't know me very well," I said.

As he nodded, the edges of his lips lifted but dropped before a half-smile had time to form. "At first, I thought you were hanging out with him to try to get to me. That it was a manipulation." Was that why he'd always glared at me last summer? "Anyway, thanks."

What was I supposed to say to that? *You've been watching too many conspiracy mob movies if you think I'm capable of that kind of manipulation.*

"Why don't you join me in the hot tub?" he asked.

Was this a parallel universe? "Are you joking?"

He frowned. "No."

"You hate me."

"I don't."

"Don't be a jerk *and* a liar."

He snorted, his amusement at me shocking me again. "I don't hate you. I thought us hanging out would help...lessen the bad blood between us."

Ha! "You are the bad blood between us. Besides—" I shot a glance over to those girls. "—I'm done with the hot tub for a while."

He followed my gaze and tilted his head in question. "Why don't you want to go back in? Do you know those girls?"

I avoided eye contact as I lied. My gaze dipped and instead studied the muscular lines of his chest. Very distracting. No shoes. No shirt. Yes, please. "I don't want to go back in because I don't want to go back in with *you*."

He saw right through me, tipping my chin up so I met his gaze. Forcing me to stare into those hypnotic blues. "Tell me what they said to you."

"They seem to think I should wear a swimsuit that shows less skin."

His jaw clenched. Would he agree with them? Say, *Well, what's true is true?* After all, my last ballet teacher told me, *"You're a little too...thick to be a ballerina."*

I waited for Adam to insult me.

"So, they're stupid," he stated.

"I'm not— Wait, you said they're stupid?"

"Anyone who sees you in that and thinks you should cover up should move to Idiotville and be voted town moron."

A familiar feeling settled in my chest. A slow, pulsing, heart-melting feeling. Dangerous. Irresistible. "Yeah?"

"And you don't need the hot tub. You're hot already."

I coughed into my hand before flipping my hair over my shoulder. Very nonchalant flirting. Tasteful. "You think I'm hot?"

"You know how hot you are."

I pointed toward myself. "Me?"

"Someone must have told you. Maybe a boyfriend."

"Nah, he never compliments me," I said. Adam's eyes narrowed, so I decided not to tease him. "Considering he doesn't exist and all."

He nodded, leaning closer. "Interesting."

I went to flip my hair again, realizing all the strands were already over my shoulder. "It's fascinating, really."

He moved closer, his eyes snatching up all my attention. "Well, then maybe I should tell you just how hot you are."

My feet stepped back from instinct, but he followed step by step. "If you feel inclined to do so."

"Evie Turner, you are so hot, I'm afraid touching you will burn me." *Oh my.* "When I saw you in that bikini..." *Mm, yes, continue. Please go on.* "You're more than hot. You're on fire."

I fanned myself. "Am I?"

"Mm." He leaned his forehead against mine, our bodies so close, our feet touched. "You should cool down."

And he pushed me into the deep end of the indoor pool.

6

STOLEN KISSES ARE SWEETER THAN LIFESAVERS

Water. Everywhere. Dark, deep water. Pulling me down as if there were some sort of suction machine at the bottom. Water flooding my nose. Ears. Throat.

Like poisonous liquid oxygen. Filling me. Choking me.

And my feet couldn't touch the bottom. They couldn't touch the bottom.

The chlorine burned my eyes until I closed them, blind to more darkness. Thrashing my arms under the water, I tried to rise, at the same time trying to find the bottom.

My feet still couldn't touch the bottom.

My body lifted and began to float, but I still inhaled water. Choking. Drowning.

Strong, warm arms wrapped around me. An instant later, my head came back up for air. I coughed out the lung full of chlorine I had swallowed and coughed and coughed some more. My throat was on fire as I tried to say, "Thank you," but my voice had yet to go back to normal. My eyes felt bloodshot from being open in the water, and my limbs were still frozen from my panic.

Adam swam me to the pool ladder on the deep end and pushed me up until I was back on the cement floor. His fingers pet my face, stroking away moisture that could have been chlorine or tears. Who even knew anymore?

"God, I'm sorry. I'm so sorry. Eve, say something." He patted my cheek lightly, but my throat continued not to work. As I hyperventilated, his expression grew tortured. "Evie, it's okay. You're okay."

If someone looked up "freaking out" in the dictionary, my picture would be twenty pages earlier under "crying hysterically."

"Breathe. Just breathe. You're okay now." He held me close, his arms so tight around me it could almost make me think he cared. "I didn't know," he kept saying. "I swear, I didn't know. I was just trying to—shit—I didn't know."

My coughing lessened; my lungs opened back up for business.

"You're sixteen and you still don't know how to swim?" he asked me.

Sixteen and still haven't been kissed. Still don't know how to swim. God, I felt so dumb. Humiliated. No wonder Adam only ever saw me as the same little girl from six years ago.

"Wh-why would you do that? Why would you throw me in?" I continued to cry, not caring what he thought of me anymore. "That wasn't freaking funny."

"You're right." He tucked a curl of my hair behind my ear with a somewhat crazed look in his eyes. Had he been worried about me? Or was it just guilt? "It wasn't fucking funny at all."

EVERY TIME I saw Adam after that, his expression was always full of caution, of carefulness. Like I was some kind of glass doll that would break from any quick movements. He lost his cold exterior around me but replaced it with something worse. Pity. Guilt. I wondered if a part of him worried I'd tell his or my parents about what happened. I would never tell them. It was gosh darn embarrassing.

Every "*Are you okay? I'm really sorry*" look he gave me added to my fury. He now had power over me I didn't want him to have. I had worked so hard to be comfortable in my skin—to no longer be seen as a little girl. Yet, I was still the little girl who could not swim.

That decided it for me. This was the summer I would learn to swim.

And maybe, one day, Adam would fall in the deep end, hitting his head so he couldn't swim back up, and

I'd have to jump in and save him. He would be the damsel in distress, and I would be the knight in the shining bikini. Or maybe I would be the villain to push him into the deep waters in the first place.

"I'm going to learn to swim today," I told my dad, two days after my drowning fiasco.

"Oh? Is Adam teaching you?"

"No, he is most certainly not."

Dad chuckled. "Evie, you do know swimming isn't an easy thing to teach yourself?"

"I realize that, but don't worry. I'll practice in the outdoor pool where the lifeguard is."

"Don't push yourself too far today."

My mother joined our conversation, glancing up from her fashion magazine. "Your father and I would be very distressed if you drowned."

Dad laughed again, winking at me. "Very distressed, indeed."

I PLOPPED my towel and goggles down on a table by the outdoor pool and rubbed my hands together, the way gymnasts did before attempting the uneven bars in the Olympics.

The water in the deep end appeared a lot less menacing in the bright noon sun. The blue sky reflected on the pool, making it seem like swimming might feel closer to flying on the hot summer day. A *great day to learn how to swim—or drown. Always best to stay positive.*

I squeezed on my red-rimmed goggles—most likely looking like the oddest sixteen-year-old girl this pool had ever seen—and stepped into the shallow end. I walked through the pool, adjusting to the temperature, until the water slapped just under my chin. I paused, chanting, *"You can do this."*

I didn't want to turn thirty in less than fifteen years and realize I still couldn't swim. I didn't want to shy away from the diving board or water park slides that shot guests out into nine feet of water. I didn't want Adam to keep seeing me as a little girl.

My arms shot out in front of me, and I mimicked Michael Phelps' forward stroke. After a few minutes, my arms and legs tired. Dog paddling to the side of the pool became impossible when I realized how wide the distance was. My leg cramped underwater. *A charley horse* now? The painful spasm distracted me, and my head slipped underwater. I quickly resurfaced, my arms working overtime as I spat out some of the water. My other leg cramped underneath me as well; from panic or overuse, I didn't know. And I didn't care.

My head was underwater again. I couldn't breathe. I opened my eyes, safe from the chlorine through my grandma goggles, but seeing the deepness below and the top of the water getting farther away as I sank freaked me out even more. My chest tightened as my body and mind prepared for my panic attack. I struggled to kick through my pain, but my arms ached and resisted helping me.

The lack of oxygen made me dizzy. Spots blurred my vision, and I freaked out even more as I realized I started to pass out. I could not faint underwater. I could die. I would die.

I had to...just keep moving and get back to the top...
... ...
"One, two, three. One, two, three." Pressure eased from my chest before something pressed against my lips instead, separating them, blowing...air. Air.

My eyes shot open, and the warm lips left mine just as I regurgitated about a liter of chlorinated water onto the cement. Regurgitated in a classy way. Very feminine. My mother would have been proud.

I wiped my mouth after my coughing fit passed and looked up to see an Adonis stretched over me, tapping my back to help my hacking. I knew it was a cliché, but had I died and gone to heaven? "God?" I asked the dirty blond-haired male who appeared only a year older than me.

His skin reminded me of light caramel. First, due to its color. Second, due to my desire to lick it.

Pale green eyes, matching the tone of Peter Pan's tights, locked onto mine with curiosity and amusement. "Actually, my name is Kellan. My friends sometimes call me Kell, but I've never gone by God. I could maybe pass for a Zeus if I tried hard enough."

In shock, I stared at the smiling, heartthrob of a boy babbling above me, unsure of what to say or do.

He shook his head, the short, dark blond curls bouncing up and down. "Sorry, I shouldn't tease you. You swallowed a good amount of water, but you should be fine. I gave you CPR and mouth-to-mouth because you stopped breathing for a minute there."

"I *died*?"

"No, no, you were fine. Just needed some air."

I blinked up at him. The sun illuminated his blond curls until I saw a halo, or maybe that was my brain's own bias turning him into an angel in front of my eyes. "You're awfully chill about saving my life."

"Don't take offense." He shrugged. "I just save a lot of people in my line of work. Lifeguard, you know."

"I do know, and I'm very impressed."

He chuckled and grabbed my hand as he moved from his knees into a hunched over position above me. "Are you ready to stand?"

Not if you keep making my knees weak. "As I'll ever be."

He lifted me like I weighed nothing and sat me down on my feet. "Want to tell me what happened down there?"

A sigh escaped me. "I drowned."

"Mhm, I did realize that. I meant, why did you drown?"

Telling this male model I still did not know how to

swim was not something I particularly wanted to do. "My legs cramped."

He tilted his head, not believing me. "Sure, okay."

I crossed my arms, and his gaze dropped down to my cleavage before hopping back up to meet my eyes. "It's true."

"I'm not calling you a liar."

"Good because I'm not one." We stared at each other in awkward silence before I turned around to walk back toward the pool. "Bye now."

"Wait, where are you going?"

I pointed below me. "Back into the water."

He pointed at the water I'd regurgitated onto the cement. "You just drank half of it."

"No need to be so dramatic."

"Why would you go back in—" His beautiful eyes widened as he wagged a finger at me. "Oh, no. You're one of those girls, aren't you? The ones who fake drown themselves so I'll give them mouth-to-mouth."

"I am not."

"You probably just got too caught up in your character and really drowned. Is that what this was? Just trying to steal a kiss from me?"

"I didn't— Wait. You did mouth-to-mouth on me."

He nodded. "I did."

My finger lifted to trail over my bottom lip. "Your mouth touched my mouth."

"I was there," he recounted it like a witness to a crime. "I felt it happen."

"I lost my first kiss," I muttered in amazement before grinning at the realization. Finally, something checked off on my summer romance bucket list. A year overdue.

"Your first—" Kellan tripped on what appeared to be air and coughed while stabilizing himself. "You've never been kissed?"

"Now I have."

"No, but that—" He made wild gestures toward where he saved me. "—that doesn't count."

"You just said girls fake drown for you to kiss them all the time."

"But not for their first kiss." A hand ran through his thick, curly hair. "Why didn't you tell me?"

"Maybe because I wasn't breathing."

"You—you're—how old are you?"

"I'm almost seventeen."

He released a heavy, relieved breath. "Thank God."

I tapped my bare foot on the ground harder than necessary. "Thanks a lot. How old are you?"

"Seventeen. You're sixteen and never been kissed?"

"Until now."

He ran another hand through his hair, this time pulling lightly on the strands. "A first kiss is supposed to be special. You can't count this."

"I sure as heck can." I had been trying to get rid of that sucker for sixteen years.

Kellan seemed to be having a hard time processing this. "I don't understand," he said. "First, you say your legs cramped, but you're prepared to get right back in the water. And now, the never been kissed thing. One has to be a lie."

I got the feeling he wouldn't leave it or me alone until he figured it out so I said, "If you must know, I'm trying to teach myself how to swim."

"You're sixteen and you've never been kissed and you don't know how to swim?"

"What a great tagline. I should put it on my business cards."

"You're sixteen and you have business cards?"

"No, stupid. Please move on."

He stood there, absorbing all I'd told him, staring at me in awe the whole time. I suppose comparing myself to a unicorn wasn't too far off. I was unique, rare, and somewhat horny. Curse my teenage hormones. "You drowned trying to swim, and you still plan to get back in to try again. Why?"

"I'm not going to just give up. It's something I need to learn how to do."

"You don't think you'll drown again?"

"I might," I admitted.

"I can't save you each time you practice."

"I'm pretty sure it's your job, so..."

"I don't have time—"

"To save my life?"

"No, I... How about you stop with your deep end swimming today and pick up tomorrow when I'm off duty?"

I tried not to feel insulted. I tried. "Is this your way of saying you don't want to deal with me?"

He grinned, his teeth white like from unrealistic toothpaste commercials. Impressive. "This is my way of saying I'll teach you how to swim on my day off."

I tried not to feel butterflies. I tried.

"How did your swimming go today?" my dad asked at dinner with the Pierce family.

Adam's head shot up at the mention of my swimming.

"Great, actually." I chewed a piece of chicken and swallowed it down a little too quick. "I found someone to help teach me." A hot someone with CPR and mouth-to-mouth expertise. A cute lifeguard who was officially my first kiss, whether he accepted that title or not.

"A new friend, how exciting."

Adam did not appear as happy for me as the rest of the table did. He stared down at his plate and cut the chicken with his knife, using twice the amount of required force.

"I missed you at the beach today, Evie," James said.

"I promise I'll make up for it, little guy."

James rolled his eyes. "I'm six now."

"Sorry, medium-sized guy."

James smiled and ate a piece of broccoli. "If someone is helping you swim, can they help me too?"

Kellan seemed nice enough to help both of us. Especially, if I peer pressured him with the whole: *You stole my first kiss, it's the least you can do.* "I'll ask him."

"Him" sent off two reactions. First, my dad choked on his wine. Second, Adam cut through the chicken so hard, it cracked the plate.

7
THE SEED OF LOVE GROWS BEST IF WATERED AND YOU ARE A DROUGHT

Time to learn to swim.

My cherry bikini still felt damp from the day before, so I opted for my less revealing bathing suit, trying not to think about the *"you should invest in a one-piece"* comment from those hot tub girls. The shiny black fabric had a couple of side cutouts from overlaying straps and a bare back that dipped to where a normal bikini bottom laid. It may have been a one-piece, but that did not make it appear any less scandalous. Especially with so much cleavage.

My fifteen-year-old, smaller-chested self would have done a happy dance. Heck, I went ahead and did a happy dance for her.

A knock on my door interrupted my dance moves. "James is here," Dad said.

I threw on my bathing suit cover-up, which was a strapless, hot pink dress with navy blue flowers. It hit me at the knees and excited me that the fierce, black bathing suit underneath created such juxtaposition in style and attitude. In the pink cover-up, I felt cute and bubbly. In the black one-piece, I felt sexy and mature.

"Ready to go to the pool to learn how to swim?" I asked James, raising my arms up and down to pump him up for our time with Kellan and shake off my nerves as well. I didn't have Kellan's phone number so I had not informed him James would join us. He seemed nice enough not to care about an extra student.

We waited for the elevator to come to the seventh floor for us. I froze when the doors dinged open and we stepped inside. Adam and his gang of guys stood there shirtless, sweating, and holding various sports balls. I recognized hippie Liam right away once he grinned at me. Flirting, even when faked to make someone jealous, was dangerous.

The boys took up most of the room. I ended up standing right in front of Adam, my back facing him. Heat radiated from his front and his warm breath tickled the back of my neck, but I ignored it. Tried to ignore it.

Liam shifted closer to me when the elevator doors closed and lowered us seven floors. "Hi, I don't know if you remember me—"

Adam cut him off. "Headed for your swimming lesson?"

"Yes," James replied, but Adam waited for me to answer as well.

"We sure are." I leaned in to inspect the elevator buttons and lights as if they fascinated me more than Adam's bare chest.

"If you need a real teacher, let me know," he said against the back of my neck. "I'll come down and join you two."

Oh, really? "I didn't think you would be interested in *babysitting* us." Ha. "Anyway, we have a real teacher." The floor numbers counted down and soon I would be free from the elevator ride from Hell. "He's a certified lifeguard," I said.

"Try not to drown. Don't want to lose your first kiss to CPR." Adam smirked, knowing I'd never been kissed. *Things change, bucko.* His friends snickered at his teasing. What was so funny about a never-been-kissed sixteen-year-old?

"Actually, he's already won my first kiss," I shot back. "And before the end of the day, he'll probably get more than one."

The doors dinged open, and I grabbed James's hand, dragging him with me as I speed-walked away after shouting, "Bye now!"

I tried not to turn around. I failed. Adam's flaring nostrils were the last things I saw before the elevator doors closed.

KELLAN'S EYES widened when he saw me show up with

young, little James. The sexy lifeguard stood in the middle of the indoor pool, waiting for us. No shirt in sight. *Hello, muscles. My name is Eve.* Beads of water dripped from his curly blond hair as he lifted an eyebrow at me.

"I should start charging for lessons." He grinned his good-natured grin. "I didn't know I'd have a crowd."

"This is James." I went to gesture to him, but he ran to the pool steps and into the shallow end of the pool, not waiting for any introductions. "Okay then."

"Is he your little brother?"

"No."

"Cousin?"

"No."

He stared at me. "Eve, did you steal this nice young boy?"

I laughed. "He's a family friend. We've been hanging out for years."

"You're the unofficial babysitter, aren't you?"

"No." I smiled over at where James splashed around, watching us and waiting for the lesson to start. "I like him. I think of him as a friend."

Kellan's smile should have won the "soft and peaceful" award for smiles. "That's really sweet."

"You're really sweet." *Get yourself together, Turner.* "I —I mean, this is really sweet of you to teach us to swim." *Just get in the pool already before you embarrass yourself.*

"How could I say no—"

I tugged off my pink cover-up the moment he cut off his sentence. The air-conditioning caused goosebumps wherever my skin was not covered by the black, strappy one-piece. Slipping my flip-flops off my feet, I stepped into the heated pool.

Kellan cleared his throat and swam over to where James and I were in the shallow end. "So, let's get started…"

"Good job, James. Remember not to let your head go under the water or bend your back." Kellan circled us as James and I attempted floating on our backs. "You're bending, Eve."

I tried to straighten, but that resulted in my neck tilting and my eyes getting a splash of chlorine.

"Settle down. Balance. That's good. Very good." Kellan's warm hand now touched my lower back under the water, holding me up. "There you go, nice and still." My eyelids fluttered open to see Kellan leaning over me, his face close to mine.

"Eve!" a deep male voice shouted my name. An answering shiver wracked my body. I knew who it was without looking. "Can I talk to you for a minute?" Adam growled.

Kellan removed his hand from me as I stood up and glared. "Right now?" I asked.

"Yes."

I huffed and got out of the pool to face an angry, scowling, hotter-than-a-summer-sun Adam.

"James, stay in the shallow end," he told his brother in a voice less harsh than the one he used for me. *At least I'm special.*

James pouted, and Kellan frowned but swam with him to where he could reach the bottom.

Water dripped from me as I got out of the pool. Adam watched me cross my arms to keep warm as I walked over to him. He picked up my towel, knowing it was the one with huge red cherries all over it, and wrapped it around me. His touch lingered.

Adam silently led me out of the indoor pool to where we could talk, his hand at my back like some kind of regency gentleman escorting a lady. The small sitting area outside was empty as most people laid on the lounge chairs by the outdoor pool.

"Thanks for handing me my towel," I said, the warm ocean breeze wafting over my back.

"What the hell were you doing?" he snapped, destroying any soft moment between us. As usual.

"Floating?"

"You say a lifeguard is going to teach you and my brother to swim, and I come down here and see my brother floating on his lonesome while you flirt with the guy!"

His combat mode triggered my combat mode. "I wasn't flirting."

"You wore that pink dress to make me think it was

an innocent swimming lesson and then walk around in this little black number like some dominatrix."

"It's a one-piece bathing suit," I defended myself.

"It looks like lingerie."

"It does not." Other than the cut-out back and a few extra straps crossing over my stomach, it resembled any other black one piece. "Other girls wear way less out here."

"I don't care about other girls." Did that mean he cared about me? Not that I cared. I didn't care whether or not he cared.

"Look, James was never 'on his lonesome,'" I said. "We were both next to him the whole time."

"You probably wouldn't have even noticed if he drowned. You were too busy looking into the guy's eyes with that dreamy vixen look you get on your face."

I poked a finger into his chest. "One, of course, we would have noticed. I would never let anything happen to James. *I'm* the one always hanging out with him. You're the one off doing who knows what with no shirt or supervision. Two, I have no idea what dreamy vixen look you are referring to. My face doesn't do that."

He took a step closer, fiery anger in his eyes burning me up from the inside like internal sunburn. Adam grated, "I know exactly what your face does because you make that expression every time I walk into a room."

"Ha! You're delusional."

"You are delusional if you think I don't know exactly

what is going through your head whenever you're staring at my chest like you want to spread hot fudge over it and lick it off."

Was my face that readable? "I don't like fudge," I mumbled.

"Fine, cherry sauce or whatever. You stare at me like I'm a cherry popsicle."

"Stop comparing yourself to lickable things!" *It's giving me too many ideas.*

His chest pressed against mine, the only sign that we'd stepped closer and closer to each other during our heated exchange without realizing it. "Why? Because you know I'm right? Or do I need to buy a bottle of cherry sauce and test the theory?"

"Right," I scoffed but stared at his chest because, my oh my, what a glorious sight. "Like I wouldn't be able to resist licking it off you?" I wouldn't. He was right. "And anyway, don't act like you don't ogle me too."

"You think I ogle you?" he asked. His gaze settled onto my lips.

"Don't you?" *Please say you do too, or I will be thoroughly embarrassed.*

He rolled his perfect eyes. "Why else do you think I've been avoiding you?"

Wait. He avoided me because he was attracted to me? Not because he still thought of me as some immature kid he didn't want to spend time with. But because being around me was...hard for him? Literally hard. I tried not to peek down at his swim shorts.

"Evie, raise your gaze right now before I give you something to look at."

Why was the temperature so freaking hot? And weren't we in the middle of fighting a minute ago?

"Just—just shut up." My breathing was hard as his chest rose up and down against mine. Up close, the smell of his sweat and sunscreen created a heady haze, affecting my thoughts.

We stared at each other, trying to even out our breathing. It helped when I stepped back, creating space between us.

Adam sighed after a minute of silence. "I'm sorry I... snapped." He rubbed his jaw. "But James is six years old. It's not appropriate for you to go around flirting with random guys in front of him."

"I'm not..." My sentence ended on a growl because, God, he made me mad.

"See? You can't even lie and say you weren't flirting with him."

Standing my ground, I said, "Maybe I was flirting with him, but he's not a random guy; he's my first kiss."

Adam gave a hoarse, sour laugh. "Mouth-to-mouth doesn't count."

"It does to me."

He smirked. "Blowing into someone's mouth isn't a kiss. Lips touching other lips isn't a kiss." His eyes narrowed on my mouth again.

"Sounds like you know a lot about kissing." The hurt and vulnerability in my voice betrayed me. "I'm sure you get kissed whenever you want. Not everyone is so lucky. Congratulations."

"Evie."

I threw my arms up in the air. "You mock me for never having been kissed; then when I've finally been kissed, you start whipping out technicalities. Is it that important to you to make me feel small and immature? Do you get off on making me feel inadequate?"

"Evie."

"Because trust me, I don't need your help with feeling inadequate. I do a fine job of that all on my own—"

Suddenly, Adam Pierce was kissing me.

And like an old kite in the strong beach wind, I felt like I held on by only a thin string.

Because his lips on mine could have made me fly away.

His hand cupped the back of my head, fingers twisting and tangling into my wet, thick locks, pulling.

Lips. His lips clashed with mine, moving, sucking, pressing, kissing. Wild. Heat. Sparks. Fire. They moved with me, deepening the kiss.

It was like that first dip into a hot tub. Scalding. But perfect. Relaxing but jolting.

I had seen movies and read books, but nothing compared to this.

This was kissing? Mouth-to-mouth seemed like child's play in comparison. Everything seemed like child's play in comparison. Why had he waited so long?

Did this mean he wanted to be with me? Was he finally realizing he had made a mistake by pushing me away?

If I kiss him for another minute or two, will he fall to his knees and beg my forgiveness and admit to always having been in love with me?

What would it take to forgive him? I wanted it to take a lot. I feared it would take a little.

His other hand, on the small of my bare back, pressed my body firmly to his. A heavy feeling settled below my stomach. Want. Need. His chest moved against mine, and I moaned. My noise vibrated our lips, causing him to groan in return.

This was the first kiss I was owed. The one he promised me at the end of our first summer together.

His lips tore themselves off mine as we huffed to catch our breath. He stared into my eyes, and the direct eye contact was like being injected with pure *swoon*. The way he fought to gain control of himself again made me feel like I was the best kisser on earth.

He cleared his throat, masking whatever emotion had been playing across his expression and defaulting to his smug façade. He said, "*That* was a kiss."

Right. Because the kiss was just to prove his point. He didn't really want me.

The kiss was meaningless to him. Just like me.

Summoning all of my acting talent, I downplayed it. "I can't say it was as reviving as my first one."

Adam smirked, seeing right through me. "Find me if you need another lesson."

8
SON OF A CONCH

I hate Adam Pierce.

I took an extra minute or two to come down from the kiss with my nemesis and walked back to the indoor pool, where James and Kellan waited for me.

James splashed around with some new, young friends in the shallow end. Kellan floated on his back in the deeper water. I sat down on the ledge of the deep end, my feet dangling in the water, to talk to Kellan and apologize for the interruption. "Sorry about all that."

He swam over to me and crossed his arms over the ledge, holding himself up with those thick biceps of his. "It's all good. I deal with jealous boyfriends all the time. Part of the gig."

"He's not my boyfriend."

He let out a relieved breath. "Thank God. He scared me."

I laughed. "He's James's brother. He seemed to think we were, uh, distracted and not paying enough attention to James."

Kellan nodded, raising an eyebrow. "Distracted?"

"Flirting," I clarified.

"Hmm." He glanced at the cement ledge he held onto. The side of my thigh touched his elbow. "Interesting how things look." My question of *Were we not flirting?* was on the tip of my tongue, but he continued, "So, that guy is just a family friend?"

"That's about the warmest description I'd give our relationship."

He cocked his head to the side and stared at me. "Do you kiss all your family friends?"

I groaned and hid my blushing face in my hands. "You saw that?"

The glass wall separating the indoor pool from the outdoor sitting area was clean and easy to see through, but I had hoped James had kept Kellan distracted.

"It was hard not to see such a passionate embrace."

"It wasn't—He just—That's not what it was. He... teases me. I told him you were my first kiss, and he said mouth-to-mouth doesn't count. Then, he kissed me to steal my first kiss from me, probably to use as yet another thing to hold over me." I kicked a foot under the water. "It didn't seem to mean anything to him."

Kellan frowned. "He sounds like a jerk."

"Sounds like one, walks like one, talks like one..."

"I do agree that mouth-to-mouth doesn't count as

your first kiss. No, let me finish." He waved away my protests. "I don't think him kissing you should count either. If he kissed you—stole a kiss—then that's not a kiss. A kiss is something you initiate and want from beginning to end." I would cling to any logic that told me Adam was not my first kiss. "Plus, first kisses are generally after first dates." Kellan smiled, placing his hand over mine and squeezing. "So, that guy's kiss doesn't count at all. Simple math."

"Hmm." I nibbled my lip before I let my mouth spurt what my heart wanted to say. "We should go on a date."

He chuckled at my straightforwardness. "You want to go on a date with me?"

"I would very much like to, yes."

He smiled. "I know the perfect place."

Penny: *Your first date!*

Me: *With my first kiss! (Kind of. It's confusing.)*

Penny: *What are you going to wear?*

Me: *The dress I was supposed to wear when we were meeting Adam at the restaurant on the first day, but they missed it. The red one.*

Penny: *Girl, if that hunk of male lifeguard doesn't kiss you in that dress, he has swallowed too much chlorine in his life.*

I grinned at my phone and set it down to unzip the bright red dress, the color of maraschino cherries, lying on my bed. The scooped neckline showed a bit of cleavage. The skirt flared out after cinching at the waist, emphasizing my hourglass figure—or rather, making my pear-shaped figure appear more hourglass-like. When I wore it, I felt two inches taller and twenty points hotter. My wild, dark hair fought me and my brush until its surrender when it finally laid flat on my head.

I checked my phone again; no new messages. Kellan now had my cellphone number, and he planned to text me when he was in front of the timeshare building for us to walk along the beach to the pier. The entertainment for the night at the pier was karaoke, and Kellan convinced himself he could talk me into singing on stage just for the fun of it.

My stomach twisted with nerves, and I decided watching TV in the living room would distract me from feeling nauseous before the date. Stepping outside my room, I found the Pierce family sitting on our couch holding frozen drinks and my parents seated across from them.

"Evie." My mother waved me over to join them.

"Um, hello. Sorry, I didn't know we had company."

Adam's eyes followed me as I crossed the room. Our passionate kiss replayed in my mind. His gaze dropped to the tasteful line of cleavage on display, then down to my legs revealed under the almost-to-the-knee red dress. *Like what you see? Who cares? Not me!*

"You're all dressed up," Maryam informed me.

"Thanks, yeah, I'm going out."

"A date?"

Adam's head shot up from admiring my legs to examine my expression as I said, "Yes. My first."

"A first date. How exciting."

"And what are you doing on this date?" my father asked. Adam nodded with him. Neither seemed aware that their stone faces matched.

"We're walking to the pier for karaoke."

My father pushed for more information. "Is that a euphemism?"

"No, it's when people sing songs and realize the correct lyrics for the first time after reading the words on the screen."

"Make sure to take your phone, just in case."

"Just in case the guy secretly works for human traffickers and decided I was the perfect prey, so he elaborately got a job as a lifeguard and taught me how to swim on his day off just to snatch me now that he's won my trust?"

"Why do you have to put thoughts like that in your dad's head?" My mother reprimanded me. "He'll never let you out of his sight if you keep that up."

I kissed my dad's cheek. "I've got my phone and my passport; no need to worry." My phone buzzed, and I opened the message to see Kellan had texted me, "*Here.*" "Okay, I'm leaving."

Adam continued glaring at my cleavage. "Shouldn't you take a sweater or something?" he suggested. "It's supposed to get colder tonight."

I lifted one shoulder, opening the door to leave. "I'll have a nice, strong lifeguard to keep me warm."

"Look, sometimes, the heart wants what it wants. And mine wants a cherry snow cone."

Kellan formed the time-out sign with his hands. "It's called a snow*ball.*"

"Oh no." I paused, and we stopped walking down the boardwalk of the pier. "Is this where our northern and southern roots tear us apart?"

He shook his head in mock disappointment. "It was bound to happen eventually."

After buying a cherry snow cone, we passed the old arcade Adam and I went to when we were kids on our last night together. The place where we had won each other the arcade rings. I stepped inside, Kellan following me.

Red and blue lights flashed through the dim arcade as winners won and losers lost. Dings and old videogame music overwhelmed my ears but still managed to make me smile. My feet carried me over to the most familiar spot, just to see if that old claw machine remained. The other games had been upgraded. Fewer classics and more spinning gambling wheels, dinosaur shooting games, and jumping electronic-simulated rope. At least Skee-Ball stayed a fan favorite.

The old claw machine from six years ago was still there. The prizes inside were more modern—stuffed pillows with emoji faces—but it was still the same shell of a game. The same knob and button I used to win Adam's wolf ring. The same prize dispenser from which Adam took out the turtle ring he'd won for me to show me that "*This is forever.*" But it hadn't been forever.

When he had seen me looking at the turtle ring, my all-time favorite animal, Adam had put his last token in before I could stop him. Because back then, he did anything to make me smile. Back then, somehow within such a short amount of time, he became my best friend.

"Do you want to play?" Kellan asked.

I shook myself out of the trance. "No." I gave him a small smile. "No, let's go to karaoke."

When we showed up, an elderly woman sang a popular country song while couples aged from four and five to eighty and eighty-two danced on the makeshift dance floor in front of the stage. Kellan pulled me into an embrace, and we swayed around to match the best of them.

A good dancer too? "How do you not have a girlfriend?"

He balanced his head over mine as we moved across the floor. "You tell me."

"You're too perfect."

He chuckled. "No, but please go on."

"You cry at the end of *The Wizard of Oz*."

"Only a monster wouldn't."

"You collect wigs. This isn't even your real hair, is it?" I tugged on his luscious curls, just using it as an excuse to feel them. Thick and wild, but soft and silky. "You...You chew with your mouth open and live with your parents."

"You caught me. A high schooler who still lives with his parents. I'm shameful."

"Admitting it is the first step."

He pulled back just enough so that he could look into my eyes as we danced. "You want to know why I don't have a girlfriend?"

"Please."

"Ever heard the expression 'nice guys finish last?'"

I snorted. "That's a stupid expression."

"Is it? Are you saying you've never been drawn to the bad boy more than the good guy?"

My thoughts went to Adam. "It's easy to be drawn to bad, but bad never changes into good. Accepting that is when someone can find good and appreciate it when it's found."

Kellan leaned his forehead against mine. "And do you think you've found good, Eve Turner?"

His lips were so close to mine. Would he kiss me?

Would this count as my first kiss? Finally official and everything I had waited for?

Loud clapping erupted around us, and we stopped swaying as we noticed the song had ended. I hooted and clapped for the old woman making her way off the stage.

Kellan nudged me. "You should sing."

I rolled my eyes. "No way."

"You said you sing and dance in school."

I was much more of a dancer than a singer. "Yeah, not randomly on a pier in Myrtle Beach."

"This isn't random—it's karaoke. Everyone is singing. You stand out more if you don't. Take it from someone who knows."

"If you know that, why don't you sing?" I prodded him.

"A little something called bad genetics. Even my shower singing is against the law in four states. My voice is medically proven to cause ears to bleed."

He was going to convince me to sing, wasn't he? Those good looks and that funny sense of humor would get me in trouble. I shifted onto my right foot, excited nerves coursing through me. Adrenaline began its slow, familiar pump through my veins at the thought of performing. "You really want me to sing karaoke?"

"Bad enough that I'll buy you another cherry snowball when we leave." His green puppy dog eyes wore me down. "Plus, I'll even call it a snow *cone*, just to keep you and your northern roots happy."

Timeshare Boyfriend

"You had me at another cherry snow cone."

"You'll do great."

I made a worried face at him as I decided to live on the edge for once. Before I gave myself the time to change my mind, I ran over to sign up for a song. After flipping through the many pages of classic songs, one stood out to me.

Five minutes later, I stood on the small stage, holding a microphone in my shaky right hand. The music started; it counted down: five, four... I glanced around the audience, catching Kellan's eye, and moved on to see Adam and a few of his friends standing in the back, watching. Adam. Did he come on purpose to mess with me? Ruin my first date? I tore my gaze away from him and back to the screen. Three, two, one.

Don't think about Adam watching.

"I-I've loved and lost and loved and lost you," I sang.

I couldn't resist looking over again. Adam stood there, in the dim, colored disco lights, watching me with an unreadable expression.

"*But I'm moving on this time without you.*"

My voice was nervous and shaky. My face heated. I tried to keep eye contact with Kellan, but I kept shifting to see if Adam's face conveyed any of what he felt.

"*I've said it before, but this time I mean it,*" I sang, my voice cracking and causing a few people to flinch.

Just stop shaking. Stop shaking. The microphone was heavy and cold in my slick and hot hands. I took a couple of steps around the stage, swaying my nerves out of my body. Letting them go. Letting it all go.

My diaphragm opened. My voice gained momentum. My face portrayed each deep, yearning emotion in the lyrics. Adam continued staring at me. Everyone in the audience stared at me now. This was my song. I felt it as I sang it.

And I sang it to him.

"You pulled me by a string, with scissors in hand,
pushing me down before I could stand.
Like an ocean wave, you crash into me,
but you always pull back.
You always pull back."

I sang about the heartbreak and the heart healing and the heart shredding. The pain and hope and shattered expectations.

My voice rang out. Loud, clear, and powerful. Booming out of the speakers. Soft and strong.

"You said it was the start when you broke my heart.
And maybe I was dumb, but now I'm numb."

Adam shifted but kept my gaze. I could no longer keep up the pretense that I looked at anyone else in the crowd other than him. Everything he did or said challenged me. Hurt me. Lit me on fire. He needed to know.

"Say goodbye to your number one chew toy.
Bye, bye, Mr. Bad Boy."

His eyes were wide.

Maybe because he could tell I meant it. I was finally done.

"You said it was forever, but now it's never."

That younger Adam who had said, *This is forever.* The grown one who had said, *Nothing lasts forever.* It no longer mattered which boy he was anymore. Because I was moving on from both of them.

It was never going to be Adam and Evie. It was never meant to be us.

"*Take a bow; you won.*

I'm done."

9
LOVE THY ENEMIES OR TRY HARD NOT TO

When the song finished, Kellan held his hand out to help me down the steps of the stage. Adam was no longer visible in the crowd.

We walked away from the karaoke and further down the pier to where non-licensed fishermen lined the dock. The air smelled like salt, both from the ocean water and the popcorn stand. The waves crashed harsher than in the light of day, reflecting the moon until the water itself looked like melted silver. We stopped to stand and stare out at the ocean, a romantic end to our date.

"You were amazing," Kellan told me.

"Thanks," I said, insecurity clear in my voice.

He touched my hip, turning me to look at him. "You have something. When you sang...you captivated everyone."

Had Kellan seen me singing to Adam? "I'm not interested in captivating everyone."

"Who are you interested in captivating?"

"You see," I began, placing a hand on his warm, muscular shoulder. "There's this lifeguard who saved my life a couple of days ago and who I technically count as my first kiss even though he doesn't."

"And this lifeguard...is he insanely attractive and funny?"

"I don't want to sound too dramatic, but on a scale of one to a perfect ten, he's an eleven."

He chuckled and moved closer, his arms caging me in until I felt the dock's railing against my back. "Tell me more."

I leaned my head forward. "He seems to think that a kiss doesn't count unless it is initiated by that person and enjoyed from beginning to end."

His gaze narrowed in on my lips. "Sounds like a wise guy."

"He's okay, I guess."

He cracked a smile.

"You know, my goal this summer was to lose my first kiss. I know that sounds silly, but I'm almost seventeen and I wanted it gone. I wasn't focused on it being special or anything like that." I leaned in, preparing for the perfect mouth-to-mouth alignment. "I'm so glad I met you instead of some random guy because now I realize it's not *losing* your first kiss. It's having one, gaining one. It is something to be given, not taken." Certainly not taken by Adam Pierce. "I couldn't ask for a better candidate." I leaned forward. "What are you thinking right now?"

He leaned in. "I hope my mouth is minty."

Boom.

Not boom like it happened. Boom like, all of a sudden, thunder boomed. The clouds opened up and drenched the pier with rain. Screams sounded as people ran for cover, down the pier to where a few shops had awnings. We ran, my cute sandals sloshing in rising puddles as fat drops of rain pummeled us. Squealing with laughter, we ran.

Once we made it under a big, raised beam over a doorway to an ice cream parlor, we stopped running and waited for it to become a drizzle. Summer weather was always crazy.

Kellan's arms wrapped around me as we huddled under the small, dry space. "I guess the rain ruined the moment?"

I looked up at him as we pressed against each other, slick and chilled, yet warm. "I always wanted to be kissed in the rain."

His lips touched mine. Soft and firm and perfect. Nothing but the sounds of heavy breathing and hard rain.

"Minty," I murmured against him, and he chuckled before deepening the kiss.

THE AFTEREFFECTS of kissing in the rain weren't all the movies made them out to be. Now, in the elevator, I stood in a wet dress, shivering.

A ding sounded before the doors opened, and I ventured down the hall to my unit. I rummaged around in my purse for the key when I heard a clearing of a male throat.

Adam and James sat in front of their door in the hallway beside my unit. Adam had an arm around James, who looked sadder than I had ever seen the constantly-smiling boy. Other than when he was stung by a jellyfish.

Adam nodded at me, his expression grim. "You're wet."

Brain, do not record that memory to play it back later. "What's wrong? Why are you guys sitting out here?"

James stared at the ground, and Adam ran a hand through his hair. "We're fine. Just needed some space. A little bro time, right?" James did not answer Adam's question.

"For real, what's going on?" No response. "James, are you okay?"

"*You...and I know...long time...done...fuck you!*" Screaming came from under the door of the Pierce's unit behind the boys.

James leaned further into Adam who stared at me, begging with his expression. "Eve, you should go change into dry clothes. You're shaking."

Were their parents fighting? "Are you sure you don't want me to stay out here with—"

Something glass shattered against the other side of the door, inside their unit. Had Maryam thrown it? James began crying, and my heart broke for them.

I unlocked my door and motioned them inside. "Come on, come in."

"I don't—" Adam cut himself off when James rushed in after me.

Adam entered, passing by me slowly. Our arms touched, mine still slick from the rain, and his hot and spark-inducing. "Thanks."

"Of course. James, do you want to watch a movie?" After pressing power on the remote, I handed it to him. He laid back on the couch looking ready for any kind of distraction.

"Are you sure we aren't disturbing you?" Adam asked, his head moving around the room, scanning for evidence of my parents. I doubted he wanted them to find out about the Pierces fighting.

"They went out on a date night. They do that sometimes." My statement caused Adam's tense shoulders to drop back in a normal position. "They won't be back until late." Another shiver wracked my body through my cold, wet dress.

Adam's gaze focused on me, dropping to my chest. "You should change."

"I'm fine."

"You're freezing. Go change; I'll take care of James."

Once inside the privacy of my room, I let out a deep sigh and shivered yet again. Crossing in front of my mirror to my dresser drawer, I paused and glanced at my reflection. Two points protruded from my dress, my nipples outlined by the wet fabric. Another thing to be embarrassed about in front of Adam. But he hadn't laughed or pointed it out. He had simply told me to change into dry clothes. Kind of nice of him.

I shook my head. Decent—not nice. Adam was not nice.

Shedding myself of the damp dress, I threw on my cherry pajama pants and matching sleep shirt. They were baggy and comfortable, just how I liked them. A couple of minutes passed as I dried my hair with a towel, before a light knock shook my door. Opening it revealed Adam.

He blinked, taking in my sleepwear and seeming to lose his train of thought. "Um, sorry, I... Do you have any popcorn?"

"It should be on the top shelf above the microwave."

"Thanks." He turned but reversed back, entering my room and lowering his voice so James wouldn't hear him. "Thank you for this, I mean it."

"Don't mention it."

He stood there, still not leaving. He glanced around the room, analyzing my unmade bed with unmistakable heat. He rubbed his chin and tore his gaze away from it only to settle on the top of my bedside table, where the turtle ring he won me six years ago sat. I rushed to move in front of him, but he was too quick.

He picked it up and held it in his hand. In his grip, it seemed so fragile. *Like my heart.* "You kept it." He seemed shocked. Of course, he did. He had literally *thrown* his away.

Because I meant nothing to him.

"I wasn't going to bring it," I said quickly. "It doesn't mean anything. It's not like I'm pining after you. I just— I like turtles."

"Still your favorite animal?"

"I tend to be loyal when I choose to like something," I said, and his jaw clenched. "Turtles are my favorite and they will be forever."

I waited for him to comment, "*Nothing lasts forever.*" He didn't. He moved the ring around in his palm, gently.

"I can't believe you kept it," he whispered, his voice one of wonder.

His astonishment angered me. "Yes, well, I did." I strived to think of a subject change. "So, your parents fight a lot?" I winced at my straightforwardness. In my effort to protect myself, I had picked at a problem of his.

He placed the turtle ring back down on my table. "Have been for a while now."

"It bothers James?"

"Not just James."

"Adam." I moved closer to him, and he didn't inch away.

"She cheats on him," he said. "He found out after that first summer here." Is that what made Adam so jaded? Watching his parents fight? "James is my half-brother."

I tried to lessen my obvious shock. "Does he—"

"He doesn't know." His expression hardened. "And he never will."

"Do they treat him the same?"

"My dad ignores him. My mom...is my mom."

"They've been fighting since he was born?" *Six* years. Still, they were together. "At least they haven't—"

"Don't say at least they haven't divorced. Everyone always thinks divorce is the worst option, especially for the children." He sat on the opposite twin bed next to mine, the room designed for two guests. "People should understand that staying together while fighting teaches the kids no relationship lasts forever way more than any separation would. If they were divorced, they could try to find a better option. Instead, they stick together and make everyone around them miserable."

Was I blind? "I hadn't even noticed them fighting."

He gave a dark laugh. "They'd never fight in front of —" he made air quotes. "—*Hannah's family*. Our moms are stuck in a never-ending attempt to impress each other. You don't know how many times I've been compared to the straight-A's Evie."

I shifted my weight onto my left leg and studied my bare feet against the cotton rug. "I'm sorry."

He stood and lifted my chin. "Don't apologize." His

fingers touching my cheek sent tingles through my veins like he was some kind of sorcerer. My breath hitched. Curse my instant attraction to him. Adam noticed and dropped his hand from me. "It's not your fault you're the perfect child," he said.

"I'm not perfect."

His lips twitched into one of those treasured half-smiles. "That's what I keep trying to tell myself."

My breath caught in my throat again. "What does that mean?"

"I'm sorry about last year. I shouldn't have—I was an ass."

"Not just last year," I quipped, and he snorted.

"I'm sorry for the way I've acted." His eyes burned into mine. *So, this is what direct eye contact feels like.* "It was tough, those summers without you." He sank onto the bed again. "When everything came out about my mom and James, a part of me wanted to hate her because she cheated. She broke our family." His fists clenched and unclenched on the bedspread. "But I love my mom...and our family was already broken."

I sank next to him and placed a hand over his.

He snorted. "Look at you. Comforting me after I've been horrible to you." He stared at our hands and shook his head but didn't pull away from my touch. "The truth is, I didn't know what I was going to do when I saw you again that summer. A part of me wanted to act like nothing had happened, like no time had passed, but then I saw you wearing that plastic ring and looking like you expected...like you expected to reunite with your soulmate, and I—I had to push you away before I disappointed you."

Classic relationship phobia. Yet another way Adam matched the antiheroes in my favorite books. "You didn't have to be so rude about it."

"I know. I'm sorry."

I stood from the bed and inched toward the door. This new sincere and honest Adam was too intense, too different from what I had seen before. I didn't know how to handle him. "Thanks."

He stood as well and moved closer. My lungs tightened as he neared me. "You were amazing tonight—your singing," he said.

"I was okay."

"Did he kiss you?"

A shocked gasp choked me. "You're giving me whiplash with these subject changes."

He tilted his head, his gaze so intense on me. Like his vision was a submarine sinking below sea level, sinking through to my very soul. "Do you like him?"

"I thought you didn't care," I said.

Tell me you do care. Tell me you've always cared. Tell me your parents are what stand in our way, but that I make you believe in love again. Tell me you like me, want me. Tell me when I sang, it felt like I sang to you. Because I did.

His gaze was on my mouth. "It doesn't matter how I feel."

I leaned in farther. Just. A little. Closer. "It does to me."

His palms cupped my face, pulling me toward him. Just when he would eliminate all distance between us, he hesitated. His lips hovered so close to mine. We stayed that way for a full minute, neither of us moving. The air around us seemed to turn to the kind of hot haze that gave people in the desert a mirage. Something that seemed so real. But it wasn't.

Even the sounds of his breath gave me more traitor tingles than Kellan's kiss.

Finally, he pressed his forehead to mine, tipping our mouths away so his almost-kiss would never come to fruition. "It doesn't matter that I think you're as close to perfect as a human can be," he whispered.

So, this is what cardiac arrest felt like.

He continued, "It doesn't matter that when you enter a room, I lose all ability to focus on anything else but trying not to talk to you, stare at you, want you." He bent and burrowed his face into my neck, his warm breath marinating me into a tenderized emotional heap. He whispered into my ear, his lips grazing the lobe as he said, "It doesn't matter that each year, I spend three hundred and fifty-one days trying to forget you. It wouldn't work between us."

"*Why* wouldn't it work?"

His deep sigh blew against my collarbone as he pulled his face away from me. "We see each other two weeks of the year, Evie. If we did this, if we got together, the long-distance would poison everything, and you'd hate me afterward. Hell, if the long-distance doesn't make you hate me, I'm sure I'd accomplish it on my own."

"You can't know something wouldn't work without trying it." I hated the way it sounded like I pleaded with him. Again. I was supposed to be done with him. Was I ever going to be done with him?

"Two weeks, then we leave each other. Again and again. It was already hard enough before I knew what it felt like to kiss you." A deep breath shook his chest. "Damn it, Evie. Imagine if we really tried this." His fingers grazed mine, his eyebrows furrowing over his pained expression. "Imagine how much it would hurt when it ended. I'm protecting you."

"You're protecting yourself. I'm not afraid to get hurt, Adam."

"But I'm terrified of hurting you." His lips curled into an agonized smile. "Evie, we're too different. I tried to be flirty and playful by throwing you into the pool, and you nearly drowned. I'm not boyfriend material. I'm not someone who would sing a duet at karaoke. If we started something, do you know how hard it would be?"

I leaned in, saying against his lips so he would hear me loud and clear, "Sometimes the hardest things are worth it."

"But sometimes what's worth it falls apart because of all it takes to keep it together."

James poked his head into my room, reminding me of a gust of winter wind pushing out the heat from a hearth. "Adam, you said you were going to make popcorn."

He stepped away from me. "I'll be right there with the buttery goodness, buddy." Adam nodded at him, and James left my room. Adam turned back to me, holding onto my hand before letting go. *He will always let go.* "It wouldn't work," he said. "Because I don't believe in love."

His aching, lonely words echoed in my ears as he walked out and closed the door. As if that ended our discussion.

I whispered to him, barely audible, "Honey, find your Bible, cause I'm about to make you believe... No, I'm about to make you have faith...in love... Darn it. Stupid wordplay."

10

LOVE LOOKS NOT WITH THE EYES, BUT WITH THE MIND, AND YOU ARE BRAINLESS

The Next Summer, One Year Later

"*On the road again*," Penny and I sang from the back seat of my mom's car. "*I just can't wait to get on the road again!*"

"Think you girls could quiet down?" my father inquired during the instrumental part. "I'm having trouble hearing the GPS."

"Sorry, Dad, but you know people can't whispersing a Willie Nelson song. We have to use our diaphragms."

"It's the law, sir," Penny added.

A week before we were supposed to leave for Myrtle Beach, Maryam called my mom to let her know Adam planned to bring a friend this year to the timeshare. My mom then asked if I wanted to do the same. Five minutes later, Penny packed a suitcase.

By the end of last summer, Adam and I were on good terms. Well, better terms. He talked to me, laughed with me, and hung out with James and me for the last two days before our families parted ways for the drive back home. I had promised to make him love me; but, with less than fifty hours left of our two weeks at Myrtle Beach, my success did not materialize.

But this was a new summer. The summer I'd get him to fall in love with me.

Did I want to be with him? The answer was unclear. But after everything, I wanted to be the one who made him believe in love. The "one." Whether he was my "one" was still in question.

I am owed a summer romance at this point.

Was it pride that made me want him still? Pride and lust?

My mind jumped back to when Adam took James and me to a trivia night at a local seafood restaurant. Adam Pierce, obsessed with documentaries and facts, knew every answer but two. As a straight-A student myself, his knowledge was a turn-on. And when I knew the correct answer for the two questions he didn't? I never knew anyone could look at me like that. Like I was everything.

"Do you think Adam's friend will be hot?" Penny asked me in a low tone so my parents couldn't hear her from the front seats.

I rolled my eyes. "Are hot males all you care about?"

She held up three fingers. "On an ordered list of things I care about, it goes: you, hot guys, cinnamon apple pie." In truth, Penny did not care about boys. She used them when she needed them but otherwise focused on herself, her closeted obsession with comic books, and her friends. Her need to talk about cute boys stemmed from her taking on the "experienced and outgoing" role of our friend group. Her favorite *Sex and the City* character was Samantha. She was truly more of a Carrie.

"Mm, I prefer cherry pie," I said.

"You prefer cherry anything. If an artist ever made a man out of cherries, you'd steal it from the exhibit and marry it."

I scoffed. "I'd at least date him a little first."

We grinned at each other.

"How do you think Adam will treat you this time around? Agreeable or arrogant?"

"I guess we will find out."

THE FIRST THING Penny and I did upon arrival to the timeshare unit was unpack our suitcases and get ready for the first meeting. Due to my lack of sneaky photography skills and his lack of public social media accounts, Penny still had no idea what Adam looked like. This would be the first time she saw what I saw. I needed her to verify why I allowed myself to be strung along for seven years. Not that I had been pining. My junior year of high school had gone well with developing crushes and dating. Still, "boyfriend" was something foreign to me and—whenever said out loud—made me think of Adam.

Sometimes, I also thought of Kellan, but we had fizzled out once the summer ended. Long-distance was no joking matter.

"Don't wear the blue, it'll make it look like you're trying too hard," Penny informed me after I tried on a dress from my suitcase and asked her what she thought.

"I am trying too hard. Why do girls have the pressure of looking pretty while guys just fuss with their hair and throw on half-clean clothes?"

"What are half-clean clothes?"

I explained, "Clothes you wear for part of a day and know you haven't sweat in, so you don't throw them in the wash. But you also know they're not clean enough to be hung with the real clean clothes, so you throw them on the floor until you need a half-day, half-clean clothes outfit."

"That was so specific and wordy, I have chosen never to question your strange habits again." Penny dug through the clothes I brought, then pulled out a black mini skirt. "Oh, I like this."

Two hours later of getting ready and putting on makeup, Penny rushed to the toilet shouting, "Shit!" I followed her in to help hold her hair as she threw up and groaned into the porcelain bowl.

"Are you okay?"

"I get delayed motion sickness." She wiped her mouth and frowned, holding onto the toilet in the form of a possessive bear hug. "That, plus, I'm lactose intolerant and obsessed with ice cream."

"I told you not to get that milkshake when we went to the drive-through."

"Yes, yes, you're smarter than me, I did this to myself, karma is a bitch—" she stopped and lurched again. "Damn it."

I prayed that 1. She would feel better within the next five seconds as we had to leave to meet the Pierces soon and 2. My parents didn't hear her cussing and put her on the Eve-cannot-talk-to-these-people-ever-again list.

Only one of my prayers was answered.

"I know you wanted Penny to come along to dinner, but she'll be fine," my mother said. "There's food for her in the unit, and she can meet the Pierces some other day. We are here for two weeks."

I knew how many weeks we had because it was also the amount of time I had to convince Adam to fall for me. Long-distance hadn't worked with Kellan, but Adam and I only lived three hours away from each other, not eight. Besides, Kellan and I were never in a real relationship, we just continued to text until the hundredth "*How was your day?*" message got boring and repetitive.

Fiddling with the ruffles hanging from my green dress calmed me as my father pulled in and parked at the restaurant. *Time to see him again.* The clack of my sandals against the pavement matched the fast pace of my beating heart.

"The reservation should be under Pierce," my mother told the hostess when we walked inside. The air conditioning must have been on full blast because goosebumps covered my skin within seconds. Some of the bumps might have been from excitement, but most of them were from the fact that a person could build an igloo in this place and it would take years to melt. I struggled to put on my long-sleeved, black shawl before we got to the reserved table.

That's how Adam saw me for the first time in a year: my right arm covered in black cotton, and my left one bare and wiggling to find the hole of the other sleeve. I blushed and nodded at the Pierce family as they stood to hug us or shake hands. Adam moved next to me and held the sleeve up to make it easier. I slid my left arm in and felt much warmer, forty percent due to the shawl and sixty percent due to Adam smiling one of his little half-smiles at me.

"Nice to see you again, Evie."

Little heatwaves shot through me from where he touched me through the sleeve. "And I, you, Adam." *And I, you*? What the heck did that even mean? He laughed, so I forgave my silly mouth and sank into the chair across from him, next to James. "And how are you?" I asked James. "You look taller."

"I am taller. Gonna be taller than you soon," the seven-year-old said, and Adam laughed again. I liked this friendly Adam.

"You won't have to try very hard," Adam teased, and I gaped at him.

"I'll have you know, I'm five foot six."

"More like five-four."

I stuck my tongue out at him, and he groaned. "Where's your friend, anyway?" I questioned. "Your mom said you were bringing a guest."

His eyes darkened as he lost his smile. Did he think I would go after his friend? Penny had already called dibs. "Running late. And yours? Or do you not have any friends to bring?" Instead of sounding insulting, the humor in his tone told me he was just teasing me. For some reason, it even sounded like flirting.

So, that's how it would be. "She's not feeling well, but she'll be better tomorrow."

"Mom said I couldn't bring a friend cause I'm too young," James said, wanting my attention back on him.

I sipped from the glass of water in front of me. "I bet you're super popular at your school."

"I'm my teacher's favorite."

"And you, Adam? How's school going?" Since he was three weeks older than me, we were in the same grade, about to enter our senior year of high school.

He scratched at the table. "Fine."

"Any thoughts about college yet?" My mother popped into our conversation, her "college" ears ringing.

"Not yet." He shifted in his chair. "I have time."

"But not much time," she warned him.

"Yes, ma'am."

How was I supposed to make Adam fall in love with me when my mother lectured him about college choices?

My dad swooped in, not even knowing he saved me. "What's it like being eighteen? Evie still has a few weeks left until she's an adult."

"It's cool. I can skydive and order off infomercials."

"The best and only benefits of adulthood," my dad joked.

"It's a shame you're not eighteen yet," Adam said to me. "We're going to go to some clubs, and I know you love dancing." He was *inviting* me? He would have willingly brought me along? This felt...new.

"You don't have to be twenty-one to get into the clubs down here?" my mom asked, again diminishing my one-on-one flirting time with Adam.

"Not if you let them draw an X on your hand."

"There you are, Taylor." Maryam waved to someone behind me. I assumed it was one of her socialite friends but turned around to see a gorgeous girl my age walking toward our table. How did they know each other?

Timeshare Boyfriend

"Hi, sorry I'm late." She marched over to the opposite side of the table, taking over the seat next to Adam. Her long dyed black hair stopped at her elbows and her nose piercing shined with a small diamond. "Hey, babe." She leaned in and pecked Adam on the cheek.

"Adam, introduce your guest," Maryam instructed.

Adam winced and swallowed but said, "This is Taylor. My girlfriend."

※ ※ ※

WHEN GRINDING your teeth at the dinner table, remember to:

1. Not be obvious about your anger or discomfort.
2. Pop some food into your mouth on occasion in order to lessen the teeth-on-teeth action that will lead to costly dental bills in the foreseeable future.
3. Not stare at whatever is making you angry or upset because staring at it will ultimately lead to more teeth grinding.
4. Not pry for information you know you don't want to know but still want to know anyway.

"So..." I began my covert interrogation. "When did you two meet?"

Gorgeous, raven-haired, nose-pierced girl—also

known as Taylor—glanced over for Adam to answer but ended up answering before him. "I'd say about four months ago."

"Four." Teeth grind. "Four months? Wow, and already vacationing with the family."

"I thought it was rushing things a bit too, but when Adam Pierce begs, there's no way to say no." She nudged him, but he sat as motionless as a gargoyle. Probably thought if he moved, I'd strike. He wasn't super wrong in his assumption.

"And you go to school together?"

"We do. We met in detention if you can believe it," she said.

"I can," I remarked, and she frowned. "Adam has always been a troublemaker."

"Nothing wrong with a little trouble." She nudged him again. He continued studying the menu we had ordered from ten minutes ago.

I leaned in and cupped my hands together. "And who asked who out?"

"Adam asked me to go to a concert with him."

"A concert?" The perfect first date for me, a singer and dancer, but whatever, I wasn't bitter. I was just sour.

"Yup. It was great. We didn't get to talk much then." Was that code for kissing? "So, we planned a second date and still didn't...talk a whole lot." She giggled. It *was* code for kissing. "We've just kept it going, learning new things each day, finding time to talk and stuff." What *stuff*? I wanted stuff.

Curse Penny for giving in to drinking a milkshake, knowing she would be sick later, and abandoning me when I needed her most. I needed her to comfort me. I needed her to shut me up because we both knew how stupid my mouth got when emotions ran high.

"And you'd say your relationship is strong?" I asked.

Taylor gave me a weird look, most likely because it was a weird question. "I'd say so."

"Awesome. Great. That's really great and awesome. Fantastic, really."

My mom let out a nervous laugh at my strange behavior and tried to steer the conversation in a different direction. "Maryam, have you heard of those new sandals—"

"And Adam, you think it's a strong relationship?"

He looked up from the menu, seeming to make eye contact with every person at the table except for me before answering, "Yes."

I let it go and steamed like a bowl of Brussel sprouts throughout dinner. When asked if I wanted dessert, I responded, "Not in the mood for sweet tonight."

Our families walked out together, after paying the bill, and said goodnight. Just before we split up, Taylor leaned into Adam and said, "I'm going to drive my bike back if you want to ride with me." She drove a *motorcycle*? Was Too-Cool-For-School stamped on her forehead as a baby? What a freaking cherry on top of the nose-pierced sundae.

Adam motioned to his parent's car. "I think I'll sit in the back with James this time."

She smiled. How could she not? A high school boy wanting to hang out with his younger brother? Be still my flaming panties. "Okay, I'll meet you back in the room then." She slept in his *room*? His room was designed like mine, so it had a second twin bed, but—but sleeping together in his *room*? Sleeping together in general?

Oh my God. Did they have *sex*? Even in my head, I whispered the word, "*sex*," unable to use full thought volume. I guess I scaled as a ten on the virgin scale.

"See you there," he said.

She leaned in for a kiss. In front of his parents. In front of me. He glanced at me before diverting her aim to his cheek.

"Love you," she said.

My chest tightened. No. No way. No dolphin flipping way. He wouldn't. Not Adam Nothing-Lasts-Forever Pierce. He wouldn't say it back.

"Love you too."

"*I don't believe in love*" my ass.

11
HELL HATH NO FURY LIKE A WOMAN SCORNED; ESPECIALLY, THIS WOMAN

"That asshole," Penny yelled in our room after hearing all the events of the dinner.

"Shh!" I threw a pillow at her, which she caught. "My parents will hear you."

"I hope Adam hears me. Ass. Hole."

"I can't believe I came here thinking I'd make him fall in love with me." My head landed in my hands. "I'm so freaking stupid. Every summer, I show up and I've learned nothing. I'm so stupid."

"You are not. The history between you two is long and complicated. Anyone would be shocked that he has a girlfriend after what he said to you last year."

I threw myself on top of my bed, face first, bouncing up and down as the springs on the mattress creaked.

"I bet she's ugly," Penny said.

"Stop. She is not. She has that biker chick chic look.

She's gorgeous and seems nice. It's not her fault Adam is a jerk."

She snapped her fingers, a classic *I have a great idea* habit of hers. Spoiler alert: her ideas were often not great. "You need a rebound," she said.

"Rebounds are for when couples break up. Adam and I didn't break up. We didn't even happen in the first place." Why did I feel betrayed when no betrayal occurred? Was I that delusional?

"Even if you two were never a couple, you were still emotionally involved for a long time. So, you need a rebound."

"How about no guys for a while in general?" I sighed, feeling sick to my stomach. "What are we doing tonight?"

She hopped onto my bed, hugging me. "Tonight, we're going to watch every Drew Barrymore romantic comedy movie ever made and eat popcorn and ice cream." She pulled back and threw her arms in the air. "Tomorrow night, we're going to sneak into that club Adam told you about and strut in like we're the hottest girls there—because we will be—and dance and laugh and break every heart in the room."

"But ice cream first."

"Ice cream is always first."

"Won't we need fake IDs or something?" I asked Penny as I drove my mom's car to the dance club.

After two hours of prep to become hot and older looking, we headed to the off-limits club around eight o'clock. Penny had contemplated giving herself makeup-induced crow's feet to appear older but backed down. Hotness over pretend aging won every time.

Our outfits consisted of short shorts and shiny low-cut tops. The gold of my top shone in the dim light of the car, so I knew it would light up on the dance floor. In comparison to my sunshine look, Penny was the personification of the night sky. Black with silver details.

"We won't need fake IDs to get into a club. They'll see that we're hot women and let us in. We're good for business."

"I don't think breaking the law is good for any business," I commented.

She shrugged as I parked. "My sister gets into bars all the time."

"She's twenty passing as twenty-one, we're—"

"Almost eighteen. A couple of months away. Same diff."

"Not same diff. We're technically still minors."

"Shh!" She threw a hand over my mouth. "Don't say the word 'minors' too loud. That's a red alert to places like this."

"But we are minors—"

"Shh!" She slapped another hand on top of my lips.

"Damn it, look what you made me do. You need a new coating of lip gloss." She dug into her purse to find a tube of it before we exited the car. "This one is cherry flavored." My face lit up. "Do not eat it," she warned. "I can't be best friends with a flavored lip gloss eater."

"I wasn't going to eat it." I was going to lick it and reapply multiple times during the night.

"We both know how weird you get around cherry things," she said as she wiped the gloss over my puckered lips. "Ah, there you go. Now, we're ready."

"I don't think we can pass as eighteen-year-olds." Still, I followed her out of the car.

"Please, the bouncer will take one look at those babies—" She pointed at my cleavage threatening to pop out of my top. "—and think you're in your twenties."

I crossed my arms, trying to cover them. "That's not how it works."

"Fine, let's talk about being in college then. If he overhears us talking about our master's degrees, he won't question us."

We stopped to stand in the back of the line. "People with masters are at least twenty-two. We are trying to pass for eighteen, that'll just raise suspicion."

"You worry too much, we'll be fine."

Ten minutes later, we stood at the front of the line.

Penny said, using her diaphragm to project, "Wow, my thesis paper is taking up so much of my free time; it's a shock I'm even here right now."

The bouncer glanced over at us, eyes narrowing. The word "big" failed to describe him. His arms were the size of my calves, and I was no skinny girl. He wore black from head to toe; even his socks were charcoal. Intimidating. I shook in my heels. I couldn't play off my shaking as due to the cold, either, because it was a hot eighty-five degrees outside. "Next," the bouncer announced, and we walked over to him.

I chanted to myself, "*Look eighteen. Look eighteen.*" I may have said it out loud by accident because he took one look at us and said, "IDs please."

Penny batted her eyelashes at him. "Are you sure that's necessary?"

He remained unaffected. "Yes."

She fanned herself. "Well, gosh, I'm flattered. Haven't been asked for my ID in years." *You're pushing it, Penny.*

My left eye twitched like it did when I lied. He noticed.

"IDs please, other people are waiting in line."

Penny handed him hers as I rifled around for mine.

He glanced down at hers then raised an eyebrow at us. "This says you're seventeen."

She sighed. "Damn, I was hoping you wouldn't do the math." She then sprinted away, around the building, shouting, "Run for it, Evie!"

"Sorry." I nodded at the bouncer before walking after her.

"What are you doing here? I said you were too

young," a male voice said from the line as I passed. Adam. Taylor hung onto him like her left leg didn't have the power to hold up the other half of her body. "This isn't the place for you."

I took a step closer, challenging him. "I'm not a little girl anymore. I turn eighteen in three weeks." I was tired of having this conversation; of trying to prove to him I was worthy or mature. I was just tired of him. I took another step closer and poked his chest with a finger. *Disregard the tingle.* "And you know what, Adam Pierce?"

His blue eyes turned to storm clouds at my closeness. "What, Evie Turner?"

"It's none of your gosh darn business what I do anymore, because the fact of the matter is, I'm too old for *you*." Strutting away, I walked around the side of the building before stopping and finding Penny.

She leaned against the brick wall, frowning. "I thought it would work. Did he not think we were hot enough?"

"It's not always about hotness. Sometimes, it just comes down to us still being minors—"

She cupped a hand over my mouth, "Would you stop saying the 'm' word?"

"Come on." I tugged her arm toward the car. "I'm sure a drive-through is still open somewhere."

She didn't budge. "We are not going to a drive-through after two hours of getting ready. We are getting into this club."

I rolled my eyes. "There's no chance the bouncer will let us in."

She rubbed her hands together, forming a plan. "Then, we'll just have to sneak in."

"Is it that important that we go to this club? It probably won't even be that fun. Dancing with strangers that seem attractive because of the dim lighting, people spilling their drinks on you, the whole place smelling like sweat and *Axe* body spray..."

"You say that like you've been in a club before, but you haven't. This summer is supposed to be about new experiences and moving on from staying safe. It's time to enter the danger zone."

I shifted my weight. "The danger zone sounds scary."

"Scary is better than boring."

Tips for sneaking into a club:

1. Don't.

If the first option does not work for you, it's time to get creative.

1. Asking to go in just to use the restroom does not work.
2. Acting like you're a bartender is risky and faulty in most cases, considering the bartenders are inside serving drinks and

receiving tips, not taking breaks outside during the peak business hours.
3. Acting like a bartender who stepped out for a smoking break isn't a horrible idea; it just isn't a good idea.
4. Scale the walls like in *Mission Impossible*.
5. Check to see if there is a doggy door you could slip through. Since you are a curvy high schooler and not a toddler on a diet, you'll be looking for a very large greyhound doggy door. Most likely nonexistent.
6. Get mistaken for the dancers supposed to go on in five minutes. This seems rare and cliché, but you'd be surprised.

A guy wearing sunglasses indoors opened the locked door, which we had tried picking five minutes earlier with hairpins and a ballpoint pen, and shouted at us, "Moon and Sun!"

Penny and I pointed at each other with questioning expressions. I did resemble the sun with my golden outfit, and Penny fit the moon description with her black and silver get-up.

"You two are late! We agreed eight-thirty."

Penny rolled with the punches. "Sorry, sir, traffic was killer."

"You're lucky our regular dancers called in sick." Really lucky. Suspiciously lucky, but I'm telling you, it

Timeshare Boyfriend

happens. "Come on, get a move on." He held the door open for us. "The next song starts in two minutes."

Penny grinned and pulled me inside. We trailed after him, down a dark hallway, before we entered the main room. The heavy bass of the song vibrated the walls and floor, the force shaking my body as well. It was so loud, I tapped my fingers over my right ear for a second and checked for blood. My fingers were clean, so the music wasn't as piercing as it felt.

A bright light blinded me before jumping back around the room and hitting different people. The strobe created a hazy adult-feel to the wide room full of dancing and drinking. Otherworldly. One second a girl and guy gyrated, the next second the light came back on to show them making out. A few sofas sat in a small corner of the room where more couples made out. Maybe this place was too grown-up for me. Wait, no. I was a grown-up. Just three weeks until I turned eighteen; this place would be my scene in under a month.

A girl ran in front of us, gagging and running for the bathroom with lightning speed.

This was not my scene.

"Maybe we should—"

"This will be fun," Penny whisper-yelled to me. "He thinks we're dancers. What if he pays us in cash afterward too?"

Dancing was my scene. I lived for moving along to music. If that's what we did, I could handle it.

I didn't want to leave before Adam saw me. He needed to realize I was an unstoppable, full-fledged woman who had no interest in him. I glanced around for the stage designated for our dancing but found nothing other than a small platform next to the DJ for people to request songs.

"Where—"

"Up you go," the sunglasses man said, gesturing to the human-sized cage suspended several feet above the dance floor.

Oh no. Heck to the no. I turned to leave but Penny grabbed my arm. "Relax. I'll be with you the whole time. If you're not having fun after one song, we'll leave. Sound good?"

"What's the holdup?" he asked.

The loud beat matched my nervous heart as I swallowed. "No hold up."

***

"Isn't this fun?" Penny squealed and threw her arms up after we danced to six songs.

I laughed, having the time of my life as well. At first glance, the elevated cages appeared scary, but it provided a personal dance floor for us, no accidental elbowing or unwanted guys copping a feel. We danced and enjoyed each beat to the fullest.

The song changed to a heavy beat, vibrating the cage's bars, which I held onto as I dropped down and pulled myself back up. Glancing at the crowd below me was the mistake I made. Direct eye contact with Adam. Because, somehow, we always seemed to find each other. My first thought: *Where's Taylor?* My second thought: *Why is he looking at me like that?*

"Why'd you stop dancing?" Penny yelled to me over the music.

My arms went over my head as I slid back down the bars, resuming my dance, which now took on a sexier tone as most things did whenever Adam was within a mile radius of me. His lips parted when my legs spread open. *Thank goodness I chose shorts tonight.* His gaze followed my hips as they rocked back and forth with each sound of the bass.

My hands ran down my torso, slow and steady, traveling down my legs as I bent over. The beat got faster, quickening before the drop. His gaze ignited, warming me through the bright, skimpy outfit.

I closed my eyes, letting each note of the music take me somewhere else, somewhere new. Dancing calmed me, energized me. Dancing in front of Adam...lit me on fire.

I looked at him again. He still stared at me, swaying side to side, following my every movement as if hypnotized like a snake with a talented flute player. I whipped my hair back and lifted my right leg, connecting my heel with one of the horizontal bars on the cage. A half split. *See? I'm a woman now.*

His mouth opened. Desire? Surprise? He knew I danced; he just didn't know how well. I lowered myself, bending my knees, arching my back, while keeping my heel caught on the high bar. My leg stretched and throbbed as my foot went over my head.

The song entered the last chorus, so I stood and decided to go for a grand finale. I spun and spread across the bars on my side of the cage.

Adam's gaze followed the finger I trailed down my neck, chest, and abdomen. Down, down, down. His face held a pained expression, and he didn't appear to be breathing. I wasn't either. Anticipation filled my chest, leaving no room for air. I dropped, my butt hitting my ankles as I supported myself on the tips of my toes.

In a classy and tasteful manner, I stuck my tongue out at him and flicked it.

Though I couldn't hear it over the music, I knew he groaned. I also knew I was officially done trying to impress him, my point made clear. I was no little girl, and he would do best not to mess with me.

"Fifteen-minute break," the sunglasses guy yelled to us before opening the cage door.

My legs felt stiff and Jell-O-like.

"I'm going to get us some water," Penny said and bobbed and weaved into the crowd, leaving me.

One minute. That's how long it took for Adam to find me. "What the hell were you doing up there?" he asked gruffly.

I licked my lips, and his gaze dropped to them for a split second. "You were the one watching me like a hawk," I pointed out. "You tell me."

That made him madder. "How'd you even get in?"

"You wouldn't believe me if I told you."

He glanced around the crowd. "You need to leave. I was serious about this not being the place for you."

"And I was serious about me being a grown-up."

He shook his head. "Do you have any idea how many guys were watching you up there?"

"I know of at least one."

He took a step closer, lowering his voice. "Go home. Now."

"You're real sexy when you give orders like that." I flashed him an evil smile. "Too bad I don't care anymore."

"I'm serious. All those guys looking at you—it's wrong."

"Jealous?"

"It's legally wrong."

I put a hand on his chest and teased him. "Yet, it feels so right."

He pulled back. "You've made your point. You're not a little kid, I get it. I've never *not* gotten that. But right now—breaking the rules, sexualizing yourself, and putting yourself in danger just to prove a point—it's the most childish thing I've seen you do."

I stood there, stunned as he walked away from me.

A minute passed before I walked to the bathroom to take a break from the noise and big crowded room.

Looking in the mirror, Adam's words clicked with me. My mascara had rubbed off slightly, leaving dull black spots under my eyes. Under the bright light, my makeup looked like a clown's with harsh blush and contour trying to make me appear older. It was childish of me to feel the need to prove my maturity.

Small tears trailed down my cheeks as I thought about how many times I tried to impress him. All the hours I had spent trying to show him I wasn't the same turtle-ring-wearing girl who couldn't swim. The summers with the unspoken goal: make Adam fall in love with me. How stupid was I? Why did I care—after everything—about how he saw me?

My eyes were red and puffy from crying. After several minutes of quiet reflection in front of my reflection, I left to find Penny. She wasn't by the bar where she said she would retrieve water, so I scanned the area next to it. Instead, I bumped into Adam again.

"Really?" I asked fate. Where was his *girlfriend* during all this?

His upset expression slipped away. "Were you crying?" He raised a hand to my cheek, grazing a gentle thumb over my sensitive skin.

"No. There's just an eyelash in both of my eyes."

"At the same time?"

"Mascara is both a blessing and a curse."

"Damn it, I told you I'm not good at this stuff." He

ran a hand through his hair and let out a noise. "Did I make you cry?"

"You didn't *not* make me cry."

His jaw clenched like he was the one in pain.

In a surprising move, he pulled my body against his and hugged me close. When was the last time he hugged me? Had he ever hugged me? What did that mean? Why did it matter? I wanted to cry again. I said I was over him. I was done. How did a single look from him manage to rewrite my feelings and throw my hesitations in the shredder?

"I'm sorry," he said into my neck, his breath playing with strands of my hair.

"I'm not a little girl anymore." A sensation prickled my eyes. *Do not cry again.* My hoarse voice gave me away. "I can do what I want."

He pulled back, his face close to mine. His cinnamon scent flooded my nostrils, making my eyes water again. "I know. You're confident and kind and funny and smart and—fuck, Evie, the way you dance is..."

His lips were on mine before someone could say, "*you have a girlfriend.*"

12
YOU CAN'T BUY LOVE, BUT YOU CAN BUY HAPPINESS

Heat. Burning heat slid through my veins like a sexy snake as his lips collided with mine. His hands pressed against my lower back, digging me into him like I might never get close enough. Molding me to him; so, if we ever separated, we might still have imprints to prove we were once this close.

This was not just a kiss of lust. He was trying to say something onto my lips. Desperately trying to tell my mouth something that sounded a lot like, "*I love you. I've only ever loved you. It's always been you.*" But the kiss was a lie.

I slapped at his chest until he pulled back. "You have to stop kissing me."

He breathed heavily, his fiery eyes focused on my lips. "You don't want me to?"

I hesitated, and he kissed me again. I claimed his

lower lip for myself, wanting to plant a little flag that said, "Property of Eve," and colonize on the plump, pink surface. After momentarily forgetting where I was, I slapped at his arm again, and he stopped.

"You have a girlfriend," I said.

We stared at each other, trying to catch our breath, when my traitor hands pulled his face back down to mine. His tongue lightly prodded me, and I opened for him on instinct. His fingers spread out on my back.

Why did his embrace always feel so monumental? Like a sunset, his arms around me felt so beautiful. So natural. So temporary.

I pushed him away again. "Stop kissing me."

"You kissed me that time."

"Irrelevant. You have a girlfriend you say 'I love you' to and you're kissing someone else? And you call me childish?"

"I just—"

"You're a cheater," I accused.

He took a step away from me. "I'm not."

"Oh God, I aided a cheater. I'm an accomplice." I cupped my face, trying to hide it from the world. "I'm a horrible person."

He unpeeled one of my hands from my cheeks and held it, placing it against his chest. "You're not. It's my fault. I kissed you."

"What are you doing, going around and kissing other girls when you have a girlfriend?"

"I didn't mean to kiss you."

"Bodies don't just do things on their own."

He took a deep breath and let his hands drop to his sides. "You're right. I'm sorry. I kissed you because I wanted to. You just...you looked so sad."

"So, it was a pity kiss?"

"Of course not. I just forgot—"

"Forgot your loving, gorgeous girlfriend?" Something sank in my chest. "You are a bigger jerk than I imagined. I know you have issues and don't believe in love or whatever, but I thought you'd at least be loyal. But no, apparently, you're just like your mother." I shut up, my eyes widening at what poison my mouth spurted.

His expression hardened as his blue eyes imitated the sea reflecting the night sky. His face turned as stony as a sculpture. He took another step closer to me, caging me against the wall. His fingers wrapped around my wrists, the same way they did in my fantasies.

He lowered my hands to my sides but didn't let go. "My mother is...complicated." He stared down at me, tenser than a millionaire with all his money on a single blackjack game. "I am not and will never be a cheater."

"But you have a girlfriend."

"It's not what you think."

My mind strived to understand how he could A) have a girlfriend, and B) kiss a girl who wasn't his girlfriend, while C) not cheating. My jaw dropped. "You're one of those swinger couples that trade partners? I thought that was only for old couples looking to spice up their sex lives."

He closed his eyes, pinching the bridge of his nose again. "The things you say." He shook his head, the sides of his lips twitching. "No. We're not swingers."

"Then what?" I waited for an answer.

To-Do List:

- Ask doctor for heart medication. Can't deal with another two weeks of Adam Pierce every year without strong heart medication.
- Don't reveal to anyone else that you know the definition of the word "swingers." It embarrasses you and everyone around you. Unless they are swingers, then they may get offended.
- Look up the song currently playing online later, because gosh, it's my jam, and Adam Pierce giving me a heart attack prevented me from dancing to said jam.

"We don't have a label," he explained.

"Don't tell me you're one of *those* guys," I shot back.

"Fine, you want to know the truth?"

"Obviously."

"You see me two weeks every year. You don't see when my dad buys me gifts he knows I don't want at Christmas only to give James nothing. You don't see me come home to my mother crying on the couch then smiling at my dad when he gets home. You don't feel the chill in the winter. Or hear the rain in the spring. Taylor is straightforward. She doesn't want messy emotions. She knows I don't do feelings and what us hanging out means."

"But you told her you love her."

He shrugged one shoulder. "They're just words, Evie."

"No. No, they're not," I said. "Don't ever say those words unless you mean them. Those words are the most important part of life. When you say them out loud, when you feel them, that changes everything." I chastised him so passionately, his eyes widened. "Do not say them unless you mean it," I said.

He blinked, hesitated, and then nodded.

"You have to tell Taylor about our kiss."

"I will."

I gave the room a quick scan. "Where did she go by the way?"

"She seemed to think I was paying too much attention to you."

"Hmm."

He looked down at his shoes. "And talking about you too much."

"Double hmm."

"Sun." The sunglass manager man tapped me from behind, motioning to me. "Break is over. Back in the cage."

I glanced up and noticed Penny, or rather "Moon," up in the human dance cage, waiting for me.

Adam grabbed my arm. "You're not going back up there." At least he said it like a question and not in a demanding, controlling way.

"This is *my* summer. I'll choose what to do with it this year."

"He's still here?" Penny asked me between songs after another hour and a half of dancing in the cage.

Adam sat on a couch across the room, switching between being on his phone and watching us. At first, I thought he stayed to mess with me. Instead, he sat in the corner, giving me space and glaring at any guys who came near the cage to hoot and holler at us.

"I don't think he's going to leave until we do," I said.

"And where's Taylor?" I had filled Penny in on everything about Adam and Taylor.

"I think she left within the first five minutes of coming in."

"He should date someone who shares his interests," Penny commented. "Someone he could actually learn to like and have fun with instead of just hooking up to emotionally escape his parental situation."

I continued moving my hips to the music, ignoring her pointed stare. "I have no more interest in Adam Pierce. I'm over being strung along. Every summer, it's been 'What will Adam think of me this year? Will this be the summer he decides to love me?' I'm done with it. I'm done with feeling like some pathetic, lovesick girl. I'm spending the rest of these twelve days doing what I want, when I want, and not according to some guy."

She laughed. "So, if he broke up with her and confessed his love for you tomorrow, you wouldn't fall at his feet and say, '*yes, take me!*'"

"I'm not a '*yes, take me!*' kind of girl." I dropped into a half split and pulled myself back up. "I'd say something like, '*is that a phone in your pocket or are you just happy to see me— Oh, it is a phone. Cool. Cool, cool, cool. Well, while you have it out, you should add my number.*'"

"That was a very long and accurate description of something you would say."

"I like being honest with myself." I spun. "I know you don't believe me when I say I'm done with him, because I've said it in the past, but I'm sure this time."

"Feelings are not something easy to switch on and off like a light. Trust me, I know."

"But it's not about feelings," I said. "One of the major things pushing us together is just heat. Lust. We almost never have deep conversations or talk about what hobbies we have in common. If you took his looks out of the equation—and the fact that I want to kiss him all day, every day—there's nothing there."

"That's a lot to take out of the equation."

"It'll be easy. We'll just be friends."

She stopped dancing. "You and Adam Pierce as just friends?"

"Yeah."

"With no benefits?"

"None."

She laughed again. "This will be the ultimate summer."

13

IF YOU LOVE SOMETHING, SET IT FREE. OR DON'T, CAUSE LETTING GO SUCKS

The next day, Adam met with Penny, James, and me to spend time on the beach. After three hours, Taylor came out to join us. It was clear she tried to take him away from us. She offered to go with him anywhere imaginable or *do* anything imaginable—which she insinuated in a very loud, seductive voice—but he chose to hang out with us. Thus, the meltdown began.

"Why the hell did I even come down here if you're not going to spend time with me?" she asked right in front of us, putting Adam in the hot seat. The sand was already hot enough.

"I *didn't* ask you to come," he said. "You were the one who wanted two free weeks at the beach. I thought I was doing you a favor."

"I didn't know about *her*." She glanced at me. I glanced behind me. Behind me was just an umbrella.

"We could be out having fun and instead you're hanging out with your boring little brother."

"Excuse me?" Adam's voice boomed. It echoed over the mounds of sand, seeming to ping off each sharp seashell and rumble the ocean waves. No matter how much of a jerk Adam could be, he *never* let anyone mistreat his younger brother. It was part of the reason why Adam and his father no longer had a relationship.

"What did you just say?" Adam asked Taylor.

James was Adam's Achilles' heel. She had just gone for the heel. "Oh snap," I whispered to Penny.

Taylor began backtracking. "I love James, but he gets in the way. You know that."

Adam's face was chiseled stone. "Apologize right now."

Taylor glanced from Adam, to James, to me. "I didn't mean—"

"James is amazing," I said.

James stopped kicking sand; his shoulders lost a bit of tension. He smiled a small smile at me. Smaller than a smile should be. All because of her.

"It's true," Penny added. "James is my new best friend. Sorry, Evie."

"Offense taken but forgiveness given," I responded, and we inched closer to where James sat, trying to surround him with support.

Taylor's pale face disappeared behind dark red splotches. "James is a great kid, but he's a kid. You don't actually enjoy spending time with him—"

"Leave," Adam said. "Now."

She frowned and scratched the back of her neck as she avoided eye contact. "I'll see you back in the room later."

"No. You have your motorcycle. Go home."

She scoffed. "You're breaking up with me?"

"We were never a real couple."

Everything seemed to boil over inside her. She flashed her teeth like an aggressive mammal. "You don't know what a real couple is."

Adam flinched at her words.

"You know I love you, right?" I asked James, who still stared down at his lap, absorbing all the things that had been said.

"Yeah," he said and took my hand in his. "I love you too."

When I glanced over at Adam, he stared at us, but it resembled what he might look like while staring at the sun. Squinting, like my closeness with his brother was an overwhelming bright light. Like there was nothing else he would rather go blind watching.

OVER THE NEXT FEW DAYS, Penny and I saw more and more of Adam. Whenever we invited James to hang out with us, Adam took the invitation as a Pierce plus one. We went to the beach, pool, and mini-golf together. At first, I thought he was lonely from losing Taylor, but he genuinely enjoyed our time together. It became harder to not think of him; so, instead, I forced myself to friend zone him in my mind. Did my mind listen to *"He's just a friend"* while my eyes devoured his bare muscular chest out on the beach? No, but it did its best.

Adam seemed to enjoy our budding friendship, and his cold exterior melted bit by bit each day. Still, warmer Adam remained bossy Adam.

"You're doing it wrong," he said after I hit the neon pink golf ball with my putter.

I wiped some sweat from my chest and pretended not to notice the way his gaze dipped to follow my action. Outdoor mini-golf in ninety-degree weather may not have been the best idea. "I believe the object of the game is to hit the ball with this club as hard as I can until it goes in the hole," I said.

He blew out an amused and frustrated breath, a classic dealing-with-Eve practice of his. "You're supposed to get the ball in the hole with the least amount of strokes possible. You're hitting it so hard, it bounces off the back and rolls all the way back down to where you started."

I nodded, giving him a *your-point-is?* expression. "The longer it takes me to make it into the hole, the more time I spend having fun. More bang for my buck." The romance reader inside of me waited for him to say something like *I'll give you a bang*, but I pushed the naughty thought away. *Just friends.*

"You're taking so long that Penny and James left us

to keep playing the course." He gestured to them three holes ahead. Their silhouettes were all I could make out, but I recognized them based on the bright orange cap James wore. "They like you more than I do, so it's saying a lot for them to abandon us after the first three holes," he remarked.

I nudged his shoe with the bottom of my putter. "You like me. Don't act like you don't. You would've left with them to move on if you didn't."

"I still might." He nudged my sandal with his putter in return. Playful and friend-like. The rubber end of his club tapped against my ankle and trailed an inch up my leg before falling back to the green-felted ground. The small action sent my heart into palpitations. Not friend-like. "I wanted to finish before dinner time," he commented.

I frowned, glancing at my red, cherry-themed watch. "It's two o'clock in the afternoon."

He nodded, giving me a pointed look. "Exactly."

I blew a stray piece of my thick, dark hair out of my face. "Whatever, I'm not that slow." I hit the ball. It skipped right over the hole and rolled to the opposite side of the felt again. "Darn it."

He stepped closer to me. "You're not even holding the putter correctly."

I glanced down, seeing no error in how I gripped it. "There's no correct way to hold this thing. You're making that up."

He placed a hand over mine on the club and positioned himself behind me. His chest touched my back, and I jumped away from him as raw lust shot through me at the small touch. The man smelled like cinnamon buns for goodness' sake. How was I supposed to think of him as *not* delicious? *Friends don't think of other friends as "edible,"* I reminded myself.

"Whoa, what do you think you're doing there, buddy?" I asked.

He sighed. "I'm going to teach you how to putt the ball so we're not spending hours on a thirty-minute course." He moved behind me again, but I stepped to the side, avoiding him. His touches made my self-control melt to the green-felted ground.

"I've been hitting it for half an hour now; I think I know how."

He leaned on his putter, looking sexy and masculine as usual. "Do you really want to be here for three hours just because you don't have the patience to learn a golf trick?"

"I have patience."

"Don't you want to beat me at mini-golf someday before we're old and decrepit?"

Grouchy, I mumbled, "I'll beat you in golf today, how about that?"

He chuckled and stood behind me. His arms wrapped around me, and his hands covered mine on the putter. "First, you need to put both hands on the grip. You keep having one down on the shaft and it's throwing you off."

I swallowed. "Shaft?"

He missed the innuendo working through my dirty mind. "The stick part."

"Right, of course."

"You also keep hitting before aiming, so make sure you align the head with the hole." Align the head with the hole? I couldn't be the only one with my head in the gutter. He moved my hands over the putter, placing both on the grip and doing a practice swing. "That's right; hold it nice and tight, aim, align the head." He removed one of his hands from mine and moved behind me to press down on my lower back. "Now, bend at the waist."

"Is this for real?" I asked before following his guidance.

With me bent over, his groin was now aligned with my backside. Dizziness and heat suffocated me at this realization, and I wobbled a bit, falling forward toward the ground. He caught me just in time, his hands squeezing into my hips, supporting me. I pushed my back against him, stabilizing myself, and he groaned when his groin bumped against me. I groaned too. Well, it came out more like a moan.

He cursed.

Yeah, I had definitely moaned. He cleared his throat. "Um, that's the correct stance." He stepped back from me. "Go ahead and try it. Aim and swing, not super hard."

My swing isn't the only thing that's hard. Shut up, Evie!

Just friends. Just friends. Amigos. Copains. Freunde. The word "friends" in other languages I needed to learn.

I aimed the head of the putter with the line leading to the hole and swung. It bounced off the back wall and rolled slowly, too slowly, over to the hole. Five more centimeters. Two more centimeters. It stopped, right in front of the gosh darn, cursed hole.

We stared at it for a couple of seconds, willing it to move, but it stayed still. Adam stepped over to it and gave it a soft nudge with his shoe into the hole. It rolled in with a joyous bouncing sound.

I jumped up and down. "I did it."

"You did." His smile? There aren't words to describe it. Pure pride. Pure...admiration? Almost like he could have loved me in that moment—if he was a boy who believed in love. But he was too afraid of feelings.

We walked over to the next hole, which appeared much more complicated as it had dips and bridges. "I should go pro." I flipped my long, wavy hair, feeling good about myself. "I bet I can beat you now."

He tilted his head; that grin took up so much of his face. "What would you bet on that?"

My shoulders lifted. "What would you want?"

Did his eyes turn molten or was that a trick caused by the pesky sunlight? "I get the ball into the hole with fewer strokes than you, and I win a kiss," he said.

I held up a finger in protest. "Friends don't kiss."

"I suppose."

"And we're friends."

He was *still* smiling. Adam Pierce. *Smiling*. "I suppose."

"And you have a girlfriend."

He shook his head. "Not anymore. And she was never my girlfriend."

"Right, she was just your 'hook up' buddy." *Wow, try saying it with a little less jealousy, Evie.*

"Actually, we never..." Adam trailed off. His smile fell, leaving him looking uncomfortable. "We both wanted distractions. I specifically wanted a rise out of my parents. Taylor's nose piercing and tattoos sadly did not spark any reaction in them. My dad already doesn't believe in my future. My mom..." He blew out a breath. "The relationship was a bit of an 'act.' But you were right when you said I shouldn't say, um, those three words unless I mean them. I need to be better. I'm ready to try." Classic Adam: changing into a better man after I'd sworn off him.

"You don't regret breaking up with her?"

"If she was here, I wouldn't be able to hang out with you guys." He twisted his putter around. "And I have a lot of fun with you guys."

"All of us?"

"A lot of fun with *you*," he clarified.

My heart melted, thirty percent due to the ninety-degree sun beating down on us. "Yeah?"

"More fun than I've had in a while." We grinned at each other for a minute before he moved closer to me.

His eyes burned into me like jellyfish stingers wrapping around my internal organs. Making me shiver. "Still interested in betting against me?" That sharp, spicy, and sweet cinnamon scent of his mixed with the humidity in the air, warming me as inch by inch he eliminated the distance between us.

"We shouldn't kiss if we're trying to be friends. It'll confuse us." It would confuse *me*.

"You're the one who acted so sure about beating me," he teased, but his expression hinted at something deeper, a yearning that matched my own. "Swallowing your words before we even begin?"

"The only thing I swallow is—" I cut myself off, realizing my words sounded sexual.

He bit his lip, appearing a bit tortured. I swore his body emitted rays of heat just as penetrating as the sun. "Please finish that sentence," he begged. "Please."

Adam Pierce begging? Scorching hot.

"What do I win if I beat you?" I asked, trying to stay focused on anything but the fact that I was close to tackling him onto the ground and making out with him until both our faces fell off.

"Two kisses," he suggested.

I fake glared at him, but he saw right through me. "I'm serious," I said.

"I'll buy you two scoops of cherry vanilla ice cream," he offered. By his expression, he knew he had me right where he wanted me. My cherry obsession was no laughing matter.

"Fine," I agreed. "I'd do just about anything for a cherry-flavored dessert."

"That is incredibly important information that I have just stored forever in my brain."

I laughed, and he placed the ball down on the small circle mark.

He flirted again, "I look forward to kissing you."

I stumbled over my words. "I look forward to licking you—licking the ice cream." His gaze stayed molten, so I clarified again, "Eating the ice cream."

He took in a deep breath and bent at the waist. His putter took two practice swings; aligning the head with the trail he wanted the small neon golf ball to travel.

This particular hole was octopus-themed and had "tentacle" bridges overlapping the green felt. The obstacle consisted of hitting the ball over one of the few bridges that led to the hole in the octopus's mouth. Dips in the felted ground made that harder to do. Aim and concentration would be most important during this hole due to all the little details that could cause a two-stroke hole to become a six-stroke hole. Every stroke counted in this bet.

Stop thinking of Adam and stroking!

Adam pulled his arms back, ready to swing, when I yelled, "Oh look!" to distract him. I shouted it prematurely, however, because he stopped just before making contact with the ball to glance over at me.

He narrowed his eyes, knowing I tried to distract him and make him lose. "I thought you hated cheaters."

"I don't know what you're talking about. I'm not cheating. Besides, it's different when it's a mini-golf game versus a relationship."

He went back to focusing on his shot. Meanwhile, I came up with an idea. Moving in front of him—out of range so my body didn't block him, but in eyesight, so my body could at least distract him—I tugged my tank top down a bit and bent to see how he lined up the putt. His eyes moved from the main tentacle bridge over to where my cleavage strained through my tight top. I wiggled a bit for his added benefit.

"Any time now, Mr. Pierce."

He growled. *Growled.* My brain stored the information that calling him mister got a positive, animalistic response. "Stand behind me, Evie," he commanded. "You're distracting."

"Who? Me?"

"Behind me. Now."

Yes, sir. As Adam refocused on the ball, I moved behind him and wrapped my arms around him. Molding my front to his back, I pressed my palms on his chest. *Hello, rock-hard pecs.*

He tried aiming again but his hands shook.

"Just concentrate," I whispered to him as he slouched over to aim. He froze in his bent position as my fingers trailed down his muscled stomach to the waistband of his shorts.

He hit the ball too hard, and it bounced off the ridge and rolled further away from the hole.

I laughed. It was almost too easy.

"You think that's funny?" He turned, towering over me. Our toes touched—such a small detail, but one that made heat bloom in my chest. He rasped, "You think teasing me and turning me on just to distract me is funny? You have no idea what you do to me."

A quick glance at his shorts told me what I did to him. I had a healthy fear of snakes but this one had my name written all over it.

"You want to know how many times I replayed our kiss?" he asked. "Or how about how much I want to throw you on this felt right now and show you everything I've fantasized about this past week? This past year?"

My gasp seemed to give him more confidence.

His warm, long fingers stroked down my shivering arms. "Do you know how many times I replayed you strutting around in that pink cherry bikini last year? Or the number of erections I had in the span of those two weeks, trying to avoid you? I constantly worried about passing out because all my blood was in my dick. And when you answered those questions at trivia, I've never been harder in my life. It was torture, not being able to touch you. And knowing you were going on dates with that lifeguard when you should have been with—" He stopped.

One of his hands took the club out of my grip and moved it away. I tried to gain back my focus, but ignoring Adam was a skill I had yet to master or even rank beginner. My body and soul quivered at his mere proximity.

"You think I don't notice the way you look at me? You don't notice the way I look at *you*," he said.

My gaze fell to my neon ball sitting on the felt by its lonesome. "This, uh, distracting me doesn't help you win the game if I'm not hitting the ball."

He stared at me for a minute, breathing his sensual cinnamon scent against my face. I inhaled it in covert puffs like it was an illegal drug and I was scared of getting caught.

"I'm not playing games," he said. Before I could ask him what he was playing, he picked up his ball and began walking away. "You win this hole."

14

PARTING IS SUCH SWEET SORROW, BUT NOT AS SWEET AS IGNORANCE

"Stop worrying," Adam instructed me. My rapid heartbeat did not listen. "I've never met someone so afraid of horses."

I scoffed and inched further away from the majestic beasts. "Probably because horses can smell fear, so they would have taken all the other horse-fearing people out with their monster hooves."

"Snuffed 'em out like a light," seven-year-old James said, and we all looked at him with wide eyes.

Even the worker who prepared a few horses for us to ride appeared surprised.

Penny's one dream activity for our vacation was to ride horses on the beach. Luckily, we had found a place close by our timeshare building that offered discounts for group rides.

"That was—" Penny began but I cut her off. "How do you know a phrase like that?"

Adam placed a hand on his brother's shoulder. "I'm sure it's nothing—"

"Sometimes, Adam lets me watch movies with him. I think it was in it."

My eyebrows rose as Adam fidgeted in the sand. "What movies does he let you watch with him?"

"Adam has watched *The Godfather* thirty-three times."

Penny laughed but I was too busy staring at Adam's cute blush. "That's nothing." Penny waved it away. "Evie has watched *The Princess Bride* at least sixty times."

"It's indisputably the best movie ever made," I remarked.

"*The Princess Bride* has horses in it," Adam pointed out. "Are you scared of those?"

"A lot of people don't realize this, but the horses were added to up the horror aspect of the movie."

Adam smiled. "You should become a politician."

"Because I'm such a natural-born leader?"

"Because you're a liar." His amused smile, one of the rarest to see out of its natural habitat, blinded me. "Plus, how can you be afraid of horses when there are so many other scary things in that movie?" he questioned. "The sea monster, the rodents of unusual size..."

My mouth dried up. From pure lust. "You—You've watched it?"

"Of course." He shrugged as if him having watched my favorite movie of all time had not just turned me on more than anything else ever had. "It's a great movie."

Breathe. Breathe. Just remember to breathe.

"Uh oh." Penny waved a hand in front of my face. "I think you just lit her loins on fire."

"What are loins?" James asked.

Adam and I shouted, "*Nothing!*" Penny laughed.

"Will it just be the three of you then?" the worker asked, eyeing me with concern. "The discount only works with parties of four and over."

"Don't worry," Adam reassured her. "Eve is going to ride the horse."

"In your dreams." I took a step back. "You'd have to tie me up to get me on that thing."

Adam replied, "I've tied you up in my dreams before so—"

Me: "What?"

Adam: "What?"

Penny: "WHAT?"

"Pretend I didn't just say that," he said, blushing again. God, why did the pink coloring of his cheeks make me want to lick him? "Please."

No can do, bucko. That memory was stored forever.

"The next group arrives in twenty minutes, so I need everyone to choose a horse and get started," the worker said.

We walked closer to the stall holding four horses. Two black, one white, and one tan.

"I want that one!" James pointed at the tan one, but Adam shook his head.

"Evie should pick first." His concern for me made a

few of the knots in my stomach untangle. A few.

"Which one do you find the least scary?"

"It's hard to say. They are each terrifying in their own way."

"Cherry is the gentlest," the worker informed us and gestured to the white one. I could not deny that after the mention of the name "Cherry," I became a bit less nervous about riding it.

"This is a sign." Adam nudged me. "You love cherries."

"Why is she called Cherry?" I asked.

The worker shifted her weight. "Well, it's a bit of an inside joke. She has a genetic disorder which means she wasn't good to breed with, so she's never..."

Cherry—as in unbroken hymen—as in virgin. "I'm going to ride a virgin horse?"

Adam and Penny laughed hysterically behind me. For a full minute.

Everyone got up on their horse, a worker assigned to each one, without any difficulty. Except me. If sweating was a competitive sport, I would have won a gold medal. The worker assigned to me tried to help me up onto the horse, but her grip on my skin was slippery. I settled back down on the ground after a few attempts.

"Breathe, Evie," Adam said, and I realized I had closed my eyes. I opened them and saw that he walked his horse to be beside mine.

The sight of him on a horse may have been enough to get me over my phobia. Mmm. I did not read a lot of cowboy romances, but *yeehaw*. All he needed was a cowboy hat and a sheriff badge. No, wait. No badge. He would be the bad cowboy who followed his own laws. Laws he made up after losing his first wife in a dust tornado. He had named his black horse after her and sworn against love. Little did he know, a bar maiden would get his heart pumping again—

"Evie?" Adam questioned, and I jumped a bit, alarming my virgin horse. "Did you blackout? What just happened?"

"Nothing." To do: give western romances another try. I still stood on the ground next to my horse, unable to get on. "I don't think I can do this, Adam."

I waited for disappointment or pushing, but neither came. He said, "Then, don't." I tilted my head, and he continued, "Don't feel pressured to do things you don't want to do. This is meant to be fun."

"But I want to do it. I'm just scared. It's…tall."

"The only thing to fear is fear itself."

I narrowed my eyes on him. "You've officially become annoying."

"Everything worth it in life is scary, Evie." He smiled again. "If you get on that horse, I promise to ride right next to you the whole time, okay?"

"And if I fall off and get trampled, you're okay with being sued?"

"I have a horse lawyer on call for this exact reason," he joked again. There was something addictive about hearing Adam Pierce joke. Or seeing him blush. Or being near him in any capacity.

"Okay." The worker helped me up onto the saddle. I bit back a shriek of alarm when the horse started trotting. Light. Slow. Terrifying.

Adam followed right next to me only a few feet away. He never broke eye contact.

"Distract me."

"Horses have two hundred and five bones."

"One, why would you choose to distract me by telling me a horrifying fact? Two, how would you know such a specific and horrifying fact?"

"One, that fact is not horrifying. It's about bones. That's like saying you're scared of yourself because there's a skeleton in your body right now. Two, I know a ton of facts about horses because I saw a documentary on them."

"One, that skeleton statement just blew my mind. Two, what is it with you and documentaries?"

"One, I like documentaries because I like learning things. Knowledge means fewer surprises in life. Two, let's stop doing this whole number thing. It's getting old."

"Fine, distract me with more horse facts."

"Horses can sleep lying down and standing up. A horse's eyes are bigger than those of other land mammals. A horse was cloned for the first time in 2003."

"Are you choosing scary facts just to mess with me?"

Instead of continuing to talk, he began humming. He hummed a familiar tune, but I could not place the song in my head. He hummed it with a calm look on his face as he watched me, and it relaxed me. I did not freak out again until Cherry's front leg sank a bit deeper into the sand than her other steps. My arm shot out and Adam's did the same until our hands met and interlocked.

We gazed at each other in alarm, maybe shocked that both our reactions had led to reaching for each other. But he didn't let go. Even though my sweaty hand was slippery and a challenge to hold onto under the summer sun, he didn't let go.

That was how I spent my horse ride on the beach.

Holding Adam's hand and listening to his humming.

THE DAYS PASSED as a blur of fun, laughter, and Adam. He stuck to James and me like glue on a kindergartener's macaroni art project. I pretended to not enjoy every moment of it. I did, however, enjoy every moment of it. Though the heat between us proved hard to ignore, the developing friendship excited me. I had missed the thoughtful, sweet, and funny Adam I had known and seen glimpses of over the years. His defensive walls fell before me, just how I had wished they would every previous summer. A question popped into my head of how long his walls might stay down.

We even did a movie night in his living room and watched *The Godfather*. "What do you like so much about this movie?" I had asked him.

"*The family loyalty.*"

"*But people keep getting betrayed.*"

He seemed a bit sad as he replied, "*Maybe it also helps serve as a reminder too.*" That he expected to be betrayed?

The boy was complicated.

Later in the week, Penny walked and talked with me on the beach, as we approached the dock where the Pierces were fishing. I had offered to join them, but Penny opted for more time in the hot tub.

"Wow, Adam sure doesn't like his dad, huh?" Penny pointed to where Adam sat, hunched over by a fishing pole as his father talked in his ear. "He looks upset."

"Evie," James yelled when he saw me close to the dock. Adam's tense back relaxed when he turned around and waved.

"Have fun with your boys," Penny said and left me as I walked up the steps and down to the deeper water section where the Pierce men stood with fishing rods. The second Mr. Pierce saw me, his expression brightened.

"I didn't know you liked fishing, Eve," Mr. Pierce said.

"No one *likes* fishing," Adam commented and moved to be closer to me. Our arms brushed.

His father pressed on. "With you here maybe someone will actually catch something today." His comment made Adam's eye twitch. "Do you know how?"

"Seems pretty easy." I shrugged. "Worm, hook, fish."

Mr. Pierce gathered his stuff and inched away from us, sitting on a bench. "Ah, sweet ignorance."

"You can use my rod." *Shut up, dirty mind!* Adam held the fishing instrument out for me.

"Pretty," I said and bent down to touch some of the fancy bait art that sat in a box with extra wire. "These would make adorable earrings."

"What—" Adam trailed off, his hot fingers skimming over the flesh of my lower back where my camisole rode up. "—is that?"

I frowned with confusion then remembered the day before, Penny had convinced me to get a temporary tattoo. I had chosen a bleeding heart. "You like it?"

"Too much." He pulled my shirt down so it was covered again. "I know what I'll be dreaming about tonight."

My eyebrows shot up. Holy Guacamole.

"Adam, quit messing around," Mr. Pierce said.

"He's not messing around. I'm distracting him," I responded, switching the fishing rod into my left hand. The movement caused the hook to scratch my leg, deep enough to make it bleed. "Shoot."

"I'll get a Band-Aid." James hustled to a little first aid bin.

Mr. Pierce looked disappointed. "Careful not to get any blood on that rod. It's an expensive one. I bought it when Adam was younger, but he dropped the hobby just like all the other ones he tried."

A soft growl came from Adam. "I never said I wanted to fish. You said I wanted to fish."

"You said you wanted to play an instrument, wanted to be a Boy Scout, wanted to learn how to climb rock walls. Think of all that money down the drain just because you can't choose something and stick with it."

"I like learning things," Adam defended himself, but his voice sounded hollow. Weak.

His father scowled at him, making my heart hurt. "You're going to college soon, what are you going to do? Flip flop between majors and never graduate?"

"I thought you already had my major picked out for me, Dad."

"The problem with the younger generation is that it has no sense of loyalty." Mr. Pierce criticized him. Adam seemed to shrink into himself with each word his father said. "You drop things the second you lose interest. It's time to grow up and take responsibility."

I inserted myself into the tense father-on-son conversation. "Isn't it better to have many interests than none?" I asked.

Mr. Pierce's eyebrows arched above the top of his

sunglasses. Shocked a teenage girl dared to question him?

Something flashed over Adam's expression too, but I didn't spend time deciphering it. Instead, I continued, "Adam is a high school boy obsessed with documentaries. That's *miraculous*. If I have a son someday, I hope he knows a million random facts like Adam. Just because someone likes a lot of different things doesn't mean he can't be passionate and loyal to one thing. It just means he has multiple passions in life. And that's amazing. Because life is meaningless without passion."

Mr. Pierce chuckled darkly, sounding like a villain from a *Disney* movie. "Oh, Eve, that's sweet. Sorry to inform you, but life is about work. Clock in, clock out. It's not about knowing useless trivia."

Growing angry now, I fought the blush in my cheeks as I rose my chin high and told him, "Knowledge is never useless."

"It is when it doesn't make you any money," Mr. Pierce joked but it unsettled me even more.

"Is money all you're passionate about?" I asked.

Again, his dark eyebrows rose over the rim of his sunglasses. "Money makes the world go round. It's why we're lucky enough to have two weeks right on the beach each year. Money should be everyone's biggest passion."

"Interesting." I turned to Adam, half-expecting him to be angry and embarrassed at my questioning his father. Instead, Adam stared at me with wide eyes and a shadow of a smile. He had one emotion painted on his face: awe. "And Adam, if I asked you what you are passionate about, what would you say?" I asked.

Adam seemed to glow—with happiness or radioactivity, I couldn't tell which, but he glowed under the lowering sun as he replied, "I'm passionate about my family."

His family. James and Maryam.

A small smile claimed my face as I nodded. "I'd say Adam has his priorities straight, Mr. Pierce."

Again, Adam shot me *that* look.

The one that made him appear in love.

But Adam Pierce did not believe in love.

THE NEXT NIGHT—ON the last night of the timeshare—Penny and I sat on the sand under the moonlight, while James and Adam threw shells into the dark waves and found sea crabs.

"Thank you for inviting me," Penny said, leaning her head on my shoulder as we watched the boys. "I've had a lot of fun."

I smiled. "Me too."

"You know, Adam isn't that bad." She pushed her shoulder into mine. "I think he's grown in the past two weeks."

A deep sigh escaped me. "I'll believe it when I see him next year and he doesn't act like I'm infected with some horrible disease. I get whiplash from his attitude changes." Still, she was right. I would miss this summer's Adam. "And I meant what I said before, we're just going to be friends. I don't want that with him anymore. I want something easy, not complicated."

"Easy doesn't make someone's heart race," Penny pointed out like the wise old woman she was not.

I stood, my right foot sinking into the soft sand as I shifted my weight. "My heart has been through enough."

"Evie, come help us," James shouted for me to join them.

Penny smiled and shooed me toward them. "Go."

James and Adam both held three shells in their sandy hands. "We're going to make three wishes. You have to, too."

I laughed, remembering back to when Adam made his three wishes after our first summer together. He'd wished for us to see each other again, for me to like him, and for him to kiss me the next time he saw me. Two of his wishes had come true. I picked up three shells from the sand and washed them off in the water.

James did his first, wishing for his favorite cartoon show to be made into a live-action movie (a classic mistake, as the live-action movies never measured up to the cartoons), for a jetpack, and an easy math teacher in the fall.

James tugged on my arm. "You next."

I threw one. "I wish...for good grades." *For my heart*

to get over Adam. I threw another. "I wish to get into a good college." *For a friendship—without benefits—with Adam.* I threw the last one. "I wish for life to be less tricky." *For an easy, uncomplicated love.*

Adam stared at me for what seemed like a solid minute then stepped forward. The ocean water lapped at his feet as he tossed all three in at once. "I wish to become worthy."

James slapped at him. "You just used all three wishes on that."

He glanced at me with a small smile on his face. "Then maybe it's sure to come true."

15

IF YOUR LOVE COMES BACK TO YOU, SHE'S YOURS…UNLESS SHE'S TAKEN

The Next Summer, One Year Later

"BABE, *she's not going to find out about us. I need you. Evie won't even touch me. You're the one who knows what I like. She doesn't even know what she's doing. She's a virgin prude. I'm so pent-up. Come over. I want to remember what a good kisser feels like.*" That was part of a voicemail I received three weeks ago from my drunk and—apparently—cheating boyfriend. He left the voicemail as a mistake, drunkenly trying to call some other girl.

My first ever boyfriend called me a virgin prude and a horrible kisser. The boyfriend who spent seven months during school telling me, "You look so pretty today," "Let's go out tonight; I want to show you off," and "Evie, I think I love you."

A liar.

All men! Liars!

My father seemed offended by my new attitude toward the Y chromosome. I did not care how he felt about it, because he was a man and I was officially done with men. Fictional men, sure, no hard feelings toward them; I was not about to empty my bookshelf of the many romances. But real men? Done!

It was a pattern. A trend I needed to shatter. *Evie falls for boy. Boy says he likes her too. Boy wakes up one day, seeming to be a different person with no interest in Evie. Evie is heartbroken and left confused and with broken pride.*

Was it so easy to fall out of love with me? To lose interest? *It's just like with Adam.*

My first boyfriend, John was supposed to join me at the Myrtle Beach timeshare before he left that revealing voicemail, which I saved on my phone to replay whenever I felt weak. John the Cheater was supposed to come to South Carolina with me and hold my hand and prove once and for all that I was over Adam Pierce.

Instead, I returned to the beach emotionally damaged and lonely. Great.

Did I still remember Adam's wish to be worthy? Of course. My dreams liked to replay it time and again, but I was done with men now. Done with being vulnerable and being the one always more in love.

Nothing lasts forever. Now, I believed him.

In a month, I would start college, so I didn't need a relationship anyway. I did, however, need some relief. John and I had not gone very far in our physical relationship—evidently, I was a "prude"—so I had been devouring romance novels like boxes of chocolates, which I had also been devouring a lot of recently. Hormones and chocolate went well together. Who knew? Everyone knew.

"Evie, it's time," my dad announced through my door.

Seeing Adam again meant nothing, of course. Nervousness? Psh. He should be nervous! Because this was a new Evie who was done with letting anyone string her along.

This summer, I was not the pathetic, lovesick teenage girl.

I was eighteen, I had ended my first relationship, and Adam Pierce was just another Y chromosome I had no time for.

THE RESTAURANT we went to lacked the finesse of earlier years, which was fine with me as I craved some good chicken tenders more than a blue cheese and carrot salad. I raised an eyebrow at the fact that when we arrived, the hostess had no evidence of a reservation under the name Pierce. Lucky for us, more tables were open than not, so no reservation was required.

"This place seems cool," I commented.

My mom frowned at the ambiance. "Not what I expected."

"You're sure this is the place Maryam told you?'" my dad asked. Mom nodded. He checked his watch. "We're early so they still have time to show up. I hope this is the place; I'm starving."

"You're always starving."

"Hannah!" Maryam's shrill voice came from out of nowhere.

My mother stood up to hug her and gush about Maryam's beautiful designer dress. Adam and James stood behind her, smiling at me. I smiled and waved back, proud at my restrained drooling over Adam's taller height, sexy shorter hair, and chiseled jawline. I could be done with Adam.

"Where's Henry?" my mom asked about Mr. Pierce, and Mrs. Pierce's entire pleasant expression dropped off the face of the earth.

"He's not coming," she grumbled, taking a seat at our table. The boys did the same. James sat next to me, and Adam sat across from me and next to his mother.

My mom waved a hand in the air like she just didn't care. "That's okay, we'll see him later—"

"He's not coming to the timeshare at all."

"Go, girl," slipped from my lips. Everyone looked at me with wide eyes.

Silence. Awkward silence. Then, the waitress showed up. "Hi, have y'all been here before?"

"Never."

"Fantastic. We've got a great chicken tender meal for under five dollars." *Yes, please.* "And our soup of the day is chowder."

Maryam made a noise, but Adam rubbed her arm. Comforting her? Were Mr. and Mrs. Pierce having money trouble and that was why we were eating at a three-star restaurant and not a five-star one? Was it because of a divorce?

"What can I get y'all?"

I jumped to order, as hungry as my ever-hungry father. "I'll take a chicken tender meal with honey mustard and a cherry Coke."

My mother attempted a joke. "Try not to gain the freshman fifteen before you've even moved in yet." The joke did not land.

"I think she looks perfect," Adam said. "What college did you choose?" he asked me, his direct attention causing me to go a bit dizzy.

"I—"

My mom cut me off. "It's actually a great school in New York—"

"Let's talk about it after we've ordered," my dad said. "I'll take the chicken tender meal as well, barbeque sauce, please."

"WE'VE BEEN BUYING Eve all new stuff for her dorm so her bedspread will match her towels and such," Mom gushed, excited with the prospect of doing some interior design. "We even got her roommate to agree to a theme." She pushed at my arm. "Go ahead and tell the Pierces what you two are doing."

"I—I have a cherry bedspread," I said, and Adam grinned at me. His grins killed me. *You are done with men.* "And my roommate has a watermelon one."

"A fruit theme. Isn't that just adorable?"

Maryam nodded. "It is. I love it."

"Are you and your roommate doing anything fun, Adam?"

Maryam answered for him, "Boys don't get as into decorating as we do, Hannah."

Adam grabbed my attention again. "Your mom said you were going to a college in New York. Which one?"

"It's just a public university that has a good performing arts program. The dance classes are supposed to be amazing." I had applied to colleges in New York intending to pursue my dream as a performer. The big city was the best place for me to do that.

"Adam is going to a public university in New York too. Maybe you could grab the subway and meet each other for coffee sometimes?"

A nervous laugh slipped out of my mouth. "New York is pretty big. I'm not sure how much time I'll have to leave campus." And seeing Adam in a season other than summer? Weird.

"He's going to Genia University, is that far from yours?"

My jaw dropped. My heart stopped. "Genia University?"

My mother rejoiced. "Eve is going to Genia!"

"Are you serious?" Adam appeared shocked but not as shocked as me.

I was a second away from going into actual shock. It was one thing for us to see each other for two weeks every year, but go to school together? *College* together? Living within a mile radius of each other? Studying in the same library?

Our mothers came to the same conclusion, "This is perfect."

"Perfect," Adam repeated, an unreadable expression on his face, though he seemed pensive.

I frowned. "Yeah, perfect."

Adam and I at the same college? Around each other year-round?

"I'm bored," James said, and we moved to a different topic. My mind had a harder time moving on from the big information it had received.

PENNY: *That's honestly crazy. There are probably over a thousand colleges in the United States and you both chose the same one?*

Me: *He does live in New York, so I guess it makes sense*

that he'd stay there to go to school. But why Genia? That was my school.

<u>Penny</u>: *I know you're upset but maybe this will be a good thing. Maybe all the sparks between you two are because you only see each other once a year during summertime. Maybe it'll wear off if you see each other in the winter with runny noses and puffy winter coats.*

I imagined Adam with a cold, waddling around in a winter coat. Still, the hottest thing I could think of. If he was sick, I could even nurse him back to health, feed him soup, watch his tongue flick against the spoon—*Stop.*

<u>Me</u>: *This is a disaster. I wanted to start college off with new friends, new experiences. I didn't want to bring old relationships with me.*

<u>Penny</u>: *Thanks.*

<u>Me</u>: *Hush, you know we'll be friends until we watch our grandchildren play around on the lawn with each other, while we rock in rocking chairs on the front porch of a house we live in together since both our husbands died in World War III. Eventually, both passing away, holding hands in those rocking chairs.*

<u>Penny</u>: *In front of the grandchildren?*

<u>Me</u>: *Those younguns needed a good scare anyway.*

<u>Penny</u>: *Have you told Adam about John the Cheater yet?*

Tell the boy who decided years ago I wasn't good enough that yet *another* boy had found me lacking as well? No.

James knocked on the door to my room, checking on me. We were headed to the beach as soon as I finished putting on sunscreen. "Are you ready?" At eight years old, James had matured in every way other than gaining patience.

Just because I was done with the Y chromosome did not mean I was avoiding little James. It just meant I was avoiding his big, sexy, funny, smart, older brother.

Penny: *Don't think you can ignore me!*

I put my phone away, deciding to text her back later. "Yup."

We walked to the beach, carrying two towels and a beach bag full of toys and games. When asked if he wanted to build a sandcastle, James replied, "No," which was bittersweet to hear. Kids grew up too fast.

We laid out on our towels and people-watched for a while, before James said, "I'm going to miss Adam when he goes to college."

Sympathy tugged at my heartstrings. "I'm sure he'll miss you too."

"He's been really cool this year."

His statement piqued my curiosity. "Yeah?"

"He acts happier and nicer. We hang out a lot."

Was this a part of Adam's trying to be "worthy?" A side effect of Mr. and Mrs. Pierce splitting up? "That's awesome."

"I think he's going to come down to the beach soon too."

Great.

Timeshare Boyfriend

I closed my eyes and drifted into a drowsy state of sleep to the sound of ocean waves crashing and kids giggling. Not sure how long I rested, but what woke me was a drop of cold liquid hitting my lips. I licked them only to receive a sweet cherry flavor on my taste buds.

"Hey there, Sleeping Beauty." Adam stood above me, holding a dripping ice cream cone. "Your ice cream man has arrived."

Yum. Also, yum for the ice cream. "That looks amazing."

"Not as amazing as the girl about to eat it."

Blood rushed to my blushing cheeks. This was a new Adam indeed. Complimenting me? In public? While holding ice cream? "Um, thanks."

I sat up on my towel and grabbed the cone from him. A stream of cherry vanilla ice cream dripped down the side of it, and I licked it from bottom to top, trying to save all I could like a good Samaritan. I looked up at him after swallowing.

His eyes blazed as they studied my mouth.

My own gaze fell to his swim trunks before shooting back up. "Are you going to swim in the waves later?"

"Are you?"

After Kellan's swimming lessons, I had successfully learned how to swim. Going into the ocean to jump waves or dive off the pool's diving board no longer filled me with fear. "Maybe."

He laid a towel next to me and joined me on the sand. "Then, yes." Yes, he would swim if I swam?

I licked my delicious ice cream again, but the summer sun melted it quicker than I could ingest the two scoops. It dripped some more, this time on my chest. The chilled cream trailed down, about to escape between my cleavage when one of Adam's fingers caught the runaway droplet and swiped it up, removing it from my skin. The air seemed to crackle, shooting invisible lightning, as Adam licked his finger. His tongue swirled, curling and scooping the ice cream from his thumb. Slow. Hot.

Holy Moly.

I coughed into my hand, trying to mask my reaction. *Done with men. Done with men.* "Why did you get me ice cream?"

He leaned back on the beach towel. "I thought you'd like it."

No argument there. "I do."

He turned on his side and met my gaze. "What other things do you like?"

Why do you care? I wanted to ask sassily, but instead my mouth blurted, "Um...I like to read."

"What do you like to read?" Now he was interested in my hobbies? *Mayday, mayday!*

"Uh..." There were always two reactions to *I read romance novels*. The first was the sweet, unassuming, *aw, so you're a romantic*, where the person pities you and thinks you're a sucker who loves love. The second was the surprised, naughty, *oh...* where the person thinks all you read is porn. Might as well get it over with. "Romance."

He nodded, a thoughtful look on his face. "Sweet or steamy?"

I swallowed a bite of ice cream too fast and coughed again. "Um, I—" *Don't answer steamy. Whatever you do, don't answer steamy.* "—I like a mix. In between those, I guess." Spicy as well. The more jalapenos in a rating, the better.

He smiled. "Nothing wrong with a little heat mixed in with heartfelt." *Or a lot of heat,* but telling him that would lead to nothing good.

"Why do you want to know what things I like?"

He leaned toward me, one of his hands connecting with my arm so he could trace his fingers over my skin. Back and forth. Even the small, tender touch made it hard to breathe. *Attraction* had never been a problem with Adam. "I want to know everything about you, Evie," he said softly.

Sparks sizzled my pores where his skin touched mine, like each molecule of my body decided to throw a personal bonfire party. *You are not interested in him anymore. Too much history. Too much possibility of heartbreak.* I inched away from him, and he stopped.

"Why?" I asked. "Why do you want to get to know me better?"

"For starters, we're going to the same college."

"Which is weird," I pointed out.

"I think it's fate."

I sat up, a nervous laugh slipping from me. "You've never believed in fate before." Was he suddenly a romantic?

He sat up as well. "People change."

"Yeah, people change, but not into a completely different person."

"They finally broke up, Evie," he said about his parents. "And it's like this weight has been lifted. I've grown a lot since last summer. I've...let go of a lot of things. The reasons I used to push you away, they're not valid anymore. We're going to go to the same college; we will get to see each other more than two weeks every summer."

"So, now it's more convenient for you to try at 'feelings?'"

Guilt pricked me when he flinched. "I like you. Listening to you stand up to my dad for me, seeing you with James, the way we laugh together. I've liked you for a long time, but I needed to work through my issues. I never wanted to risk—"

I tore my gaze from his intense one to watch James playing in the waves. "It can't be that easy." There was no way. I would not accept what I'd been waiting to hear for years just because I heard it. It was too late.

I've been hurt too many times.

He leaned in again, his face two inches from mine. "It wasn't easy, but it was worth it."

I threw my arms up. "Gah!"

"What?"

"I can't hear this right now."

"I know it's taken a long time for me—"

"This is an '*X-Chromosome Marks The Spot*' summer," I shouted.

He blinked. "It's a what?"

"It's a no men, no feelings summer. I'm focusing on me."

"I would like to focus on you too."

Typical. "The summer I've sworn off love, you finally decide you want me?"

"I've always wanted you." He frowned. "Why have you sworn off love?"

"Why does there need to be a reason?" I asked, but the shaking in my voice betrayed me.

He pressed his luscious lips together, thinning them. A disapproving look from Adam; nothing new there. "My mother told me a few weeks ago that you had a boyfriend this year."

"And?"

"And did he do something to cause this change in you?"

"He didn't do anything you haven't before," I shot back.

A dark eyebrow rose. "What does that mean?"

"He made me think he cared about me. Then—suddenly—he didn't. Remind you of anyone?"

Adam's jaw ticked. "I hate that he hurt you. I hate that I hurt you."

Deep sigh. What was the point of any of this? Could I

not enjoy the beach without drama? "Maybe love doesn't exist," I said. "Maybe everyone is doomed to be hurt in the end."

"Evie, you *love* love. How can you say that? What did he do?" Adam saw the flash of vulnerability in my expression before I had time to hide it. "Damn it, I could kill him for making you feel this way."

"I'll give you his address."

"I'll call a hitman."

"Speed dial?"

"How else am I to promptly avenge you for everyone who has hurt you?" he remarked.

"Will you hire a hit on yourself?" I asked. "Because you've hurt me."

This time, it was his turn to release a deep sigh and stare off at the ocean. "Evie." He looked back at me. "I don't want to hurt you. This summer, I want to heal you."

I struggled to breathe. "The moment has passed, okay? Two years too late. Three years even."

He stood from the towel, towering above me. "It's never too late."

"I'm serious, Adam. I'm over you."

"So you say." He pulled off his shirt and kicked off his sandals, about to join his brother in the waves. "If it's true, it won't matter what I do."

"What the heck does that mean?"

He shrugged again, a small smile forming on his lips, mischievous and hopeful. One of my favorite combinations. "I guess we'll both have to see, won't we?" *Heart, stop pounding.* "I'm happy we're going to the same college together. I think it'll be good for us."

Stay strong. "There is no us."

"There's always been an us."

16

HEARTS OF GOLD SINK THE FASTEST

"Stop trying to seduce me."

He shot me an innocent expression while he flexed the muscles in his arms. "I don't know what you're talking about."

I pinched the bridge of my nose the way he used to do around me all the time. "I know what you're trying to do. You can't just walk around shirtless everywhere for days on end."

"It's the beach; everyone is shirtless." He gestured to other shirtless guys our age playing beach volleyball on the sand near us. We sat back in beach chairs with our feet in the sand while reading. God, why couldn't he be on his phone or something? Watching him reading did things to me, but watching him reading while shirtless? My toes curled in the sand.

"Yeah, but you're—" *different*, I wanted to say. The sight of other shirtless guys? Sure, not bad. But Adam?

Timeshare Boyfriend

My thighs clenched together whenever I saw him. "Shiny."

He blinked. "I'm shiny?"

"I—I meant..." I meant that he was extra distracting considering he had applied sunblock right before my eyes. Rubbing it into his chest, getting it nice and slick, taking his time. I crossed my legs, trying to ease some of the ache. "You're shiny as in you are sweaty."

"Sorry." He chuckled and ran a hand through his dark hair. "It's hot. I can't help it." He trailed a hand down his muscled chest. His fingers traced the ridges I dreamed about touching, kissing, licking...

"Hot," I repeated, mesmerized by his body.

"Really hot." His hand moved even further down, over his happy trail, to the waistband of his swim trunks. My heartbeat quickened. My mouth dried. "You're looking pretty hot too, Evie." His hand stopped moving, and I struggled to get my breathing back to normal.

I fanned myself. "The sun is kind of intense, I guess."

"Want me to rub some sunscreen on you?"

An alarm went off in my head. "I don't think that's a good idea."

He leaned toward me. His arm touched mine due to the proximity of our beach chairs' armrests. "So, you'd rather get skin cancer than let me touch you?"

I rolled my eyes. "I'm not going to get skin cancer."

"With the depletion of the ozone layer, your skin is

vulnerable to more harmful rays than normal. Plus, sunscreen also decreases risk of heatstroke."

"Let me guess, you saw it in a documentary?"

He picked up the bottle of sunblock and shook it with a flirty grin. "Look, I'm just saying if you want to be safe, you should let me rub this on your body. Preferably all over. For safety reasons."

Trying not to smile, I opened my book back up to distract myself from him. The romance novel had a covert cover of a crystal heart, which helped me feel less embarrassed reading the spicy scenes in public. The book did not help me calm down, however, considering I was in the middle of the second big sex scene. My cheeks burned and a part of me worried if it was due to the throbbing between my legs or the sun beating down on me. As I read, I kept imagining Adam as the main love interest. *He would moan my name into my ear before trailing kisses down my neck, down my chest, down, down* — "I am going into the water," I announced, shooting up and out of my seat.

I let the water lap at my legs, cooling me down. Around John the Cheater, I had been calm, collected, and comfortable. And—mustn't forget—a "prude." Around Adam, every moment felt like too much. Sensory overload. My body ached for him. I hung onto every word he said and every action he took. For years. *Why are you so dumb, Evie?*

The waves in the ocean appeared calm until they merged with or hit another wave and crashed into crystalized white foam. Like diamond pudding. One of the oldest parts of the world, the ocean was beautiful but scary at the same time. Like love.

I turned from the water and glanced back to where Adam sat in his chair. An old man with an old dog stood beside him, talking to him, as Adam bent in the sand to pet the furry creature. My heart warmed at the sight. The dog half-jumped on Adam and tackled him further into the sand, but Adam continued to laugh and pet him.

Around ten minutes later, I returned to our beach chairs where Adam sat, engrossed in his book. "Must be a good one," I commented.

Adam looked up and had such a terrified yet guilty expression on his face that I did not know how to react. I leaned over to check the cover, only to realize it was my book he was holding. The romance novel hotter than the summer sun.

"What the hell is this, Evie?"

"I— You shouldn't just take another person's book like that."

"When you said you liked steamy books—but this is...*three* guys?"

"Four actually," I muttered, and his eyes widened so much I worried they would fall out. "It's not like she is having sex with them at the same time. It's just a reverse harem book so multiple guys like her." He stared at me in silence. "Don't look so afraid," I said, offended.

"I'm not afraid."

"Really?" I crossed my arms. "Cause you look ready to scream and run."

"Is this what you're into?"

"Not in real life." I looked down at my feet and kicked some sand. "I just like how all the guys like her and make her feel wanted."

His dramatic expression softened. I could see the question in his eyes: *Did your boyfriend not make you feel wanted?*

I leaned over to snatch the book from him, but he moved it out of my reach like some kind of ninja.

He flipped through a couple of pages, still in shock. "You've been reading this right next to me. In public."

My fists clenched. There was no way I would let him embarrass me about the books I enjoyed reading. "Yeah, so?"

"So?" His eyes scrunched shut. He leaned forward, his expression the definition of intense, and dropped his head in his hands. Groaning, he said, "I find that so fucking hot I can barely look at you right now."

Hot? He found it hot? "You don't think it's weird?"

"Did your jerk of a boyfriend know you read this kind of stuff?"

God, no. I planned to take it to the grave. "No."

Adam nodded. The edges of his lips curled.

My eyes narrowed on him, suspicious. "What are you smiling about?"

His smile was now a full-fledged grin. "I know something about you he didn't."

"Because you stole my book, not because I opened up to you," I huffed.

He waved a hand in the air. "Details." He opened the book again and scanned some of it.

I slapped at his hands, but he dodged me. "Stop reading it."

His blue eyes met mine, reminding me of the wild ocean waves several feet away from us. My heart stuttered at the absolute challenge and heat in his gaze. My core clenched.

"Make me," he dared.

I stood from my chair and towered in front of where he lounged in his. "Last chance to give it back."

Adam flipped a page and began reading out loud, "*'Harder,' Wanda screamed. Jace slowed down his thrusts to tease her.'* Wanda and Jace? Are real people even named that?"

I jumped onto his lap, and he stopped reading the book in surprise. My legs straddled his waist as I reached for the book. He raised it over his head and behind him. The weak beach chair tipped back from our combined weight, and I fell forward onto him. A cloud of sand puffed onto us from the impact of our bodies hitting the ground.

"Fuck, Evie." Adam gazed up at me in astonishment. "You broke the chair."

I continued to lay on top of him. Our chests pressed against each other—thank you, gravity—and my legs still spread around him. "You wouldn't give me back my book," I said.

He wiggled below me but gave up when he saw I had no plans to move anytime soon. "So, you decided to tackle me?"

I stared at him. He stared right back. Then we both laughed so hard, the movement vibrated our bodies and the broken chair below us. We laughed until we could not breathe and then we laughed some more.

After a few minutes of laying on him, trying to suck oxygen into my lungs, I felt something twitch below me. Specifically, something pressing up against me, between my legs.

Something stiff that rubbed directly over the throbbing bundle of nerves I had been ignoring the last couple of days.

My hips rocked forward on instinct. *Friction.* Oh. Oh, wow. Like a light switch flicking on violently.ABrupt and blinding, pent-up desire seemed to spear right through my belly. A breathless sigh escaped me. "*Oh.*" Tingling pleasure wracked my body as I moved over him once more, pressing his hardness where I throbbed.

Adam closed his eyes, exhaling as well. Then, those long lashes flicked open once more. "I'm sorry. I swear, I didn't mean to—"

My hips pushed down on his bulge again, grinding, as I mindlessly shook from the sensation. *Right there.*

"Um, Evie?" He cut off when I undulated against him. "Fuck, you need to stop."

My nipples hardened through my bikini top and poked his chest. The throbbing at the junction of my thighs jumbled my mind, my every thought. "Feels good."

"Perfect. Feels perfect." His eyelids fluttered closed again. He thrust up, rubbing harder against that perfect spot. He shook his head, opening his eyes again. "No, stop. We're in public. Oh God, we're on a public beach right now. You need to get off me, baby."

I took a deep breath to calm down and settle my heart rate. *He called me "baby." He is hard under me. So hard.* "I thought this was what you wanted? To seduce me."

"I want more than lust with you, Evie," he said, his eyes blazing up at me, two blue flames. "I want all of you."

But giving someone all of you meant being open to getting hurt. Broken. Betrayed.

I pushed myself off him and out of the broken chair until I stood. Unsure of what to say or do, I asked, "Can I have my book back now?"

Adam looked around the beach at the people near us and lowered the book down to cover his crotch. "Could I get it back to you in a couple of minutes?"

The problem with distancing myself emotionally from Adam was that it was impossible when he popped up everywhere I was, being charming and flirty and caring. He knew I planned to spend time with James and followed along wherever we went. We rode go-karts, visited the aquarium, and went to a water park. At the water park, my bikini strap broke, flashing my breasts to the world. He covered me, holding my bare chest to his as he walked us over to where his T-shirt was for me to put on.

Thus, I had to buy a new bikini. And Adam offered to buy one for me. And there we were, a day later, in a beach shop searching for swimwear together—no James this time.

Alone together. Looking at glorified waterproof lingerie.

As we walked through the racks, Adam reached out and cursed while he touched something that looked like a micro bikini fit to only cover nipples.

Clearing his throat and looking uncomfortable, Adam asked, "See anything you like?"

"They're expensive."

"Don't worry about it. I'm paying." He smiled at me again. God, his *smiles*. "Get whatever you like."

A red bikini stood out to me. I fingered the pretty straps, contemplating it.

"Baby," Adam said into my ear, standing closer behind me than I realized. "If you wear that in front of me, how am I supposed to not fall at your feet and beg for mercy?"

"Mercy?"

"Beg for mercy, a kiss, a smile, anything," he said.

Funny how this summer, when I finally decided to stay away from him, he said all the right things. "I'm going to try it on."

An idea breached my thoughts, and I knew it was wrong. I knew it was the opposite of what I should have done. But I couldn't help myself.

"Want to help me try it on?" I asked, glancing up at him from under my stubby lashes.

Adam made me feel desired. John the Cheater's voicemail still echoed in my ears. *Prude. Virgin. Frigid. Doesn't know how to kiss. Doesn't even know how to touch me.*

Feeling sexy did not mean I had to be emotionally vulnerable. Some of my friends had hookups or friends with benefits. Maybe I could scratch an itch with Adam before starting college, without it turning into a possibility of being hurt again. *Stupid, stupid Evie.*

"You want me to help you try on the bikini?" he rasped.

"It's got so many straps. I'm sure I'll need help in the fitting room." A lie. It was a normal bikini with normal straps. Heh, I lied so well, someone might think I had a Y-chromosome.

Adam's eyes narrowed; his lips pursed. But his

excitement to see me in the bikini overpowered his suspicion of whatever game I was playing.

Considering how empty the beach store was—everyone traveled to the beach with a swimsuit, sunglasses, a surfboard, etc., so they didn't need to buy them—Adam and I easily slipped into a dressing room together undetected.

Closing the door, I moved to stand in front of the mirror. Adam's back was against the wall, giving me all the space he could. As if suddenly, he *didn't* want to help me try it on.

"What is this, Evie?" he asked.

This is me being a grown adult woman, reveling in feeling unattached and sexy and not *vulnerable*. This was me feeling wanted. Finally.

"I'm trying on a bathing suit because my old one's strap broke. Remember?"

"Do I remember covering your bare fucking chest with mine and feeling your nipples poke into me while trying to make sure no one saw you without a shirt? No. Remind me."

I took my time, removing my shirt and shorts in front of him. My bra and underwear covered me just as much as any bathing suit, but it still felt especially naughty for him to see me like this.

No boy had ever seen me like this.

My shorts fell to the floor.

His gaze devoured me so quickly, taking no time to chew or swallow, he nearly choked.

As my hands moved behind my back to remove my bra, he licked his lips, hyper-focusing on my every movement. Heat enveloped me, locking me in a cage of lust. He cursed, his hand sinking to pull at his mesh shorts, rearranging his growing erection.

Just as the fabric slipped to reveal my bare chest, he closed his eyes.

He. Closed. His. Eyes.

"What are you doing?" I asked. This was my time to finally feel like the sexiest person alive. What high school boy—college boy, now—closed his eyes when a naked female chest was on display? "Open those eyes."

"No."

"No?"

"I won't," he grunted.

"Why not? Am I that unattractive?"

"Damn it, Evie. If I see you naked, I'll be ruined for all other women."

Tingles. Such familiar tingles. "Excuse me?"

"I don't know what kind of power play this is for you or what you want from this, but watching you strip and knowing it's because of something more than you wanting to strip for *me* is not the reason I want to see you naked for the first time."

"Does it really matter what the context is?"

"Yes," he said. "I'm thinking it has something to do with your ex." His eyes were still closed. The boy had more self-restraint than me. My own gaze could not tear away from the bulge in his shorts.

"And?"

"Did you have sex with him?" he asked.

I stumbled at the shocking question. "Why do you want to know?"

"To understand."

"Or do you want to know so you can tease me about it? *Oh poor virgin, no one has wanted to touch you?*"

His lips separated. His eyebrows furrowed. But those eyes stayed closed. "Evie."

"He cheated on me. Does that make you feel better to know? He cheated on me because, apparently, I'm a horrible kisser and a frigid prude who is so unsexy that her boyfriend had to find passion elsewhere. He cheated on me because I wasn't good enough. But I don't need to tell you that because you realized that years ago."

Adam was hugging me. I didn't know how he moved so quickly and with such precision with his eyes closed, but he yanked me into him, holding me. Cradling me. "Baby, I'm so sorry."

"Aren't you happy?"

"Why the fuck would I be happy about some asshole hurting you?"

Because Adam had hurt me too. Once. "Because you were right all those years ago. When you told your friends I was 'nobody's type.'" So long ago, and yet it still stung.

"Hell, Evie, that was a threat to them to stay away from you. I thought that was obvious."

What? "Obvious?"

He held me tighter. "You really thought I could say no one would want you? When I fucking panted after you every time your back was turned? When I asked James to relay everything you two talked about each day just so I could know how you were? What your life was like. Or when I hid my mom's tanning lotion because I didn't want you to change a single thing about yourself. You're perfect to me. You've always been perfect to me."

Stay strong, Evie. Remember all the summers you humiliated yourself by clinging to him? Guard yourself.

"I'm so sorry. For everything I've ever said to make you feel unwanted." His fingers dug into my spine like he was desperate to reach inside me and pull out all of my sadness. I loved it. "You were *never* unwanted."

A hot tear fell down my cheek. "I'm not going to fall for you just because you're being nice now," I said.

"Shh, baby, let it out. I can feel you holding it in," he said as he rubbed my back. "Let it out."

I gripped his shirt, the tears breaking through the barrier now, flooding my face. I had no luck with guys. I wanted love more than anything, but it never made itself available to me. Did I somehow jinx myself? Was it a curse I needed to break?

I wanted not to be vulnerable, but detaching myself from my emotions was never a talent of mine. It was a talent of Adam's.

"I've got you." He soothed my sobs with his

comforting touches. He hummed that same tune he hummed back when he calmed me while riding the horses.

I was topless; yet, the moment was not about lust. My relationship with Adam had never *only* been about lust.

It was more.

His embrace felt like a vacation home. Familiar, utterly relaxing, and right. And temporary.

17

THE HEART WAS MADE TO BE BROKEN AND SEDUCED BACK TOGETHER

The morning after my embarrassing cry fest on Adam's shirt, he knocked on my door, holding chocolate-covered cherries and the DVD of *The Princess Bride*.

Adam said he wanted more than something physical with me, and I was starting to believe it. The ordeal with John the Cheater had severely affected my confidence, and Adam spent every moment of our time together trying to re-inflate my ego. He told me how good I looked, how smart and funny I was; he told me how lucky he felt to be around me. He talked about how excited he was to go to college together.

But the fact was, my heart could hardly take two weeks each summer of Adam. How was I supposed to handle fall, winter, and spring around him too?

"Adam and James are here for you," my dad called to me through my door.

I checked my makeup one last time. Though I did not wear mascara and lip gloss a lot, I liked the way it made me feel more confident when I did. Plus, the lip gloss was cherry flavored, so that made it hard to stay away.

"Hey, guys," I said, walking out of the unit to join them in the hallway where we waited for the elevator. Tonight, Adam planned to take James and me to karaoke. It brought up an old memory of when Adam had told me we could never work as a couple: *I'm not someone who would sing a duet at karaoke. I'm not boyfriend material.*

He seemed to think he was boyfriend material now.

"James, are you going to sing tonight?" I asked, ruffling his hair.

He snorted. "No way."

I hit the elevator button to take us to the ground floor. "I think singing is manly."

James frowned. "Yeah?"

"Yeah?" Adam repeated.

I bit my lip, amused by Adam's thoughtful expression. "Yeah."

"Are you going to sing tonight?" he asked me.

The elevator dinged, and we exited when the doors opened. We walked for a minute before I answered, "I don't think so."

"Why not? You're amazing."

I thanked the dim lighting for hiding my blush. "I

don't feel like standing up on a stage by myself right now."

Adam nodded, his eyes swirling with anger. "Don't let that guy mess with your self-confidence. He's not worth it."

James jumped into the conversation, noticing he didn't know what his brother talked about. "What happened?"

Adam stared at me, a silent question in his eyes. My answer was a shrug. He then turned to James. "A jerk broke Eve's heart."

James's jaw fell. "Who?" He narrowed his eyes, looking so much like his older brother in that moment. "Tell us who, and we'll take care of him."

I laughed. "You're eight, James."

"We'll make him swim with the fishes," he added.

I slapped Adam's arm. "I told you to stop letting him watch mafia movies."

Adam put up his hands. "He's uncontrollable; I don't know what to do with him. I tried taking the remote away and he said, 'Let me watch ten more minutes and I'll make you an offer you can't refuse.' I swear, my heart stopped beating."

"What was the offer?"

James started, "I'd give you two more alone time—"

Adam cupped a hand around James's mouth, not letting him finish.

Walking down the small pier to karaoke, we passed the old arcade where Adam won my ring. We gave each other a knowing look and smiled. This whole pier, beach, and timeshare held so many memories of Adam and me, good and bad. I was glad we now focused on the good again.

Were we a couple? Of course not. But we were friends.

James ran to get popcorn when Adam and I sat in the seats set up around the karaoke stage. It was still early, but a little girl already stood up there singing a popular pop song. We watched her, and I tried not to show a big reaction as Adam wrapped an arm around the back of my chair. His long arm stretched around my shoulders, his hand falling just above my chest, over my collarbone.

"Do you remember when you sang karaoke in front of me?" He spoke in my ear so I could hear him over the young vocal cords and loud music. "On your first date with that lifeguard guy."

I rolled my eyes. "You know his name."

"You shined up on that stage. You belong up there." The hand resting above my chest moved to play with my hair. "You should sing tonight."

"I don't know..."

"You can't let what John the Asshole did stop you from having fun."

I arched an eyebrow. "How do you know I'll have fun singing karaoke tonight?"

"Because I've never seen you smile as much as when you're performing."

"You've never seen me perform. Not really."

"Your mom sent my mom a video of your winter showcase for your dance class."

"She *what*?"

"I may or may not have watched it over fifty times." He grinned, and it speared me right through my vulnerable chest.

"I'm not going up there to sing karaoke alone."

He pouted.

"Pouting doesn't work on me." It did work on me, but I hoped saying that would make him stop it.

His face inched closer to mine. "What does work on you?"

Anything that involves you. "Sing with me." He would never sing with me, and I wanted to rub that in his face as a sign he hadn't changed. I needed to create a barrier between us. If I showed myself he still was not willing to take jumps for me, I'd let him go. Finally.

I needed to let him go and give my heart some rest before we went off to college together.

"Sing with you?" he repeated.

Ha, say "no." I dare you. "Yup."

He gave me a half-smile. "Okay."

What? "What?" No, he was supposed to say no. N. O. Adam Pierce did not sing karaoke. He didn't comfort heartbroken girls or compliment them. Why was he acting this way? It made it so much harder to build up walls around him.

Any emotional barrier I constructed turned into an

easily penetrable sandcastle. He was an ocean wave, always able to distort my seashore shape and texture and wipe away any traces of what was there before him.

"What song do you want to sing?"

"Are you serious?" I asked. He was joking. There was no way. "You'll sing with me?"

Adam tangled his hand in my hair, palming the back of my skull and pulling me closer to make direct eye contact with him. "I'd do anything to make you smile, Evie."

I cleared my throat, trying to also clear the rogue butterflies filling my stomach and intestines and other organs designated as no-butterfly zones. "I'm going to choose something cheesy."

"I love cheese," he said. "Specifically, gouda."

Now he was being cute and making cheese jokes? How was I supposed to resist the desire to kiss him and grope him like a crazy woman when he referenced gouda? *Get control back. Make him say no.*

"You'll hate the song I choose," I said, but his next few words blew me away.

That small, mischievous yet genuine smile. The soft warmth in his eyes. All of him pierced me as he replied, "I like you enough to make up for it."

Less than twenty minutes later, we stood on stage. The screen read, "*Summer Nights*, from *Grease*." The countdown began: five, four, three, two—

Adam grabbed my hand and held it.

One.

His voice rang out, surprising me when I realized this boy could sing. He sounded so good, I was half a second late on my cue. His voice was rich, deep, and powerful. It blew my flipping socks off.

Had a man with musical talent ever turned someone on as much as me right now?

We sang about meeting on the beach and falling in love. Playing in the water, in the sand. I danced around the stage, my feet unable to stay still while I listened to the fast-paced song. The audience clapped and hooted with enthusiasm as Adam joined in the moving back and forth. He did his best John Travolta impression, and I laughed harder than I had in a while.

I grinned. He grinned. And it was magic.

His hand never let go of mine.

When the music slowed down, so did my heart. Everything faded around us until all I saw was him.

He leaned in. I leaned in. We stopped singing. Breathless. Starstruck. I stared at him, waiting. Not sure what I waited for.

Someone yelled from the crowd, "*Kiss!*"

I placed a hand on his chest, unsure if it was to push him back or pull him forward. His hand cupped the back of my neck. And we were so close. Close enough to—

He kissed my forehead, stepped back, and bowed with me. That small, single kiss on the forehead had my heart beating out of my chest.

As we stepped from the stage, I began walking to

James, but Adam stopped me. He pulled me with him to the side of the crowd with the most privacy.

His breathing still a bit heavy from all the singing and dancing, he stared down at me. "It's us, Evie. You know it is."

~~~

Penny: *Sounds like the boy finally knows what he wants.*
Me: *I need time away from relationships.*
Penny: *Babe, you're just hurt. You don't mean that. You've loved Adam forever.*
Me: *I do NOT love him.*
Penny: *Oh, are we at the lying to each other stage of our friendship? I didn't get the memo. If we're lying, then yes, you NEVER loved him. When he walks around in his bathing suit, you NEVER act like it's porn.*

It was porn. His muscular chest was no joking matter.

Adam: *Here.*

His message reminded me that I promised to work out with him in the timeshare gym this morning. Dancing during school required muscles I needed to keep for auditioning for shows in college. Cherry Twizzlers had messed up my goal weight. I planned to build up my endurance again to be ready for Genia University's dance department.

Adam groaned when he saw me walk into the small, abandoned gym. For some reason, being on vacation—

with the beach just outside—led to a gym not often used.

I held in my moan at seeing him shirtless. This boy needed to become a model already. *Geezus.*

Adam spoke first, cutting through the sexual tension with a dull, plastic knife because, gosh, it was still thick when he inquired, "Where are your clothes?"

"I could ask you the same thing."

He wore nothing but baggy gray shorts. *Thin* baggy gray shorts. *Hello, tongue, get back in my mouth.* My workout clothes consisted of a modest black sports bra and some spandex shorts.

"I don't know if it's safe for me to look at you in that while I work with heavy machinery." He gestured to the big weights sitting against the mirrored wall.

Do not take that as a compliment. Do not blush.

Trotting over to the treadmill, I swayed my hips with a little something extra before stepping onto the workout machine. "Then try not to look at me."

"Impossible."

After half an hour of running while Adam watched my every bounce, I stepped off the treadmill and switched to the yoga mat. He finished up his set of one hundred curl-ups—no wonder his abs were so abb-y— and walked over to me. "Need any help?" Drops of sweat trailed down his chest, stealing all my attention.

The heat in his expression did many, many things to me. Naughty things. Things that felt grown-up and forbidden and life-altering.

This boy will change your life if you let him. Was I supposed to let him?

I pulled my knee up to my chest, thinking maybe the bones of my leg would block the loud beating of my heart from his strong hearing. "Just stretching."

"Let me help you."

He knelt between my legs and held my leg up for me. He then pulled it back out, so it pointed straight, and lifted it in the air. He did not stop until he pushed it up, up, above my head.

I groaned at the screeching muscles. "There." I took a deep breath as I hit the perfect stretch position.

He stopped and moved his hand over my calf, massaging it. A moan escaped me, and his fingers dug in harder, working out the knots. My tense muscles relaxed, and I let out a husky, "Oh!"

His eyes locked onto mine, both of us knowing what that *"Oh"* sounded like. He let down my right leg and did the same thing to my left, pushing it up and holding it there as I groaned. He massaged further up my leg now, to my thighs. Another one of my breathy sighs captured his heated attention.

Taking both of my legs, he pushed them toward me until he leaned over my body, using a fraction of his weight to help me fold my legs over me.

"Ugh." My muscles tensed up and pulled for two seconds before releasing into the stretch. "Yes."

"Fuck, Evie, those sounds..." Adam's eyes were shut

tight as he laid on top of me, helping me hold the stretch. "How are you so damn flexible?"

"I dance. I have to be."

I moved my legs into a split stretch, opening them wide to him. His breathing became heavier as he massaged my inner thighs. Heck, my breathing got heavier too.

His soft, warm fingers pressed into muscles. Liquid heat ran through me, down to where the most tension built from his closeness. My hips bucked on instinct when he hit a pressure point I didn't know existed. "Oh!" I let out another embarrassing noise, but Adam seemed to like it.

"These are your Fuliu and San Yin Jiao pressure points," he said as he massaged my lower calf. "They're known to increase blood flow and arousal, but it hasn't been scientifically proven yet. What do you think?" He dug his fingers into them, and my body trembled.

"What the heck kind of documentaries are you watching?" I responded in a hoarse and breathless voice.

He released a dark and pained chuckle. "And this area right here—" His hands moved down to my ankles. "This is supposed to increase sexual pleasure. Does that feel right to you?" He pressed.

My eyes rolled back. A strangled noise erupted from my throat.

He groaned and leaned between my spread legs to look at me. "Do you have any idea what you do to me?"

His groin aligned with mine, proving just how much I affected him. My hips thrust up again, searching for more pressure from his erection placed between my legs. "Fuck, Evie. Don't do that. This is about you."

I couldn't help myself. A fire started deep, below my stomach; an ache throbbed through me. A tingle of an itch needing so badly to be scratched by no one other than him. John the Cheater was wrong about me being a prude. I just didn't want to touch him. But Adam? I wanted to sink into his body and never leave.

I bucked my hips up again, making contact and rubbing myself against him through my spandex and his thin, cotton shorts.

He made a sound against me, vibrating my lips with his disapproval, but he was overcome by whatever was ruling my body parts as well. He dropped his waist down, pressing against me harder. He moved in small circles, adding to the fire and electricity running through my veins.

"Adam," I cried out, feeling the need, the yearning, the absolute craving increasing with each ragged breath I inhaled. "More."

Harder. Faster circles. A hand moved up to my chest to cup the side of my breast through the sports bra. He thumbed my nipple as it tightened for his touch.

My body shook. "Yes."

He leaned forward and claimed my lips with his. The kiss was the turning point.

It was the kind of kiss that gave a mermaid human

legs at the end of a movie. It transformed me. The kiss both gave me legs to stand on and knocked mine out from under me.

I wrapped myself around him, pulling him down harder. We moaned into each other's mouths.

Adam rolled us over on the mat. His fingers played with the bottom of my sports bra, preparing to slip underneath. My nails scratched down his back. He kissed my neck. Hot. Hard.

So hard.

I called out his name again.

"I know." One of his hands slipped under the waistband of my shorts. Flesh against flesh. His fingers stroked my wetness, quickly finding the best spot to rub tight circles and drive me wild. My body vibrated and hummed for him. Never had anyone touched me there. Never had anything felt so good.

"I know," he repeated, as if in pain, before kissing me again.

His fingers on me were unreal. I felt the sparks, like Pop Rocks in my brain, in my blood. So close to something.

"I want you. So much," he said before kissing me once more. "But I want all of you. Not just this."

I pulled his face down to mine again and devoured him.

He tore his mouth away and stared at me. "Say you want me for more than just this."

I closed my eyes and gripped the wrist of his hand,

which still occupied my shorts, urging him to continue his strokes.

"Say you'll be with me, Evie."

How could I say anything when I was so close? "Please. Please."

But his hand snuck out of my shorts. "You're not even looking at me."

I opened my eyes and saw his hurt expression.

"It can't just be *this* between us." His gaze struck through me, puncturing my lungs. "It was never meant to just be this."

"I—I don't want another relationship right now," I said. "I can't. It wouldn't be good for me." I had already spent years in a boy-induced haze of *Will this be the summer Adam loves me*? I could not keep doing this. There was college, my future, to think about.

We stayed there, laying against each other for a minute before he unwrapped my limbs from him and stood.

"I plan to be good for you," he said. "I want us to be friends at Genia."

"It's a big university, we may never see each other anyway."

He held out a hand to help me up, but I did not take it. I stayed on the ground. He shot me a small, almost timid smile and walked over to the gym exit. "If I know fate, it'll find a way to push us together."

18

FRIENDS WITHOUT BENEFITS

*F*all

"If you're in this class, you auditioned to be here, and we saw potential in you," the ballet professor said in a light Russian accent with a heavy scowl. My first impression: this class would be hard. "Ballet is vital to being a dancer, it teaches skill and endurance, but it also helps you find what is in yourself that cannot be taught. If you do not meet our expectations, you will fail. There is no such thing as a sick day in dance. Only two broken legs. Is that understood?"

We all nodded. Her words came across less as rules and more as threats.

"All right." She moved to the center of the room and gestured for us to move forward. "First position."

The class moved quickly. Ms. Petrov had a thin stick, which she whacked against the ground whenever she reprimanded someone over technique. She whacked it often.

After forty minutes of the hour-long class, Ms. Petrov called for a five-minute water break.

My sore throat and sore limbs cried their silent thanks to her as I walked over to my backpack and water bottle.

"She's a hard ass, huh?" a girl nudged me after taking a long sip from her pink-tinted bottle. "Do you think it comes from ballet or being Russian?"

I let out a laugh, hoping if I acknowledged her as funny, she might want to be my friend. So far, the people I knew at Genia consisted of my roommate Sarah and Adam, though I had yet to see him.

A boy leaned over to us, joining our conversation. "A little bit of both."

"Are you both dance majors?" I questioned, changing the subject from our professor.

"Yes, are you?"

"Yeah."

Activate lull in conversation.

"I saw you dance," the guy told me. "You're good."

I blushed. "Thanks, but I think everyone here is good."

The girl laughed. "Ms. Petrov disagrees." She nodded at the boy. "He's right though, she smiled at you a couple of times during the warm-ups. Prepare to be labeled as the teacher's pet."

I frowned. "I've never even talked to her."

"Petrov doesn't need to talk to you to like you. She watches and decides if she likes what she sees." He smiled at me again but addressed both of us. "My name is Finn." He reached out a hand to shake. Not a normal college boy thing to do. It made me like him.

"Dianna."

"Eve."

"Break is over!" Ms. Petrov yelled and started her music again. We followed her instruction, fearing being hit by her long stick if we didn't. "I will now list off your partners for the final winter showcase, which counts for fifty percent of your grade." Ms. Petrov was very matter-of-fact and reminded me of every scary Russian stereotype ever wrapped into a fifty-year-old woman holding a long stick.

When my name was called out with Finn's, we smiled at each other.

"How was your first day of classes?" I asked my roommate when she trudged into the room and threw down her bookbag.

She jumped on her watermelon bedspread. "Boring. They went over syllabuses—syllabi?—the whole time. Plus, I'm only in one science class, the rest are all mandatory freshman classes and have nothing to do with my major." She pulled her black hair out of her ponytail and shook it out on the bed. "I thought college would be more exciting."

I held back a laugh. "To clarify, college would be more exciting for you if you were in more science classes?"

She tossed a pen at me. "Molecular biology is a party, Eve."

"A party is a party. Didn't you find that flyer for one tonight?"

"You're right." She flew around the room, in search of the neon piece of paper. "It's at nine tonight."

"That's pretty late—"

"Eve, you're going."

"I have some homework—"

"This is our second night of college, we're going to this party." As far as I could tell, Sarah was a genius with a short attention span who lived in a constant state of distraction. "We need to celebrate."

I laughed. "Nothing has happened yet to celebrate. It was just our first day of classes."

"And they were rough, we need a break."

I laughed again but hoped my roommate wouldn't turn out to be a party animal.

"I bet there will be cute guys there."

I blew out a breath. "That's the opposite way to convince me."

Her grin grew. "Cute girls too."

"I'm not dating anyone this semester. I want to focus on my studies." *And not get hurt.* I pulled out my history homework and placed it on my desk. "And I'm attracted to boys."

"Well, I'm attracted to both. And anyway, there will be music there. Plenty of dancing for you." That did sound fun as long as it wasn't ballet. "They'll have food and people to make friends with, so we don't become two loners together, sneak a cat into the dorm, and then become cat ladies."

I grinned. "Fine, I'll go."

Sarah danced around the room in joy. My first thought watching her was, *Petrov would hit her stick at Sarah's un-pointed toes.*

***

THE PARTY WAS in full swing when we arrived at ten o'clock. Sarah believed in being fashionably late. The apartment building was a block away from our dorm, but easy to find due to the loud music pouring out of the windows. Walking in the room, however, was much more difficult due to the huge crowd of people shoved into the small space. It reeked of alcohol and weed. Music pounded from speakers, vibrating the floor. Green and red flashing lights illuminated the rooms like rogue Christmas decorations. Sweat beaded my forehead the moment I stepped into the hot, noisy room.

Sarah dragged me through the sea of people to the small kitchen counter. Tall bottles of alcohol sat on the granite. Nothing appealed to me.

We chatted with a few strangers for fifteen minutes or so, and I started to dance in the corner of the room.

After the second song, during a turn, I made eye contact with Adam Pierce.

He was here.

He was really here.

College together.

He grinned when he saw me and moved like a man on a mission. The crowds parted for him until he stood in front of me. The tips of our shoes brushed against each other. He leaned in and yelled over the music, "You're here."

He wrapped his arms around me in a hug, trapping me in a cage of sensual heat. My body lit on fire for him instantly at the mere feeling of him against me. Did he spray himself with hairspray? Was his skin part gasoline? The boy was flammable. Around him, there was such a high chance of getting burned.

"Looks like fate found a way," he said, grinning in a way that numbed my mind and paused all of my thoughts. He appeared utterly carefree.

It was the sexiest thing I'd ever seen. And I'd seen him shirtless. Maybe I was drunk—*you haven't had any alcohol, Evie.* Maybe he was just that hot. Maybe it was Maybelline.

My heart did dolphin tricks at his closeness. "You're hot." *Mouth, why?* "I mean, it's hot in here."

"You're hot," he said. "Dance with me."

I knew it was a bad idea: moving our bodies against each other like touching was simple. Like it wouldn't result in a major need for more touching until all bases of touching were accomplished. But Adam's eyes were like quicksand. Irresistible. Possibly deadly. "Okay."

Sarah shot me thumbs up as she saw Adam lead me into the crowded living room where a few couples danced. I needed to remember to fill her in on all things Adam. She loved drama as much as she loved molecular biology, so she'd probably pop popcorn.

Adam's hands found my waist as he pressed our bodies together and moved to the beat of the song. "How was your first day of classes?"

I shook at his mouth touching my ear. How did he make such a simple question sound so sexy? "I only have ballet and history on Mondays, so it was fine. I'll be busier tomorrow and the rest of the week."

"I missed you, Evie."

I shook again. Our dancing qualified more as grinding, which was fine with me. His warm palm pressed into my lower back; my skin tingled through my dress. "I saw you a month ago."

His lips on my ear moved down my neck, planting kisses. Kisses powerful enough to destroy my self-restraint. Plus, he smelled like spicy cinnamon vanilla. My mouth watered.

"Too long," he said. "I want to see you every day."

"I told you, I don't want to date my first semester."

His kisses became harder, heavier, up my chin. "We should be friends until then."

I moaned when he hit a sweet spot just under my ear. His tongue flicked out, and I melted to the floor. Thankfully, Adam's muscles had muscles and they held me up to continue the pretense of dancing. "Friends? You—You're kissing my neck right now," I said.

He lightened his kisses until his lips brushed like a ghost's caress over my skin. "I'm trying to stop." With considerable effort, he pulled back and pressed his forehead against mine. "I lose all thought when I'm around you. I can wait until the spring semester." His pained expression told me it hurt him to do so. "Just... Can I have one kiss? To tide me over?"

"You know we go wild when we kiss."

His eyes darkened. "I know."

Stop staring at his lips. "When we kiss...it's hard to stop."

"Just one."

My head went dizzy. My heart stopped beating. "One."

Wrong decision.

His lips met mine.

Hot. Urgent. Breathless. Slow. Fast. One of his hands went up and tangled in my hair, tugging lightly, adding to the fire. I grabbed his shirt and pulled him toward me. I needed this. Needed him. Needed him to need me

Timeshare Boyfriend

with the passion of a thousand summer suns, so he might feel a fraction of what I felt for him.

I nibbled his lip, and he groaned. He flicked his tongue against mine and gripped my hips so hard, I made a mental note to check for sexy, Adam-shaped bruises.

Suddenly, there was a wall behind my back, and he pressed me into it. We were in the bathroom. When had that happened? His hand, still on my lower back from dancing, drifted further down. Down. *Yes.* He cupped the top of my butt and squeezed, *kneading* me, adding to the pounding ache between my legs.

He pulled back, eyes glassy and lips swollen. "Stop. We should stop. I said one kiss."

I grabbed his head and dragged him back to me. Lips on lips. Hands raking over each other. More grinding to the loud beat vibrating the bathroom door. He stepped between my legs as the pesky limbs lifted to wrap around his waist.

"Fuck, Evie, stop."

"Don't want to."

He panted against my mouth and stared at my lips. A moment of silence and heavy breathing passed as he made his decision. "Then, don't."

The kiss was everything. The heat between us had built to a dangerous, explosive level, and now I needed some release. I needed him. Now. Now.

He sat me on the sink's counter so I could spread my legs for him to settle between. He thrust against me, and I shouted, "*Yes.*" My body was at the point of no return. I needed his touch on me. I wanted him so bad, it hurt. I wanted not to hurt anymore. "I need it. Please, I feel—"

"I know exactly how you feel." He closed his eyes and breathed hard against me. "I can help the ache to go away, just tell me that's what you want."

"That's what I want." I bucked my hips up, rubbing his erection against me.

"If I kiss you again, I'm going to make you come. Do you understand?"

My legs pressed his lower body into mine harder. So hard. "Yes, please."

"Once you come in front of me, there will be no chance at us being 'just friends' after that. Do you understand?"

"I understand. I understand."

"Fuck it." His lips were back on mine. Pop Rocks in my veins. His right hand moved down and bunched up the skirt of my dress.

"Please, please, pleasepleaseplease—"

The heel of his hand pressed against me through my panties, and my head dropped back, hitting the glass of the mirror. A low moan tore through me, setting Adam off.

"Fuck, look how wet you are for me." He pushed the panties aside and circled his fingers around the throbbing bud between my legs.

Something rose within me. Something powerful and dizzying and all-consuming. "I..."

"Close already?" He kissed my lips and used his left, less preoccupied hand, to pull down the material of my dress, revealing my white lace bra. "Fucking white, like I could forget." He tugged the cups down.

I didn't have time to respond because his head dropped to my breast, and the sensation made thinking impossible. Loud moans and shouts climbed out of my throat. It took all my willpower to bite onto my hand and muffle them.

Adam's lips and tongue and suction made my brain leave my body. All I felt was pleasure. All I could think was: *Yes. Yes. Yes. More. Harder. Right there. Oh, there. Yes. Close. So close.*

He lifted his head from my breast. "No one has touched you like this, have they? I'm the first." I slapped at his head for him to go back to sucking. He chuckled. "And I'm going to be the last." He licked one of my nipples, before scraping his teeth across it and quickening the circles he traced between my legs.

"Adam!" I screamed as my body shook in convulsions, each spasm rewarding me with more pleasure than I had ever felt. *A partner really does help...* "Oh, God."

He kissed up my neck, whispering into my ear, "That's it, Evie." Another shiver ran through me as my body slipped into erotic bliss. "Beautiful." His words caused the throbbing to start again, but he pulled his hand out of my panties and straightened my dress for me. Staring at me with a blazing blue fire in his eyes, he gruffly commented, "That was the hottest thing I've ever seen."

"Just friends" turned to dust in my brain's vocabulary.

DEAR DIARY,

I've never kept a diary before, but I thought I'd try it since it's my first year of college and everything. I'm going to be honest, I got lazy. The first week here at Genia has passed, and this is the first time I'm writing in here.
    1. My classes are good so far. I ended up in a class with Adam. We're in a study group together, so that's cool. But we'll get to him later. Ballet is tough. Finn likes to practice outside of class so we can get everything right. I agree because it cuts into my "seeing Adam" time, and the less I see Adam, the less time I break my rules and try to jump his bones. But we'll get to that.
    2. I like my roommate. I think we're becoming friends. I miss Penny, though. I text her now and then, but these first few weeks have been busy with getting used to the homework load and such. Sarah is much more direct than Penny. In comparison, Penny tells me to get my rocks off

Dear Diary,

with Adam, while Sarah tells me to buy a vibrator and handle it myself.

3. The food is bad. Why are my parents paying thousands of dollars for variations of grilled cheese, a salad bar, and tacos? Taco Tuesday, Taco Wednesday, taco every day ending in "y."

4. Let's get to Adam now. I keep making out with him. I try not to. I really try. He'll come over to my room to study for the English class we have together, but we end up on my bed, kissing like Sarah won't walk in on us, which happens once every two days. He hasn't touched me in the same way he did that first night even though I'm dying for it. I read my spicy romance novels and think of him as I attempt to lessen my need. It never works. I also built up the nerve to order a vibrator (mostly due to Sarah). It's supposed to be delivered in discreet packaging tomorrow.

Pledge of the week: I'm not going to kiss Adam, and I will get all my homework done a day in advance.

19

FALSE ADVERTISING AND TRUE LOVE

"It's here!" Sarah cheered and threw the mailed package at me. I fumbled—a dancer, not a football player—but caught it before it fell to the ground. The package felt light in my hands. "Now you don't need a man for pleasure."

"Just because you talked me into buying a vibrator doesn't mean I'm going to stop being interested in guys." Though as I said it, I searched for a pair of scissors to open the package with the excitement of a child on Christmas morning.

"Yeah, but maybe now you'll realize you don't need to feel dependent on Adam for pleasure. Now that you're in college, you need to be more sex-positive. You can make yourself feel good."

"I've, uh, done things before."

She rolled her eyes. "Not vibrator things. Hurry up and open it. You got silicone, right?"

I blushed so hard, I felt dehydrated. "You know way too much about this stuff."

"No such thing. But if you're this insecure about it, don't look in my top drawer. You're not ready to see what's in that."

"Here I go." I cut open the package and spilled the contents on my bed. I stood there in silent shock.

Sarah burst out laughing. She laughed for a good five minutes.

The vibrator was the size of my pinky finger's length and girth. I thought it was going to be big. Like human male sex appendage big. What the heck? "I thought it said eight inches."

"It must have said centimeters." Sarah guffawed again and fell back on her bed. "It's just for clit stuff I guess." She giggled, gasping for breath. "The look on your face when you saw it."

"It's not funny." This thing cost me fourteen dollars, plus shipping. Gosh darn it. "I thought it was going to be big."

"Aw, it's okay." Sarah got up and tapped me on the head. "You know the saying 'size doesn't matter.'" She snorted and walked over to our door. "I'll leave you two to get acquainted."

<hr />

"You look..." Adam started and trailed off a bit as he opened the door of his apartment. "Well rested."

I may have been down fourteen dollars, but I was also down five batteries. "I've been sleeping better lately."

Adam raised an eyebrow. Could he tell I had pictured his face while trying out my new favorite toy? Could he sense my satisfaction? Either way, my whole face blushed under his gaze. "That's good."

"It is good," I said a little too loudly and marched into his place. "So, what's for dinner tonight?"

After over a month of eating bad food at the dining hall, Adam invited me to his apartment for dinner. He cooked. This became a Friday night—and sometimes other nights too—tradition. I would accuse him of adding aphrodisiacs to the food, but I knew deep down that it was not the food that made my clothes feel too tight and my skin feel too hot at these dinners. It was him. He wore a chef apron; I tried not to jump his bones. Give and take. I did not know if it was the apron or the fact that he wore it over his boxers and nothing else, but it was hard to stay away.

This was us when he made fettuccine alfredo last week:

Him: Can you taste this sauce for me real quick? Is there too much Parmesan?

I leaned forward, and he placed the wooden spoon at the entrance of my mouth. I licked the white, creamy sauce from it. It was delicious, like everything he made. I released a deep, breathless, "Oh..."

The next thing I knew, I was pinned to the kitchen counter and sucking his face off.

My bad.

Tonight, the kitchen smelled like tomato sauce. Mmm. He also wore his chef apron with nothing but cat-themed boxers on. Extra *mmmm*.

"You should just become Italian already," I said.

He chuckled. "I don't think that's how ethnicity works."

"You are an amazing cook who specializes in Italian food, loves *The Godfather*, and I'm just now learning this from context clues involving your boxers, but you like cats." I used the excuse to feel the fabric of his boxers. Soft compared to the hardness underneath. "I'm sure they'll take you in."

He removed my hand from his naughty parts and returned to stirring the noodles in the boiling water. For a college apartment of four boys, their kitchen was surprisingly clean other than a few dishes occupying the sink and a coffee stain on the counter.

"I didn't know liking cats was an Italian stereotype," he said with a smile, looking at me with way too much soft affection for me to compartmentalize. *Just friends.* Friends with a kissing problem.

"All I know is, the Godfather sure loved petting that cat he held the whole time."

He froze over the stove, his head lurching back toward me. A ragged sigh and groan came from deep in his chest. He put the stirrer down and yanked my body against his. He rasped, "You just made a Godfather reference. I find that so hot."

"You find everything I do hot."

"Correct." He kissed my forehead, honoring my *no kissing* policy, which I tended to be the one to break when around him. "But on the subject of cats, I have something to tell you."

"Don't make an 'I'm a pussy person' joke. It's beneath you."

"I wasn't going to." He blinked. "I'm a bit shocked that you can say the word pussy but won't cuss. It's doing things to my head."

I pressed myself against him, my hand trailing down his chest. "Which head?"

"OKAY," Adam took a step back and released a breath. "Follow me."

He led me to his bedroom, and I wondered if my new vocabulary word had gotten to him enough to break my rules. He opened the door, and a white fluff ran out.

"What the—"

Adam picked up the huge cotton ball of an animal and held it up to show me. The cat snuggled into him, and I felt temporary jealousy over the attention.

"I adopted a cat." The pitch of his voice took on a tender quality that had my panties wanting to fall to the floor because every part of me, even my clothes, could not help but fall for him. "Her name is Snowball Scarface, but she's been going by Snow."

My heart skipped as he petted her and kissed her head. "Why Scarface—" I cut off when the cat turned her face toward me. The kitty was missing an eye. "You adopted a one-eyed cat?" Could he do something not cute? Please. It overwhelmed me.

"Shh." He pretended to block her ears. "She's insecure about it." I snorted, but the cat proved him right when she lunged for me with a loud hiss and an outstretched claw. "No, Snow." Adam held her back before I became one-eyed too. "This is Eve. She is a friend. No scratching her." That was all I got? A "friend?" *Calm down, Evie, he's talking to a cat. Not a person.* Also, it was my rule that we stay only friends.

The cat meowed sweetly against his neck, burrowing herself into the crook of his shoulder.

"She seems nice," I remarked, half sarcastic and jealous.

"I've always wanted a cat, and since I have my own place—and the guys agreed to it—I get to have one." He set her down, and she ran at me with a battle cry. He picked her up again, and she calmed.

"I don't think she likes me," I pointed out.

"She is just jealous she's no longer the most beautiful girl in the room anymore."

My heart melted, and my smile returned.

The cat glared at me with one eye.

"Here." Adam sat Snowball Scarface on the couch in the living room. "You two get to know each other while I finish making dinner."

He left us, and I sat three cushions away from the hissing monster. Her face said it all, "*He's mine, bitch.*"

I leaned over and whispered, "Let the best pussy win."

I got scratched.

I COULD NOT STOP MOANING. "Oh, God. This is so good." I took another bite of the tiramisu Adam had made me for dessert. "You're so perfect," I said.

He sat close to me on the couch with an arm wrapped around my body. "Then date me."

I swallowed the sugary goodness, coughing on some of the cocoa powder. "You know I can't. I don't want a boyfriend during my first semester. I don't have time for a relationship."

He leaned over and trailed his lips down my neck, while one of his fingers played with my hair. "You have time to eat dinner here and study with me. You have time to hang out with your guy friend from ballet."

I frowned, leaning away from him. "I do not 'hang out' with Finn. We practice our dance for the show. It's a huge part of our grade."

"Sure," he said.

I craned my neck to meet his gaze. "Are you jealous?"

He broke eye contact and stared at the TV. "What are we doing, Evie?"

A soft pang dinged in my chest. "What do you mean?"

"You say you don't have time for a relationship, but you already spend all your free time with me. You say you need to focus on your grades and classes, but you have all A's." His fingers touched mine but were gone just as quickly. "Why do you keep pushing me away?"

"I'm here all the time. I'm not pushing you away."

"You're right." His expression darkened. "You're using me for pleasure but not willing to commit to me. Do you like Finn? Is that it?"

"I do not like Finn," I said in a loud voice. "Why do you keep coming back to that?"

"Why don't you want a relationship?"

I moved farther away from him and closer to where Snowball Scarface lay, napping. "I was just in a relationship, remember? I was cheated on." My voice cracked the way it always did when I was about to cry or when I lied. "I'm not looking for a repeat."

He stared at me, and I wanted to throw a blanket over my head to hide. Whenever he looked at me, he acted like he saw my thoughts typed out on a teleprompter. "You just lied."

"No, I didn't," I lied again. "I was cheated on."

"Yeah, but that's not the whole reason you don't want a relationship. What is it?"

I stood from the couch and inched away. "Can we not do this right now?"

He sat there, staring me down. Then he stood,

walked to me, and framed my face in his hands. He rubbed his thumbs over my cheeks, reading more of my thoughts like emotional brail. "It's not that you don't want a relationship. It's that you don't want a relationship with me."

"I—It's not—No."

He dropped his hands from me. "Then, what?"

"I'm scared, okay?" I took a deep breath, but it refused to stay inside. "This has been so great. Talking to you; touching you. It's been perfect. But...it's like that first summer." He tilted his head, confused. I continued, "Everything was perfect and then you showed up five years later and broke my heart, again and again. You've changed into this different person, but how do I know that it's real? That this you is the real one. How can I know? I'll only know when you break my heart again, and I don't think I will be able to heal from that."

He remained silent, his eyes never leaving mine.

"What if we get together, and you realize you made a mistake again?" My jagged breathing and wet cheeks made me cry harder. "I couldn't—I wouldn't be able to—"

"Shhh." He hugged me into his body, clutching me tight and molding himself against my every curve like a bulletproof vest. Protecting me from himself? "I'm sorry. I'm so sorry I've made you feel this way. You don't need to be scared anymore. I promise."

"I don't know if—"

"I'll prove it to you. Give me time, and I'll prove it to you. Please."

EACH DAY that passed after I opened up to Adam, I had a harder time staying away from him in a sexual or romantic way. I studied, staring at notecards, and started thinking of him. I sat in class, listening to a boring lecture about a textbook chapter I had already read, and started thinking of him.

The moment of unraveling came on spooky Halloween night. The moment I saw him, deep down, I knew I would break my rules.

He dressed up as Westley from *The Princess Bride*, the all-time best-made film. He must have asked Sarah and/or illegally checked my search history to find out I planned to dress up as Princess Buttercup. The matching costumes led to a few mistakes.

The first mistake: I muttered, "Fuck," when I saw him in the head-to-toe black, carrying a thin plastic sword.

Knowing I never cussed, he grinned his sexy little grin at me and quoted the most romantic line of the movie, "As you wish."

After a lame Halloween party, Adam invited me to watch a scary movie with him. I said, "I don't like scary movies."

He whispered in my ear, "I'll keep you safe."

In the living room of his apartment, Adam turned on the TV and placed the disc into the DVD player. "I know you don't like scary movies, so..." The screen flashed "*The Addam's Family*," before he hit play and it began.

"You know me," I said, a familiar warmth spreading across my chest.

He pulled me onto his lap and sat us on the couch. "I do." His fingers trailed up the tops of my thighs. They opened for him on instinct. A familiar ache settled below my stomach. "I know you pretty well by now."

"Yeah?"

"I know that you are a bottomless pit when it comes to maraschino cherries." He held me tighter. "I know you want to appear easygoing, but you are obsessive when it comes to organizing and color-coding your weekly agenda. When you get a ninety-five on a test, you spend the first hour upset at what you got wrong rather than what you got right. I know you always hold the door open for the person behind you and say 'I'm sorry' when someone bumps into you like it's somehow your fault. I know you've got the biggest fucking heart, Evie Turner."

My heart and breathing grew heavy. *Adam.*

"You know what else I know? I know when I kiss you here—" He kissed just below my ear where he knew I was weakest. "—you make the sexiest little sound. And when I do this—" He nibbled on my earlobe, securing a small shriek from me. "Your whole body shakes for me."

"You seem to know a lot."

"I pay attention," he said, staring into my eyes. "Did you like what I did to you before?"

Without having to clarify, I knew exactly what he was referring to: that night at the party. His hand in my panties. I fanned myself, hot and tingly. "I-I didn't *not* like it."

He kissed my neck. "Do you want me to do it again?"

Please and thank you. "I—"

"Hey, guys. Happy Halloween." Adam's other roommate, Tim, came out of his room and saw us on the couch. "What movie are you watching?" As the winner of the most-annoying-roommate award, Tim saw nothing wrong with dropping into the chair near the couch to join us. "I love *The Addam's Family*."

Adam dropped his forehead into the crook of my neck in defeat. He then raised his head. "Evie, it's cold in here. Are you cold?"

"I—"

"Tim, could you toss Evie that blanket behind you?"

I caught it and unfolded it over us until the blanket laid over our laps and down our legs. I started to move off Adam's lap, but he kept an iron grip on my waist, telling me not to leave my position on top of him.

Adam turned the volume up on the movie and laid his hands over the tops of my thighs under the blanket.

Just when I thought, *He wouldn't*, he began drawing circles over my legs. A legitimate Buttercup costume on the internet cost too much for me, so I purchased a "Sexy Buttercup," which had a skirt with a high slit in the middle meant to show off my legs. Adam used the slit to his advantage.

He pulled the fabric of the skirt aside, touching my bare skin. His circles were now higher up my thigh, moving inward with slow precision. My legs opened for him again, and I shut them as I tore my gaze from the screen and glanced at Tim, who was oblivious to us.

Adam noticed my hesitancy and kissed the back of my neck again, calming me. "Is this okay?"

I nodded. He pressed my thighs open enough to let his hand between my legs, and my lower limbs let him, welcoming him. I leaned back into his chest, and he kissed the side of my chin.

Under the blanket, I was on fire.

His fingers started their circles over my sensitive bud, and my eyelids slipped shut. His other hand traveled further down to where my entrance was, and he pressed a finger against it, not penetrating but the pressure was enough to make me gasp in a loud breath.

Tim looked over at me, a curious expression on his face.

"Sorry, I—" Adam continued his torture beneath the blanket as I spoke. "—just love this movie so much," I managed to say through the sensations building inside me.

The stiffness of Adam's crotch dug into my lower back, turning me on even more.

Pleasure washed over me in crashing waves as his fingers sped up the circles. I was half-sure I went cross-eyed.

"Are you okay?" Tim asked, seeing my struggle but not understanding.

"Great." My words still didn't convince him to turn away from me. Adam's finger pressed over my entrance more and more. Press. Lift. Press. Lift. My hips twitched for him to push in and ease some of my ache. So close. "Watch the movie," I told Tim just as Adam slammed the finger inside me.

I came. Hard. My breathing stopped. My body spasmed.

And it was hot.

So freaking hot.

Softly bucking his hips up against me, Adam whispered in my ear, "You're so tight, squeezing my finger like that."

I clamped a hand on his thigh as I struggled to remain silent. Ecstasy bombarded me.

"Only I do this to you," Adam said softly, still circling his fingers on me as I came down from the ride. "I'm never going to hurt you or make you feel unwanted. We're in a relationship, Evie. The sooner you admit that, the sooner you'll feel this good every fucking day."

20

A HEART OF FOOL'S GOLD

*W*inter

ADAM: *Come over tonight.*

Me: *I'm meeting with Finn to go over our dance until late.*

I waited twenty minutes for a reply.

Adam: *Oh.*

That took him twenty minutes to type?

Me: *Are you jealous?*

Adam: *Should I be? You're the one who doesn't want a relationship with me. Maybe it's because you want someone else.*

My breath paused.

Adam: *Sorry, I didn't mean that. Please ignore me. I'll pick you up from practice.*

But he did mean it. Pushing Adam away to save myself from being hurt was hurting him.

How much longer could we go on like this?

"You want to practice the jump again?" my ballet partner, Finn, asked me. Our winter showcase was four days away just like the rest of our final exams in other classes.

"No, I think we've got that part down. I do want to practice that spin and lift in the beginning though."

Ms. Petrov glided around the room, giving notes to the dance partnerships for improvement.

Finn and I practiced several minutes more until Ms. Petrov circled us like a vulture. "You're doing great, Miss Turner." She tilted her head at Finn. "Mister Mason, if you were with a less skilled partner, your lack of timing may go unnoticed, but Miss Turner performs every movement as if she felt it coming. Dance more like Miss Turner."

She walked away.

Finn rolled his eyes. "I guess having you as a partner didn't end up helping me the way I thought it would."

I flinched a bit, and regret swarmed his face.

"Sorry, I didn't mean it that way."

But it seemed like he did.

"He said that to you?" Sarah growled. "I'll kick his leotard-ed ass."

I sipped from my cup of soda and placed it on the dining hall table. "I don't think he meant it like—"

"Like he wanted you as his partner just to get a good grade and now regrets his B-minus self being around your A-plus work? Cause that's what it sounds like."

The dining hall was crowded today for lunch. I glanced around just to make sure Finn wasn't within hearing range. The hearing range was a couple of seats away and no more because the level of chatter became deafening when everyone ate a meal at the same time.

"I guess it does sound pretty jerky."

She twirled her fork into her spaghetti. "You should tell Adam. I'd pay to watch him beat Finn's leotard-ed ass."

"Why do you keep calling it that? He doesn't wear a leotard. It's more like spandex tights and a T-shirt."

"'Spandex tights-wearing ass' doesn't have the same ring to it."

"You're not wrong."

"Speaking of Adam..." She smiled her sly smile. "Are you still acting like you two aren't a couple?"

"We're not," I said. "Technically."

"Technically, I'm not good at math but you don't see my TA giving me bad grades."

I blinked with confusion. "What comparison was that?"

"Cause I'm fucking my TA, and you and Adam are—"

I slapped my hands over my ears in a rash, immature action. I swallowed down the *la, la, las*. "We're not."

She threw a piece of iceberg lettuce from her side salad at me. "Don't lie."

"I'm not. I've never..." I did a hand gesture that made no sense; yet, she still got the message.

"You're a *virgin*?"

I waved my hands in the air for her to be quieter. Yelling the word "virgin" on a college campus created the same shock and panic as "bomb" on an airplane.

"I convinced a virgin to buy a vibrator. Wow, I am amazing."

"Don't say it like it's a big thing."

"It is a big thing. A nineteen-year-old virgin in college? You're a unicorn."

I blew out a breath. "I *am* horny."

"Wait, so you and Adam haven't had sex?" she asked, and I nodded. "No wonder he looks so on edge."

That made me frown. "What do you mean?"

"He drops you off at our room and while you look like you're floating on your magical unicorn clouds, he looks like he's treading water and trying not to drown. Do you ever..." It was her turn to make a hand gesture. "Help him out?"

And risk humiliation if I messed up somehow? John the Cheater's voicemail raced through my head again, "*She doesn't even know how to touch me.*" "Um, no."

Timeshare Boyfriend

Her eyes widened. "That boy must be taking a lot of cold showers." She blinked. "Or some long hot ones, if you know what I mean."

I did. The idea of Adam in the shower touching himself to thoughts of me... *Stop, Evie.* "I want to try, uh, helping him out. I'm just nervous."

"Start slow."

"Mhm, mhm. Like what?"

She laughed but offered me some advice. "Touch him over the pants. Guys love that."

"That's all?"

"You don't want to leave him with even worse blue balls, so taking him out of his pants and finishing the job would probably be best."

ADAM: *Look what James sent me.*

He forwarded the video of us singing "Summer Nights" at karaoke last summer.

Me: *Seems like a lifetime ago.*

Adam: *Back then you wouldn't agree to date me. Oh, how things change.*

Me: *I still haven't agreed to date you.*

Adam: *Yet. I don't know if you know this, but this first semester is coming to an end in two days. I believe your rule is "no dating during the first semester of college."*

Me: *You have been very patient.*

Adam: *It's been easy, knowing what I have to look forward to.*

His sweet words gave me confidence.

Me: *I think you deserve a reward.*

Adam: *What kind of reward are we talking about here?*

Me: *I guess you'll just have to find out during our study time at the library.*

"Are you ready?" Finn inquired, and I put my phone in my bag. We met for one last practice. The night before the showcase, we planned to rest and save our energy, so this was our last shot at getting everything perfect before the big performance.

"Yeah, sorry, let's do this."

We played the music and began the dance routine. The song lasted for five minutes. After the first two, Finn slipped in his cues again.

"Everything okay?"

"Of course," he responded as if he did not know he danced two measures off.

"Why don't we slow it down?" I suggested, and his eyes became stony. I had bruised his precious ego. Uh, oh. "I just want to make sure I'm getting everything right for our big show."

He scowled at the ground. "You heard Petrov, you're the perfect one."

"No one's perfect."

We started the song again; this time Finn's movements were rougher. Less soft and less what Petrov wanted from us.

I twirled, he leaped.

I jumped, he caught.

Then, he released. Early and higher up than we planned.

In the moment of falling toward the ground, instead of freaking out, I stretched my legs out and flexed my feet. I landed on a twist of my ankle that stung but otherwise I was okay. Finn stared at me, expressionless.

This time, I could not mask my glare. "Why did you drop me?"

He put his hands up in defense. "I didn't mean to; it just happened."

Liar, liar, tights on fire. "Dance partners need to trust each other."

"I do trust you," he said.

But I don't trust you. "Don't drop me again."

"I said I didn't mean to—"

"I could get hurt. For real. Dancing injuries end careers all the time."

"I swear I won't drop you again, okay? It was an honest mistake."

I WORRIED about Finn and our performance for the rest of the day. He wouldn't sabotage me on purpose, would he? To make his dancing seem better in comparison?

My ankle still felt twinges of slight pain, but I had danced through worse before. I held out hope that he would get himself and his ego back together before the big show in two nights. The performance counted for half our grade. I planned on ending my first semester with all A's.

Including an A in English, which turned out not to be my strong suit. Who knew Shakespeare was so difficult to read and analyze? Everyone. Everyone knew, but it was a required class for freshmen like Adam and me.

I showed up early to the library for studying with Adam so I could get work done before he got there. There was no way I would focus once he showed up ready to receive his reward. After an hour, he sent me a text.

<u>Adam</u>: *I'm hard.*

<u>Adam</u>: *I meant 'here,' damn autocorrect.*

My phone buzzed again before I responded.

<u>Adam</u>: *Maybe both though, depending on what my reward is.*

<u>Me</u>: *Fifth floor, study room 5124.*

The room was secluded and older, so instead of having the glass see-through walls around it fully, it only had one. The table also sat low and had wooden sides that went all the way down, so that people studying outside the room, in the main lounge area, could not see below the waist of whoever sat there. They simply saw a floating torso and a table.

Adam may have noticed the seclusion and

resourceful appearance of the table when he walked in to join me because his eyes darkened, his smile growing. "Hey there, beautiful."

I shifted on the chair, nervous. "Howdy."

Considering I was a northerner who went down south two weeks out of the year, there was no reason for me to say "Howdy" other than nerves. Adam saw this and worked to put me at ease. Instead of bringing up his reward, he got right down to study-business.

He sat next to me at the table and pulled his books out of his backpack. We went back and forth reciting Shakespeare quotes while the other fought to remember which play they were from.

"Ready?"

He closed his eyes. "Yes."

We studied for close to forty-five minutes before watching Adam with his eyes closed led to some dirty thoughts on my end. Not to mention, his knee kept knocking against mine under the table. Every cell of my body vibrated each time our legs connected.

I read from the play, "I would not wish any companion in the world but you."

He bit his lip. His sexy, soft lip that knew how to kiss me until my toes curled. His knee knocked against mine again, and I held in my groan. "*The Tempest*," he answered.

"Right."

He scooted his chair closer to me this time. Feeling

the heat, too? "I pray you, do not fall in love with me. For I am falser than vows made in wine."

"Easy. *As You Like It*."

He placed his hand on my upper thigh. "Very good," he purred, his breath hitting my cheek. When I opened my eyes, his face was an inch away from mine. The ache between my legs grew.

"I think we're going to ace this exam," I said. The beginning of our college hangouts started under the pretense of study nights; so, after using that as the constant excuse to see each other, we knew the material all too well by the end of the semester.

Adam squeezed the hand on my leg. "You're so sexy when you know Shakespeare quotes, Evie."

Take control. I rested my hand on his knee. "You're sexy too."

"Yeah?"

My hand trailed up his pant leg, settling higher on his inner thigh. I glanced down and saw the slight bulge forming in his jeans. Game time.

"Looks like someone is a little pent up," I said.

He gave a nervous, throaty chuckle. "I've been hard for the last three months."

"Only three?"

"Since the second you came all over my fingers for the first time, my dick has been in a constant state of torture."

How dare he make me laugh during my planned seduction? "You've been very patient with me."

His gentle hand grazed over mine as he said, "I would wait forever for you, Evie Turner."

Correct. Answer.

I brushed my lips against his, light and teasing. "I think it's time for your reward."

He moved up to kiss me, but I pushed his shoulders back, so he knew to let me play for a while with no interruption on his part.

My hand moved over his erection, tracing the zipper on his jeans. He groaned—deep, low, and tortured—at the contact. "This is my first time doing this. I want to be good at it," I whispered as my fingers undid the button and worked the zipper down centimeter by centimeter.

"Baby, all you have to do is touch me while I try not to come. You'll be an expert, I know it."

As I opened his jeans, his bare cock sprang up, no barrier of underwear to hinder my seduction.

"Laundry day," he explained in a hoarse voice, his eyes glued to my hand.

I'd never seen one in real life before, but the books I read prepared me. I circled my thumb around the tip of him while my right hand wrapped around the base. Squeezing had the desired effect.

"Fuck." His head dropped back then shot back up when he remembered the people on the other side of the study room glass wall could see us from our stomachs, up.

A little reward and revenge after Halloween night under the blanket in front of his roommate.

"Evie, just like that," he grated. Grinning, I licked my hand and stroked him. Up, down. Harder. Faster. "The way you feel... Shit, I'm not going to last long."

My confidence skyrocketed.

I took it up a notch.

Sliding down from my chair, I knelt between his legs, on the ground, where no one could see me. To the outside world, Adam would appear to be studying on his own. My hands continued their stroking as I asked in a teasing voice, "Am I doing this right?"

He shuddered with anticipation, watching me below him. "So right. Too right." A bead of moisture glistened at the tip of him.

"Do you like me on my knees, Adam?"

Before he could answer, my tongue flicked over the tip of his arousal, and he let out a low moan. I kept my grip and motion at the base with my right hand, swallowing as much of him as I could. I bobbed my head up and down, sucking and not enjoying it. Why did anyone willingly do this? I was about to stop and pull away when he flipped out.

"Fuck, Evie!" He thrust into my mouth like he had never known such pleasure. "Fucking dreamed of this."

This was why I did it. For his pleasure, his reaction.

I flicked my tongue against the tip again, and he jumped in his seat. "How do you know to—" He cut off, his eyes rolling back. "That's it, baby. Fuck."

I felt powerful. A sexual heiress with a fortune in steamy secrets.

He trembled.

The creaky sound of the study room door opening pierced through the atmosphere. Both of us froze. I let him out of my mouth and kept my hands to myself, telepathically telling him to get rid of whoever had just walked inside.

"Hey, can I study in here?" a feminine voice asked him.

"*Say no*," I told Adam through our mental connection. He still sat, frozen, not knowing what to do. The sound of books being placed on the table filled my ears. *No.*

"Thanks, everywhere else is full."

Everywhere else was not full. There were hundreds of rooms and places to study in the library. Understanding clicked in my brain. She had seen Adam all alone and wanted to join him. She wanted to flirt with my man.

I wrapped my hand back around his shaft and reopened my mouth. Adam made a cautious sound in the back of his throat and inched away from me on his seat. He gave my head a soft pat as if to say, "*No, no. Not now.*"

"*Yes, now,*" I mouthed at him from under the table and resumed my suction skills. I circled the head of his cock with my tongue, and his whole body jumped.

"Are you okay?" the girl questioned him.

He nodded and grunted when I picked up the pace. My head bobbed in his lap, and I wondered if she could hear the quiet, sexy sounds. *He's mine.* He gently pulled at my hair to try to get me off him, but after I took him deeper in my mouth, he began pulling me toward him instead.

"Are you sure?" the girl asked again. "You're sweating."

"I—it's hot," he responded. His eyes went crossed as I hollowed my cheeks. "So hot."

"I know, right? They should invest in an air conditioner." I could tell she wanted to make my Adam laugh, but he was too far gone. "What are you reading?"

I nearly giggled with my mouth full at how annoyed Adam looked by this girl. "Shakespeare."

"Work or pleasure?"

A soft whimper came from his throat as I squeezed the base of his shaft. "Definitely pleasure."

His whole body started shaking. Trembling with the building need to climax. He pressed a hand over his mouth, throwing his elbow on the table. As he came with a muffled grunt and several twitches of his hips, I had never felt sexier or more powerful. *So, this is what it means to be a man-eater.*

"Do you have a favorite Shakespeare play?"

Was I supposed to stay under the table the rest of the night until the random girl left? I had not thought this through.

"I like 'Hamlet,'" he answered her and shot me a *what-do-we-do?* look.

"If you ever want to read Shakespeare together, I have a—" She was asking *my* Adam on a date? Heck, no.

I crawled out from under the table and sat back in the seat next to him. Her jaw dropped, and she gaped at me, horrified and realizing what she had interrupted. "Sorry, he's taken." I leaned over and zipped up his pants for him. As she gathered her books and ran out, Adam stared at me with awe. On his face, it looked a little like love.

"I'M FREAKING OUT, PENNY." I called my best friend on my cell phone out of instinct. Anxiety and nerves wracked me as I waited backstage to perform my partner dance at the winter showcase.

"Calm down. You've danced in front of crowds plenty of times before."

"Never for half of my grade." My voice went quieter. "Or danced with a guy who dropped me two days before."

"But you landed on your feet." Listening to her calmed me, warmed me like a cup of sentimental tea. "If it happens again, you'll land on your feet."

Someone tapped my shoulder. Ms. Petrov motioned to me that I was next to go on stage.

"I've got to go."

"Good luck. And Adam's there, right?"

I took a deep breath. He was there. Or supposed to be there. Was he there? "I think so."

"Good." I heard her smile. "I'm happy for you two."

"We're not officially dating," I repeated.

"Yet," she used the same word as Adam.

I hung up and proceeded to wiggle my body, shaking off the nerves and negative feelings. This was my time to shine. This was my chance to show I had *it*. The *it* Ms. Petrov saw in me. The *it* I wanted to see in myself.

The partners left the stage, and I walked out to meet Finn in the center as he came from the other side. A quick glance out at the audience revealed that Adam and Sarah sat in the front row, holding bouquets of flowers.

My heart dropped into my stomach, quickly digested. Every one of my anxieties melted to the stage floor. Adam grinned at me as I took my first pose.

The song played, and we danced.

The first four minutes were perfect. Every move matched the music, and Finn and I danced in sync.

Then, I ran and jumped toward him. He caught me, lifted me. Up. Up. Above his head. And dropped me.

Fear.

Fear as I fell six feet.

I did what I could. I spun in the air, trying to make it

appear like part of the plan, and stretched out my legs, hoping they would land straight and safe.

I touched the ground.

Pain. Horrible pain. Shooting pain from my ankle, up my leg. I stumbled and dropped into a split to play off my inability to stand on it.

Two more measures of music played as I stayed in my split, lifting my arms around gracefully to the soft beats.

The stage lights went down.

I sat there, struggling to stand, when a slim figure came over to me and threw my right arm over her shoulder. Ms. Petrov helped me hop on one foot off stage, using her whacking stick to stabilize us both.

"I'm going to kick that guy's leotard-ed ass," Adam growled as he held my hand in the hospital room.

"What did I tell you?" Sarah pointed out her premonition coming true.

I held onto the five bouquets they had given me and waited for the doctor to permit me to leave. He told me my landing fractured my ankle and that I needed to walk in a cast and on crutches for six weeks. "At least it'll be healed right when the spring semester starts. Right in time for classes," I grumbled.

"That's my girlfriend, ever the optimist."

"Girlfriend?"

Adam grinned, pushing a hair back from my face. "Your first semester of college is over, baby. It's time we made this thing official."

Being dropped should have increased my trust issues.

Yet, as I stared up at Adam's beautiful and sincere face, all I felt was giddy hope. The kind I felt that first summer.

Finally, I was his and he was mine.

Don't drop me, Adam.

DEAR DIARY,

I realize it's been a while since I last wrote. I'm worried I bought this diary for nothing. I just couldn't say no to the shiny bedazzled cherry on the front. It's adorable.

My ankle hurts a little less, but it sucks to look down at my cast. It itches. All the freaking time. I would love to admit I didn't lose a pencil or two down it, scratching. Alas, I will not lie to you.

Since winter break started, Adam texts me every day. He even came down for Christmas. I asked my parents if it was okay, and he brought James and slept over in the guest room. Did I try to sneak him into my room at night? Yes, yes I did. And did it work? My dad would say no, as he caught us hand-in-hand in the hallway. Adam and I turned our handholding into a fake shaking of hands goodnight, and he stayed in the guest room for the rest of the night. It was also hard to sneak around with James in the house too.

Dear Diary,

I love James, but he's a cock blocker.

Example:

The guest room bathroom wasn't connected to their bedroom, so now and then, I'd see Adam in nothing but a towel around his waist, leaving the shower to walk back into his room.

The night before Christmas, I walked to my room and passed by just as the guest bathroom door opened and a waft of steam exited it. Out came Adam in his small white towel.

I moaned at the sight.

A wicked grin stretched across his face. He was just as pent up as I was. The last time we touched—other than a simple kiss—was that last study night before finals.

I jumped him. Catapulted onto him, wrapping my strong legs around his waist and yanking his head to mine for a passionate kiss.

He pulled me into the bathroom with him, which was still steamy from his long shower, and kissed me against the door after he closed it.

The kiss was wild and breathless and crazed. The sexy, soapy smell of him drove me wild.

Then, my hand randomly reached for his towel. Don't know how it happened, but it did.

His towel fell to the ground, revealing him in all his glory. I was about to sink onto my knees to praise the male sex God in front of me when James opened the bathroom door that neither of us locked.

Dear Diary,

Adam and I stood there with our mouths open, dumbfounded until I, a genius, shouted on the spot, "I was helping him find his penis—I mean, *pants!*"

DEAR DIARY,

He is perfect. We are perfect.

Spring semester was blossoming tulips and blossoming *feelings*. Strong feelings.

But, sometimes, I worry about going back to the timeshare this summer with him. I know it's not cursed, but it's where Adam Pierce became an expert in breaking my heart.

I know he cares for me, but he hasn't said he loves me. We haven't had sex.

Things could still change.

I don't want them to change.

We are perfect together. We really are.

I'm worried about this summer.

21

LOVE IS PATIENT, LOVE IS KIND, LOVE MAKES YOU LOSE YOUR FREAKING MIND

The Next Summer

"Adam!" I screamed, running and launching myself onto him.

He caught me with a chuckle and wrapped my legs around his waist, so he could hold onto me for a long, hot kiss. Shivers ran through me as I clung to him. He pulled back enough to say against my mouth, "I missed you, Evie." *I missed you, Evie.* Such simple words, but they vibrated through me like an emotional earthquake.

"Stop being gross," James yelled over at us as he carried bags from their car into the timeshare building.

Adam had texted me when their car was five minutes away, so I had run down from my room, and paced back and forth through the parking lot until he jumped out of the passenger seat of a black car and ran toward me.

"Nice to see you, Eve," Maryam greeted me, wheeling her suitcase toward the entrance of the building.

I let my legs drop from around him as I blushed. "Sorry, I kissed you in front of your mom."

He tipped his head back and laughed, looking so free and charming. I wanted to smother his lips with mine. "Don't ever apologize for kissing me." He took my hand in his as we walked to the building's elevator. "There will never be a context where I won't want it."

Challenge accepted. "You'd be fine if I kissed you at a funeral?"

"Kissing is a way to celebrate life."

"How about a sex addiction rehabilitation center?"

He ruffled my hair as we entered the building. He held the door open for me. "You caught me. If we were ever both in for sex rehab, I wouldn't want you to kiss me."

"What's sex rehab?" James asked, four feet in front of us, standing next to the elevator. Maryam also stood behind him.

My cheeks heated faster than a hot plate.

"James, is that my hat?" Adam distracted him. "I told you to stop taking my stuff."

"It's not." James took off the cap and pushed it into the back pocket of his jeans. "It's mine."

"I'm serious, no more going through my clothes."

The elevator dinged, and we loaded onto it, the discussion safe from sex rehab.

I helped the Pierce family lug in suitcases and followed Adam into his room. The Pierces had an upgraded three-bedroom unit, so James and Adam both had their own private rooms.

I sat on Adam's bed and bounced on the mattress, as he unpacked. "We're in a relationship at the timeshare. That's never happened before."

He bent down to give me another peck on the lips. What started as an innocent kiss didn't end as one. His shoulders were tense when he went back to unpacking. "I don't know how I'm supposed to walk around in public with you in a bikini within touching distance for the next two weeks."

"I packed one I think you'll really like, but I can't wear it out on the beach."

He frowned. "Why would you buy a swimsuit you can't swim in?"

"It rhymes with wrong."

He threw a few pairs of shorts in a dresser drawer. "Song?"

"No."

"Long? The bathing suit is long?"

Damn, a lot of things rhymed with wrong. "Think 'th' to begin the word."

He groaned when he understood and ran a hand through his dark hair. "Fuck, Evie, you're going to prance around in a thong bikini in front of me? Are you trying to make me lose my damn mind this summer?"

His mind? No. What did I want to lose this summer? My nearly twenty-year-old virginity.

◦◦◦◦

I TUGGED Adam into my family's unit and led him into my room. I didn't get to close the door before my father said, "Evie, come back out. Your mother and I need to talk to you."

Adam met my gaze with a question in his eyes, but I waved him into my room. I closed the door behind him and trotted over to where my parents sat in the living room. "Hey, Adam and I are going to watch a movie in my room—"

"With the door closed?" Mom asked.

"Leaving it open destroys the whole dark, movie theater aesthetic."

"She's turning twenty in three weeks," Dad said. "She can close the door if she wants to."

"Thanks, Dad." With his approval, I turned on my heel to leave.

"Wait, I'm not finished." He motioned for me to sit in the chair across from where they were on the sofa. "Though we realize you're an adult and you have a right to your own privacy, we need to have a talk before that can happen."

I shot a yearning glance to where Adam waited for me in my bedroom. "A talk?"

"You see, your mother and I—"

My jaw dropped. "You mean a sex talk?"

My parents shot each other uncomfortable looks. My mother took the metaphorical microphone from him. "We want to make sure you know what you're getting into."

"I'm nineteen. Isn't it too late to give me the sex talk?"

My dad's eyes narrowed as he leaned forward. "Is it too late?"

I was worried if I said, "yes," he would march into my room, grab Adam by the shirt collar, and tell him to make an honest woman out of me.

"What? No." *World, swallow me whole, please.* "Not in that way, I meant—"

"We don't want you to have sex," my mother said.

My heart stopped. "Ever?"

She waved her hands in the air, erasing her last statement. "I do want grandchildren. But for now, if you must, make sure to be safe."

"Can you be safe by yourself? Or do you need us to buy you, eh, buy you..." Oh God, listening to my father try to say "condoms" killed any young sex drive I thought I had.

"I'm fine. I haven't—I'm fine."

They nodded with solemn expressions.

I wanted to die as I walked back to my room and

joined Adam. Humiliation had been stamped across my forehead. He opened his mouth to ask me what happened, but I didn't give him time. "I don't want to talk about it."

We watched the movie for a while, cuddling on the bed before he started humming that same tune he hummed around me summers ago. I meant to ask him what song it was, but his hands started playing with my hair. Tugging, stroking, massaging my scalp. I let out a moan and shut my mouth the next instant.

He raised an eyebrow.

I shook my head and turned my attention back to the movie. As hard as I tried to focus on the film, my thoughts could not turn away from the subject at hand. "Why haven't we had sex yet?"

His mouth dropped open. "What?"

"We've done everything else."

"Not *everything*."

"But every time we get close to having actual sex, you stop us." I pushed myself up to look at him. "Why don't you want to have sex with me?"

His expression remained stunned. "First off, get the idea that I don't want to have sex with you out of your head because that is the most wrong thing I've heard in my life. More wrong than someone saying the ocean is orange."

"I'm sure somewhere in the world, there's an orange ocean. I know a pink beach exists."

He pulled my body closer to his on the bed, holding

me. "I want you, that should be a given. But sex is a big step."

"And you think we're not ready for it?"

"Evie." He gestured to me. "You're a virgin."

My jaw clicked. "You won't have sex with me because I'm a virgin? You do realize I'm going to remain a virgin until you have sex with me, so that defense does not hold up in my court of law."

He pulled away from our embrace and swung his legs over the bed. He sighed. "Stop saying I don't want to have sex with you. I want to—"

"Then, why haven't we?"

"Do *you* want to?" he questioned me. "It's not something you can take back."

"Really? I didn't realize trading in my virginity didn't involve a return policy and a receipt that expires five weeks after my purchase." I huffed but turned serious as I laid back on the bed. "I want to lose my virginity to someone I love, who loves me too." I didn't need to hear it from him, but I needed to feel it. I needed to know what we had was real.

His eyes widened at the word love. He used to have a problem with it when he was younger. But before we had gotten together, he told me he worked through his issues and hang-ups around the subject.

"I know we haven't said it yet, but I—I like you very much," I said.

His stiff shoulders relaxed. "I like you very much, too."

"And I'd like to think before these two weeks run out, we might...try it."

He rubbed another hand over his face. "You want to have sex within the next two weeks?"

"I'm not going to carry a calendar around, but yeah."

"I don't know if I can." He appeared distressed, so I patted his hand. "Taking your—your vir..." God, it was like my dad and the word "condoms" all over again.

"If I wasn't a virgin, would you have sex with me right now?" I asked.

His eyes hooded and raked over my bare legs.

"Unbelievable." I stood and paced in front of the bed. "Why is virginity so stigmatized in modern-day society? It shouldn't be harder for me to convince my boyfriend to sleep with me than it is to go out and find a cult that wants to sacrifice me."

"I'm worried you'll regret it. It's something you can't take back, and I'm worried you'll regret choosing me."

My heart slowed. *Adam.* I nudged his chin until he looked at me. "If there was ever a person I'd never regret being with, it's you...and maybe Tom Holland."

His head shot up. "That actor guy? Really?"

"Maybe I should go find Tom, he may not have a problem with taking my v—"

Adam growled and yanked me by my hips. I fell into a straddle position over him. "Don't joke about that."

"I'm not going to regret you. You're going to have sex with me, Adam Pierce." I tangled my hands in his hair and whispered onto his lips, "Whether or not I have to seduce you to get it is mute."

A small smile appeared on his face. "Were you trying to say moot?"

One of my fingers pushed against his lips. "Shh. Time to mute yourself." I kissed him. "If you can't get condoms, let me know. My parents will buy us some," I joked, but Adam turned whiter than my bedsheet.

THE NEXT FEW days were full of failed seduction attempts. Adam was strong-willed. I was also not the best at seduction. My winking came across more as having an eyelash in my eye. My skills with makeup and doing anything with my untamable hair sucked just as bad.

Sarah: *If he can resist you for longer than a day, I'll be blown away. Did you bring Mr. Vibe with you?*

Penny: *Give him Hell, baby. Literal Hell. Light that boy on fire. But not literal fire.*

"Excuse me," I said in a breathy voice as I brushed past Adam on the way to the pool steps. There was plenty of room for me not to press against him, but I took advantage of the situation. We were both in swimsuits, so our bare stomachs touched, causing the usual sensual sparks.

From the corner of my eye, I saw the one person

who occupied the hot tub get up and leave. Perfect. "Come in the hot tub with me," I said.

Seeming to realize I was up to something, he replied, "I don't know..."

I crossed two fingers behind my back. "I promise not to seduce you."

"Evie, I just saw you move your hand to cross two fingers behind your back."

"That's cheating. You're not supposed to notice that."

He let out a deep, frustrated sigh. "I want this summer to be about us becoming closer. We've been hot and heavy lately, and I want us to be able to just have fun too. I don't want your focus on sex to ruin our summer."

I flinched. "You think sex with me would ruin our summer?"

"No." His voice turned soft. "No way. I'm saying you don't need to spend every minute we're together pushing for it. It should happen naturally." He cupped my cheek, tender and caring. "It'll happen when it happens."

A squeal distracted me from my failing seduction, and we both turned to see what had caused it. A man kneeled in his swim trunks in front of the towel rack and held a ring box up to a girl who cried above him. "Yes, yes, I'll marry you!"

The few people in the indoor pool clapped. The romance lover inside me cheered for them, but my critical side wondered why the man had chosen the indoor pool to propose. The beach seemed much more romantic and was a two-minute walk away. Plus, only two feet away, a toddler was no doubt peeing.

"That was..." Adam began but trailed off.

"I know, I think he could've done better. Where are the flowers? The doves? The choir singing behind him?"

Adam blinked. "Do you really want all that? It seems kind of—"

I said, "romantic" as he continued, "silly."

A pang sliced through my chest. *He still thinks I'm silly? Immature? Even after all these years?* "You think wanting some romance is silly?"

He hesitated. "I don't— I mean, a singing choir? Doves? Doesn't that seem a little much?"

"I was half-teasing about the choir, but why not? Proposals are meant to show how much you love the other person."

"Why can't you show that each day? Why does one small moment call for every romantic, cheesy thing in the book?"

I took a step away from him. "You think romance is cheesy?"

"I just think a proposal doesn't have to be public and a grand affair. It seems embarrassing."

"What does being embarrassed matter if it makes the person you're with happy?" I asked, my voice scratchy and raw.

We stared at each other for a bit. I no longer felt in a seductive mood.

***

Adam and I both sat reading on my balcony. The sounds of ocean waves crashing and seagulls squawking were a welcome distraction from my own thoughts. Did Adam really not believe in heartfelt gestures? In obnoxious romantic displays of affection? It bothered me more than I wanted to admit. If I had been anyone else, it probably wouldn't have mattered, but I loved romance. I wanted it. *And he has already said before that he doesn't believe in love. What if I give him my heart and he throws it over the balcony again?*

Closing my book, I dropped all pretenses of reading and people-watched from our high view. Everyone seemed smaller from the seventh floor. Sadly, our troubles didn't.

Deep, man-made lines in the sand caught my eye. A man was digging a message for someone, with a heart around it. He had finished: "Jason and Rach" Two letters left and it would make Rachel's day, maybe even week.

"That's so sweet," I said and turned Adam's attention to the message being carved into the grains of sand.

"He dug too close to the water," Adam commented. "One big wave is going to wash it away."

"Yeah, but it only takes a second for it to mean something."

He shrugged and returned to his book. "People carve messages into the sand all the time. It's unoriginal."

"Nothing is completely original anymore." I stared down at the man in the sand. "I happen to like unoriginal."

"You don't think it's sad? Every summer, people write love messages in the sand, and they're blown away by wind or washed away by water. If anything, it shows that love is temporary."

I flinched away and stood from my chair. "Do you think we're temporary?"

"What?"

I stepped back into my unit and closed the sliding glass door.

We did not talk for the rest of that day.

Around nine o'clock at night, I received a text message from Adam. "*Come out to the beach. Follow the red light.*"

The truth was, even though I was upset, I had missed talking to him for those seven hours. I got dressed and grabbed my sandals for the beach. The red light he referenced was a small glow coming from near the waves. The closer I got, the better I saw him in the darkness. He stood on the sand, holding out a small necklace with a glowing heart pendant. It was battery-operated and adorable. Romantic. He probably hated it.

"What are you doing out here?" I asked him.

"Getting back on your good side? I thought we could take a romantic moonlit walk on the beach."

My eyes were drawn to the pretty red glow of the jeweled heart. My favorite color. "Is that necklace for me?"

"It is." He circled me and placed it around my neck. "I'm sorry for what I said."

"I just—People always bash romance for being cheesy or cliché. I get that you don't think it's important, but—"

"But it's important to you." His arms wrapped around my waist and pulled me against him. "So, it's important to me. Love has always been...hard for me, so dating someone so into it is tough. But it's worth it if I get to be with you."

"I don't need a bouquet of roses each week." I tucked my head into his chest and trailed my nose over his neck. *Mmm, my boyfriend smells good.* "But I wouldn't mind a message in the sand now and then."

His forehead touched mine. "Our names don't need to be written in the sand," he whispered. "They're written in the stars."

I released a breathy laugh against his lips. "Wow, now that was cheesy."

"On a scale of one to ten, was it gouda or cheddar?"

"Monterey Jack."

"Mmm, spicy."

22

THE HEART WANTS WHAT IT WANTS AND SOMETIMES IT WANTS ROMANCE

My hands went down to my ankles, and he lightly slapped them away. I growled. "Eff. You."

"Careful, you might hurt my feelings."

"Adam," I cried. The small bites and welts on my legs and feet called out to me. I needed to scratch. Scratch. *Scratch*. "Let me—"

"No. Damn it." Now he was the one growling. "This is all my fault."

"You bet it is, you bastard."

During his planned romantic walk on the beach, I had gotten bitten by sand fleas all over my feet and legs. He'd had the good sense to wear jeans, so the extent of his bites was two or three on his feet. I was the proud owner of over twenty-eight bites, which all screamed, "*Scratch me!*"

"See, this is why I shouldn't be romantic. I always

end up failing." He frowned and stroked his thumb against my palm as we sat beside each other in my empty unit's living room. "Now, can I leave you alone long enough to get some anti-itch cream, or are you going to start scratching the minute I leave?"

"I'm not going to *not* start scratching."

"I wish I had handcuffs or something."

My heartbeat accelerated; my face went up in flames. Adam handcuffing me? Geez, Louise, Mr. Febreeze.

He narrowed his eyes at my expression. "Why did your whole face just go red?"

"I don't know what you're talking about."

He looked back down at his phone and scrolled through the informational article. "The internet says you shouldn't go back on the beach for a couple of days before your bites heal."

No more beach days? I had just gotten to the timeshare a couple of days ago. "What does the internet really know?"

"There are other things we could do," he suggested, but his eyes lacked enthusiasm. Instead, they were filled to the brim with guilt. "What about an amusement park?"

"Yeah, that sounds—" I cut myself off and immediately bent over to scratch my bites.

He grabbed my hands and pinned them over my head on the couch. "What part of 'no scratching' do you not understand?"

"What part of 'I will break up with you if you don't let me scratch' do you not understand?"

He chuckled but a bit of fear sank into his expression. "Empty threat."

"Sure about that?"

He let go of my hands, and I raked my nails against the pink, puffy skin on my ankle. Relief. Sweet relief. My eyes all but rolled into the back of my head at the addictive ecstasy.

Adam let out a low groan. "Damn Eves, the face you're making right now..."

Nail against bite had never felt so good. I moaned when I moved my scratching to my calf.

"Don't moan. It's confusing my body." He secured my hands again, and I fought back tears. "I'm sorry you got bitten. I feel so guilty."

"Hey, look at me," I said. He met my gaze, and I leaned up and kissed his nose. "You should."

"I'm serious. I'm ruining our summer. I can't even do one romantic thing right." His eyebrows scrunched down in frustration. "I get you a rose, and you prick yourself with the thorns. I take you on a walk on the beach, and you get bitten. What if I can't be the boyfriend you need—"

"Hey." I touched his worried face. His sad eyes reminded me of someone filled with dread. Like he had just had a premonition of a catastrophe. It scared me. "This isn't your fault." I tried to lighten the mood by changing the subject. "Now, what does a girl have to do around here to make her boyfriend scratch her legs? A blowjob? Is that it?"

Adam's jaw dropped. He glanced over to the door of my parents' room. Remembering my parents were out at brunch, Adam ran a hand through his hair and cursed. "Never say 'blow job' around me again. I'm going to have an erection for the next ten minutes."

"Only ten?" I bit my lip. "I wonder what word would make it last longer." I contemplated more dirty words to tease Adam with. "Penis."

He narrowed his eyes on me, seeing through my plan. "Stop."

"You're right. Penis is too medical." I leaned in, whispering, "Cock."

He blinked and grimaced in pain. "Stop, Evie."

I bit the inside of my cheek to keep from laughing.

He shook his head, leaving my room to get me more anti-itch cream.

"Aw, you're no fun."

***

FOR THE NEXT FEW DAYS, Adam did everything he could to be the perfect boyfriend. I could not go back to the beach, but he took me to the pool and read a book beside me on the lounge chairs. He walked with me to the shops along the pier and bought me cherry vanilla ice cream. We smiled and laughed, but a sinking feeling made itself at home in my heart.

He tried so hard to make me happy, but in the moments he did not catch me watching him, he had never looked sadder. I knew a part of it was guilt over ruining my time at the beach for the rest of our week, but it seemed deeper than that. He looked scared, and I couldn't figure out why.

I tried to make him feel less guilty by showing him I did not need the beach to have fun. It helped when James and I begged him to come to the amusement park with us, which was thirty minutes away from our timeshare building. The anti-itch cream helped with the bites, and I gained the self-control not to scratch.

At the amusement park, Adam bought me kettle corn and watched me with blazing eyes when I dropped some pieces into my cleavage and fished them back out to eat. We rode bumper cars. I, of course, chose a sparkling red car with a lightning streak on it, a classic sign that it was the fastest of the fast. I proceeded to bump him every chance I got, making him lose his mind. When he lost his mind, he seemed most like the real Adam. No walls.

"Oh my God, it's a stuffed turtle." I stopped in my tracks when I saw my favorite animal hanging with other giant stuffed animals above a ring toss game. My future sleep companion was four times the normal stuffed animal size and, unlike real turtles, had the cute complexion of a piece of bubblegum. Its sparkle-filled eyes were as big as quarters.

I ran over to the game for a closer look at how to

win the adorable turtle with my name on it. Under the wooden roof, a huge square-shaped table sat in the middle, covered with clear and green bottles. "How much to play?" I asked the worker who appeared about our age, give or take a year.

The worker smiled at me. "Two dollars for three rings. Five dollars for eight. But I could slip you an extra free one for a pretty gal like you."

"Three rings for two dollars? It's going to take at least twenty rings for me to get a hang of it and win." Instead of helping my aunt's office as an unpaid intern over the summer, I should have gone for a real, money-paying job. *Sure, dance major.*

"Sorry, those are the rules."

Adam and James jogged up behind me. "Evie, you can't just go running when you see something you want to do," my sexy boyfriend scolded me. "That's how people get lost."

The worker scanned them up and down. "Are these your brothers?"

Adam's thick forearms bulged as he crossed his arms, surveying the worker with just as much critique in his eyes. "No."

"You guys, they have a pink stuffed turtle." I pointed up at it. "Look how cute it is. I need it."

"Babe—" Adam glanced at the worker to make sure he heard "babe" and understood our relationship. "—no one wins these games. They're rigged."

"I assure you, they are not rigged," the worker commented, and I took his word for it.

I pulled two dollars out from the back pocket of my shorts and handed it over. "Three rings please, and that extra one you offered earlier too if that's still on the table."

The worker grinned at me. "Sure thing, cutie."

A deep growl sounded behind me, but I didn't bother to turn around to see a glaring Adam. I had seen jealous Adam enough in my life to know what he looked like.

The worker counted out four small, red plastic rings in front of me, laying each one down on the counter that separated me from the table of glass bottles. "Good luck."

I flipped my hair. "Don't need it." A chuckle came from close behind me this time. Adam loved when I got cocky. I loved when he got cocky too. Wink, wink.

I took a deep breath to concentrate and threw one of my rings at the tops of the bottles. A soft crunch of glass breaking informed me that I did not win on my first try. The glass bottle I aimed for now had less of a top.

"It's called a ring toss." Adam's hands settled on my hips as he positioned me in front of the closest bottles. "Toss them, don't throw them."

I kissed the small ring and tossed it in a soft underhand motion. It bounced off the first row of bottles and fell to the ground. "Nice going, Adam. You wasted my second shot with your advice." I threw the last two and lost. "Dang it."

His hands went back on my hips. Heat radiated from his front, which pressed against my back, and moved through me in waves. Distracting. "I told you not to play this game. It's impossible to win."

I pointed at the reason I played. "I would give my first-born child for that stuffed turtle."

Adam laughed again in my ear, deep and throaty. "Evie."

"I'm only forty percent joking."

The worker gestured to Adam. "You're the boyfriend, I assume. Aren't you the one who is supposed to win her the prize?"

I rolled my eyes at the gender role stereotype. "I can win it myself, thank you."

I pulled out another two dollars and turned to smile at Adam, but he stared at the stuffed pink turtle with a serious look on his face.

The worker picked up on it too and prodded him again, no doubt trying to get a hefty commission from us. "Not even going to try to win it for her?" The worker blew out a low, judgmental whistle. "I guess some guys just aren't that romantic."

Before anyone could take another breath, Adam slammed two dollars onto the counter for more rings. The worker handed him three of the plastic circles. Adam frowned as he counted them. "This is three."

"Two dollars for three rings. Five dollars for eight."

His frown deepened. "She got four."

"I gave her an extra for being such a pretty thing." He winked at me.

A deep guttural sound came from Adam's chest.

"Hear that, Adam?" I teased him, poking his side and trying to get the scary look off his face. "He thinks I'm pretty."

"Then he must be blind," Adam said. My jaw dropped at Adam's statement before he continued, "Because you're fucking beautiful."

My body tingled.

Adam tossed a ring toward the front row. Failed. Middle row. Failed. Back row. Failed.

"You can't go through them so fast. Do them slow and try to adjust to how the last one went," I said in his ear behind him.

The edges of his lips curled into a side smile. "Now you're the one giving advice?"

"You could try aiming for the side rows," the worker suggested.

Adam's smile disappeared. "It's cuter when she does it." He dug out a five-dollar bill from his wallet and handed it over for eight rings.

He aimed, using every possible angle, and he failed and failed again. He cursed and turned to me. "Like I said, no one can win these games. Look." He tossed another ring over the bottles. It bounced and fell between the spaces of the bottles. Another loss for the home team.

The worker glared at Adam and picked up a ring. He demonstrated a throw. The ring flew in the air and dropped down over a bottle's top. Winner, winner, chicken dinner. Unless he was a vegan. "Like I said, they're not rigged."

Adam returned the worker's glare.

Toxic testosterone flooded the atmosphere and choked me as Adam threw another five-dollar bill on the counter.

23

ALL IS FAIR IN LOVE AND WAR AND THREATENED TESTOSTERONE

Though I loved that he tried to win me the stuffed animal, I worried about what losing so much did to his self-confidence.

I hugged him from behind. His masculine, spicy cinnamon scent played with my nostrils. "You don't have to win me the turtle."

"You want the turtle, you're getting the turtle."

"Y'all will be here all night," the worker teased, and every muscle in Adam's back tensed as a direct result.

I massaged his shoulders. "Don't listen to him. I don't need the turtle. I have too many stuffed animals as it is. My bedroom is basically Noah's Ark because I have two of every species."

"A real boyfriend would be able to win his girlfriend a prize," the worker commented.

Adam's left eyelid twitched, and he dug out another five-dollar bill from his wallet.

"Adam, you need to stop," I repeated as he played and lost and played and lost. "I don't need it."

"But you want it."

"I also want the ability to fly." I pulled his gaze away from the ring toss, forcing him to make eye contact with me. "Let's just go do something else."

"I need to do this, Evie." The desperate look in his eyes caused a cold feeling to settle in my chest.

A couple of rounds later, he had spent over forty dollars. His wallet was noticeably lighter and sweat dripped from his forehead.

"Adam, it's over." I grabbed his hand and squeezed it, but he would not look at me. "Stop. You've spent way too much money already."

"I just...wanted to do one thing right." He tore his hands away from me and ran them through his hair, clenching the strands. "I can't even win you a stuffed animal."

When I saw his emotional walls coming up, I wrapped my arms around him so he couldn't escape. "I don't need you to," I whispered to him and cooed.

He released a shaky breath and shook his head. "I can't do this, Evie."

The cold feeling in my chest became freezing. "Can't do what?" Win a ring toss? Be romantic?

He stared at me and pulled me into a hug.

We ended the day at the amusement park on the Ferris wheel. He kissed me at the top, but it felt different than before. His lips moved with such slow precision, like he was memorizing the feeling. It was desperate and real, and it clicked something inside of me. Adam wasn't just scared he couldn't "do romance" or be the perfect boyfriend. He was terrified.

~~~

I LAID on his bed and watched him clean his room up a bit. A day after the amusement park, I convinced Adam that we should have a movie night. Deep down, I knew I needed to convince him he was perfect the way he was and that his expectations of himself as a boyfriend were too high.

When he had first let me enter his room, he had run forward and slammed a dresser drawer shut, as if hiding something. *Porn?*

He tossed shorts from the floor into drawers and scanned the room to check if he had left out anything embarrassing like a pair of underwear on display. I did not find his underwear embarrassing, but maybe his hesitancy had something to do with when I walked in, found a pair, and said, "*Mm, can I keep this as a memento?*"

I propped my head on my hand. "What other embarrassing things are you trying to keep from me?"

He rolled his eyes but continued tidying up. "Nothing."

"Do you keep a diary? I'd like to see that if you have it."

"I don't keep a diary." He smiled. "Why? Do you?"

"I started one. I'm not very good at making myself write in it though."

He tucked a strand of hair out of my face. "And do you mention me in this diary of yours?"

"Much like the number of licks it takes to get to the center of a Tootsie Pop, the world may never know."

He chuckled and walked to the door. "I'm going to grab us some drinks. Cherry cola?"

"Please." I stretched out further on his bed when he left me alone in his room. I knew snooping was wrong, but my mind kept going back to the drawer he had slammed shut when I walked in. He said he had nothing left to be embarrassed about—an obvious lie—so what could it be that he hid? Porn? *Does he have a fetish?*

My feet led me over to it as I listened for when Adam came back. *You shouldn't break his trust like this.* Still, I could not help myself. I opened the mystery drawer. My heart rate doubled, and I stopped listening for Adam.

At the bottom of the drawer, sitting on the wood, was the wolf ring I had won him our first year at the timeshare. The one he had thrown off the balcony and into the ocean.

"Evie, what..." Adam stepped back into his room, holding two glasses of soda.

"You kept it." Tears blinded me, but I still managed to see him. Heck, with my eyes closed, I could see him.

He was everywhere. He was everything. "I thought you threw it away."

He put down the drinks and moved in front of me until his cinnamon scent caressed me, warmed me. "I could never throw it away." His thumb caught my runaway tears as they chased down my cheek. "Our second summer here, when I threw it off the balcony...I was trying to forget you. Move on. Make you move on. Looking at you and knowing I couldn't have you, knowing I was broken—"

"You are not broken," I told him, but he did not listen.

"I searched for the ring for hours after I threw it. The waves had picked it up and the current moved it so quick, I thought I'd never find it, but I wouldn't give up." His fingers touched mine as I held the small ring that would fit neither of us at our ripe old ages of twenty and nineteen. "It symbolized my favorite summer. It was the only part I had of you, and I couldn't lose any more of you. Once I found it, I was able to breathe again."

A light bulb clicked on in my brain. A switch flicked by his words.

He was insecure about romantic gestures and "perfect" relationships. He did not believe he was enough. But *this* proved him wrong. He had kept the ring. This was our romantic peak. This was the part where I proved how I felt about him. This was the point of no return.

I loved him. He loved me. Every moment had built up to this one.

"Adam Pierce, you are such a romantic," I said, and all of the tension in his face melted away.

His smile was pure and light and, boy, was I going to kiss the Hell out of him.

My lips crashed against his lips. Fierce and powerful and hungry. Wanting to suck his very soul out and keep it for myself.

The kiss was aloe on fresh sunburn.

It was hurt and pain and fire and healing and scars. It erased and highlighted every moment before it.

It was everything.

With a strong yank, he jerked me to him. Hard, needy, and sexy as hell. One of my hands clutched at his shirt and the other dove underneath to feel his hot skin against mine. Everything blurred. Environment. Situation. I nibbled on his lips. He groaned and pressed against me harder.

Suddenly, I was falling back onto the mattress. It bounced me up and down. Weightless and heavy. Airy and aching.

He crawled over me, undressing me as he went. Shoes, check. Socks, check. Shorts, check. *Thank you, God and Victoria's Secret, for sexy underwear.*

I laid there half-naked, grabbing at his shirt and pulling it over his head. "More. I want to see all of my perfect, romantic boyfriend."

My hands struggled with his belt until it loosened,

and he shoved down his pants. His body vibrated with a desperate urgency that mimicked my own. Limbs tangled with limbs.

Our kiss was frantic.

My legs wrapped around him, and he grinded against me, both of us releasing moans at the contact.

His fingers toyed with my tank top straps, silently asking permission.

"Do it," I moaned.

He pulled the material down, freeing my breasts. He let out another tortured sound. "No fucking bra." His mouth dropped to one of my nipples and teased it before letting it pop out of his mouth to add, "You walked around all day with no goddamn bra on?" His lips went back to the tip of my breast. He watched my reactions with fiery eyes. My back arched, and a loud sound came from me when his teeth brushed over a sensitive area.

One of his hands shot up and covered my mouth to quiet me. "My mom is gone but James is still in his room. You can't be too loud." He smiled at me, knowing full well how loud I got when on the edge of sexual bliss.

"Me?" I shot back and rolled us over on the bed until I straddled him. "Baby, we might need to get you a gag." I circled my hips and rocked against his erection. Reaching between us, my hand slipped under his briefs and freed him. I lowered myself down his body for a better look.

His cock stood straight, swollen, and glistening. Freaking masculine and calling out my name. My fingers wrapped around him, and my head bent down to pleasure him. His groans and breathy intakes rivaled my own in volume. At one point, he grabbed a pillow and bit into it, muffling his reaction to my bobbing head and flicking tongue.

"Shit, Evie if you keep that up—"

I kept it up.

"Stop." He guided my mouth off him and rolled me back over. "Your turn." He guided my lace panties off, and I spread my legs, grabbing at his hair. Lips, tongue, fingers—

"*Yes!*" I shouted, clinging to him like a starfish.

He tossed a pillow to me to muffle my sounds of pleasure. A familiar rising feeling settled below my stomach, twirling and twisting. He circled his tongue over me and curled his fingers just right to rub at a hidden spot.

"*Oh.*" My core spasmed. Pleasure ran through my veins, thick and hot and overwhelming. As my body settled down, his fingers and tongue picked up their pace, readying me again. "Adam, please." I had no idea what I pleaded for anymore. I just wanted more. I would always want more from him.

"Give in, baby." He lapped and sucked at me, plunging his fingers in and out, again and again. Faster. Harder. *The man has unbelievable rhythm.* "I can feel how close you are, squeezing me so tight. I could lick this pretty clit every day." His words shook me to my core. So did his tongue. "Be a good girl and come for me." *Oh, God.*

My body shot up from the mattress as my tense muscles released at the same time. When I fell back, I was boneless yet still aching, needing, and wanting him. Oh God, I would never stop wanting him, would I? "Please."

He nodded, the heat blazing in his bright eyes. His fingers eased out of me, leaving me empty and yearning. I bucked when he aligned our hips. His erection rubbed between my legs; so hot, his flesh seared me.

My head fell back at the sensation. A light ripping sound infiltrated the room, and I opened my eyes to see Adam rolling on a condom. As he settled back over me, I pressed against him, moaning and trembling for more.

"Are you sure?" he asked me in a husky, pained voice that said he wanted me to be sure so bad he could die. If he didn't push inside me soon, I'm pretty sure I would die too. "You can't take it back."

"It's not something I'm losing; it's something I'm gaining." I tugged his head down for one more kiss. "I choose you. I want you." I closed my eyes and braced myself for the pain. "Do it, Adam."

Nothing happened.

Then, a fingertip under my chin. "Look at me, Evie."

I did, exhaling.

And he sank into me.

Tight. Full. A stinging sensation caused me to

flinch. He frowned and began retreating, but I wrapped my legs around his waist and held him there. "No, keep going."

He leaned his forehead against mine and probed deeper. "I hate that I'm hurting you."

It did hurt. The ripping pain seized me. Looking into his eyes made it worth it.

His lips were parted as he sipped in breath after breath. His hooded eyes glazed over in pleasure after he thrust fully inside me.

When I clenched around his full length, his eyes rolled back in his head for a second. Interesting. I bucked up, my inner muscles squeezing as a result. A moan came from him that I had never heard before. It was mindless and animalistic and damn sexy.

"Fuck, Evie, don't move." He held himself there, letting my body become accustomed to the size of his invasion. I clenched around him again. His head fell into the crook of my neck and shoulder. "Fuck. What are you doing?" he asked.

He pulled out and thrust back inside. It still hurt, but—as long as I paid attention to him—the pain was bearable. Plus, if I made him come, it would be over, and the next time wouldn't hurt as much.

"Feel good, baby?" I questioned. Guys liked dirty talk, right? That was what magazines and my select choice of novels told me. I tightened my inner muscles around him again.

He yelped out a groan. "How are you doing that?"

Sweat beaded over his forehead. "Makes you feel even tighter. And you're already so...fucking...tight." With each thrust, he seemed to go a little bit more mindless.

I relished in my newfound power and continued teasing him.

"Evie, I'm already holding on by a fucking thread." He growled at my manipulations and moved one of his hands down to rub over the swollen bead of nerves throbbing with my every heartbeat. Pleasure overwhelmed me at his touch. This time my clenching around him happened naturally.

"Adam." No way. Virgins didn't come during their first time. That was a lie built into movies. That did not happen— "Oh." The circles his thumb drew changed direction and moved faster over me. Dots of color. Behind my eyelids. Pulses between my legs.

Adam lifted one of my thighs. The change in position caused him to sink deeper into me, hitting a spot I had only read about.

A riptide. Forceful, terrifying, and all-consuming.

We came at the same time, moaning and groaning, and yelling each other's names onto the other's lips.

Before we drifted to sleep, I whispered to him, "I love you." The response I received back was a light snore.

DEAR DIARY,

Something interesting about losing your virginity: once the hurt goes away, the ache becomes that much more unavoidable. Translation: I want sex now. All the time. Specifically, sex with Adam. Oh my, sex with Adam is addicting.

We haven't seen each other for a month, but school starts back up for the fall semester in a couple of days. I'm curious what part of him I'll be most excited to touch when I see him, his lips or his...not lips.

He called me a week ago to see how things were going. I replay the memory of that call every chance I get.

"My internship is going well. I just got home from my aunt's office," I said, putting my cellphone on speaker. I unzipped the back of my work dress as we chatted, and the fabric fell to the floor of my room.

I grabbed my pajamas when he asked, "Did I just hear a zipper?"

A grin stretched my lips. "You did."

"Getting dressed or undressed?"

"I was about to get in pajamas."

"About to?" He groaned into the phone, and his breathing went heavy. "So, you're standing there now, not wearing anything?"

I left my pajamas on top of my dresser. "Now, I'm laying back on my bed not wearing anything." I stripped off my undergarments. Didn't want to be a liar.

He released another husky breath.

"What are you up to right now?" I asked.

"Lying in bed in my boxers. Thinking about you lying in bed naked. Fuck." He groaned into the phone, and an answering throb started between my legs.

"And where are your hands, Mr. Pierce?"

His breathing accelerated much like my beating heart. "You know exactly where my hands are right now, you sexy minx."

"Oooh, I like that nickname. 'Sex goddess' may be more realistic, but minx is cute and acceptable."

After giving in to our urges and expelling some tension, I fell back on my mattress and sighed. He released the same sound.

"I miss you."

"I miss you too. But, we'll be back at Genia in less than two weeks."

We talked for close to half an hour before hanging up.

"Love you," I told him, holding my breath for a response.

Dear Diary,

"I'll see you soon, baby."

24

THE COURSE OF TRUE LOVE NEVER DID RUN SMOOTH, BUT WHY ALL THE SPEED BUMPS?

Fall

FIRST THING I REMEMBERED? Adam arrived at my dorm room with open arms. I dove for his hug and kissed him like I was a soldier going off to war.

The most recent thing I remembered after the kiss began and the world around us faded to nothing? Sarah threw water on us as we made out on my bed.

"What the hell?" Adam wiped water from his face and pulled away from me. "Sarah?"

"Why'd you throw water on us?" I asked her.

She stood in front of my bed with an angry expression. "I leave the room for ten minutes and come back to you two groping each other. You didn't even notice I'd walked in."

"I was distracted."

"I could tell." She flipped her short black hair and grabbed another one of her bags to unpack. "I thought you could both use some water to cool down."

I sat up, away from Adam. "That's fair."

Adam led me out of my room and into the dorm's hallway. I leaned in to kiss him again, but he stopped me. "I don't think that's smart for right now." He chuckled. "Every time we kiss, we lose ourselves."

"I think that's hot," I commented.

He squeezed my hand. "It's hot until we forget where we are, and I start stripping you in a public place."

"That might be hot too," I mumbled. His smile widened.

He pecked me on the lips. Like a chicken. Once. *Activate pout mode.*

"Want to do dinner tonight?" he asked.

"I promised Sarah we'd eat and catch up tonight. What about tomorrow? Dinner after our first day of classes?"

His smile slipped away. "I can't. I have a shift at work."

"You still have to work at that café?" Mr. and Mrs. Pierce had both hired lawyers to negotiate an expensive separation that threatened Adam's college fund. During the past spring semester, he got a job at a coffee shop to help pay some of his tuition and housing. I missed him when he had to work.

The light in his eyes dimmed. "My parents are still divorcing. So, yeah, I've got to make money to pay for books and rent and such."

"I wouldn't think you'd make much money as a barista."

He shrugged, glancing away from me. "The tips are good."

His lack of eye contact made me suspicious. "Do you flirt with girls to get bigger tips?"

Ding, ding.

Fight number one.

Evie Turner occupies the right corner; her arms crossed over her chest. She stands at five foot five and weighs a number of pounds she'd never tell the likes of you. Her most well-known move is the pouting, puppy dog face, which often can bring her opponent to his knees.

In the other corner is Adam Pierce. A lad with muscles to spare and a fierce glare that can turn an unsuspecting person into stone. He stands at six foot one and weighs one hundred and seventy-five pounds.

Evie makes the first move with a "Do you flirt with girls to get bigger tips?" Adam flinches back but recovers with an uppercut of "I wouldn't say I flirt." She dodges and performs a "What would you call it? Seducing girls who aren't your girlfriend with your eyes and mouth?" Pierce falls back— But, oh, folks, he is right back up. With quick feet work, he backtracks. "Babe, you know I don't care about any of them. I just ask about their days and wink a bit. You're my girl-

friend. It shouldn't matter what I say to them as long as you trust me. Don't you trust me?"

His *"Don't you trust me?"* knocks Turner, and she stumbles before returning her deadly shot. She knees him with an *"If I flirted with random guys for tips, you'd go crazy. It wouldn't be about how much you trust me. Plus, you shouldn't flirt with girls when you're taken anyway. It plays with their emotions."*

K. O. Ding, ding.

We stared at each other, huffing, until he blinked and surrendered. "You're right, I'm sorry. No more flirting for tips."

I smiled and ruffled his hair. "You're so whipped."

"Let's see who is whipped when you're handcuffed to my bed tonight."

Holy guacamole.

"Welcome to modern dance." The professor appeared in his forties and wore head to toe black except for a green silk pocket square. "I am Professor Sedaris. This class will not be a walk in the park—" *Can't catch a break.* "—but it will be a walk through the self. You will learn things, feel things, and portray those feelings on stage. Modern dance is often described as avant-garde. It is creative and breaks all the rules of classical dancing such as ballet." *Differs from the one class I excelled in? Of course.* "Prepare yourself for a tough semester."

Was I sweating through my leotard? Great. Just checking.

"That was my welcome speech. Let's get started."

Our stretches were the same as other dance classes, but the warmups shocked me. To get to know each of us, Mr. Sedaris instructed everyone to perform an impromptu dance solo. "Show us who you are through your movements. Show emotion. I don't want a happy, easy dance. I want *real*."

The song *"You Can't Always Get What You Want"* by The Rolling Stones popped into my head.

When it was my turn, I danced with each movement holding meaning.

I finished with the perfect landing on one foot and bowed, a grin on my face. My grin fell away when Mr. Sedaris frowned, curling an unimpressed lip at me. He glanced down at the attendance sheet. "Evangeline Turner?"

"Yes, sir." He stared at me. Was that not what he wanted? "I mean, that's me. I mean, here?"

"Miss Turner, your moves are all executed perfectly."

I released a nervous breath. Maybe the professor just had a resting disapproval face? "Thank you."

"Next time, try dancing with emotion," he said, as if it was a simple instruction and not a statement that shattered my ribs and broke my heart inside my chest.

"He sounds like an ass," Sarah said after swallowing her bite of cheese pizza. We had decided to stay in our room for dinner as we suspected the dining hall of poison on the first day. Several slices of pizzas later, it was like summer break had never interrupted our friendship. "In fact, it seems like every dance teacher you have is just unnecessarily rude."

I sat on my bed and picked up a new slice of cheese pizza. "To be honest, I'm kind of scared of this class now."

"Can you drop it?"

I shook my head. "It's a part of my major."

"Any TA to help you out and secretly fall in love with you so you get an A?"

"Mr. Sedaris doesn't use teaching assistants. He said they feel like a part of a system, and he wants flow, not structure."

Sarah snorted. "What a fucking dance thing to say."

A sinking feeling made itself at home in my chest. "I wish Adam was here."

She stood and jumped onto my bed. "Don't make me slap you." She stole my pizza instead, which was just as violent and hurtful. "Just because you have a boyfriend does not mean you need him to solve your problems or make you feel better. You have me."

"You're right, sorry."

Still, the desire to call and tell him about my day plagued me regardless of all the feminist bones in my body. I snuck away after dinner and a movie to call him.

He was supposed to pick me up after seven so we could sleep over at his place together. It was now seven-thirty.

I got sent to voicemail.

"*Hey, you've reached Adam. I'm busy, so leave a message. I may or may not get back to you.*"

Beep. "Hey, babe, it's me. Um, just wondering why you aren't here yet. I thought we were supposed to hang out after my dinner with Sarah. Text me, I guess." What else was there to say? I didn't want to sound clingy, demanding, or mad about him being late. "Um, okay, bye."

The rest of the night, I watched movies with Sarah. Eight o'clock. Nine o'clock. Voicemail at 9:05PM: "*Hey, Adam. Me again. I wanted to make sure everything is okay since you haven't called me back.*" Ten o'clock. I waited up for him to call or text me if something was wrong. At some point, I stopped looking at the clock and my eyes slipped shut.

AT NINE O'CLOCK in the morning, I woke up in a jolt of confusion, wondering why Adam had never called me during the night. My cell phone indicated that he had, but my phone had been on silent, betraying me. Darn it. I snuck out of the bedroom so I would not disturb Sarah—who still slept like the living dead—and went into the hallway to call him back.

He picked up on the third ring. "Sorry, Evie, I totally

forgot about last night. The café called me in for a late shift since someone backed out, and I couldn't say no to the extra money. I meant to call, but I forgot we had plans."

My first instinct was to feel insulted that he forgot about me. My second instinct was to figure out when I could see him next because I missed him. "You're working again tonight, right?"

"Yeah, it's going to be dead boring."

"What time?"

He sighed. "From four to midnight."

Too late for me to see him. "Midnight? What people order coffee at midnight?"

He chuckled, low and throaty. God, I missed him. "We are talking about college kids, here, Eves."

"Sorry, I just feel like we've only seen each other once since we got back."

"That's because we have. It's only the third day since moving in."

"You're right, I'm being silly."

"No, you're not." He comforted me. "I miss you too."

Tingles. "Talk to you tomorrow?"

"Of course."

I smiled. "I love you."

A short pause before, "See you soon."

After hanging up, I stood there and counted in my mind how many times I'd said *"I love you"* with no response. The first was after our first time, but he had fallen asleep. The second and third were over the

Timeshare Boyfriend

phone and ended with a variation of "*Talk to you later.*" Now this. Four times.

"What does it mean when your boyfriend won't say 'I love you' back?" I asked Sarah when I returned to our room after brushing my teeth.

She threw a pile of books into her backpack. "It generally means he doesn't love you." At my flinch, she rephrased, "Shit, no, not— Wait, is Adam not saying 'I love you?'"

I fell back on my bed. "Correct."

"Are you sure he is not saying it on purpose? Maybe he didn't hear you or something caught his attention right after you said it."

"It feels like it's on purpose. He—He's had issues before when it comes to believing in love and such. I know his parents were a toxic couple who fought a lot, but they're divorcing now. Ever since they separated, Adam has been a much happier person." Other than the jealousy and the need to be the perfect boyfriend. "I thought everything was fine, emotional attachment wise."

"Did he go to a therapist or something to work through his issues?"

I bit my lip. "All I know is one summer he didn't believe in love, and the next he said he had worked through his issues and wanted to be with me."

Sarah's face looked like an ice cream cone dipped in thick concern and sprinkled with dread. "That seems a little too easy."

My worries grew when three weeks passed, and I saw him less and less. When he wasn't working, I was rehearsing. We would text and call, but it wasn't the same. It dragged me down even lower than I already felt. And Mr. Sedaris had me feeling pretty low.

"Stop," the modern dance professor said and pointed me out to the rest of the class during a practice. "Miss Turner, what do you think you are doing wrong?"

"I don't know, sir. I'm not planning out the movements; I'm letting them come to me naturally like you said."

"But there is a new problem arising." He narrowed his eyes on me and tilted his head to the side. "You are bottling up your emotions, not letting them free, not letting them out in the dance."

My voice cracked as I defended myself. "I'm putting in emotion."

"But there is something deeper going on in you that you're not showing in your dance."

"I—"

"It is hard to let down our walls, Miss Turner, but it is the only way you are going to pass this class."

"Unless I figure out what he wants from me, I think he might fail me," I told Adam over a short dinner before his work shift a couple of days later. Snowball Scarface laid under Adam's chair at the dining table. "I can't fail. It's a mandatory class for dance majors."

"It'll be okay. You are a great dancer, I'm sure you will impress him soon."

Negative emotions filled my chest. A sea of *I can't* and *what if* and *I'll never*. I took a deep breath and locked it away to deal with later. "And how about you? How was your week?"

He sipped from his soda. "Busy with work and classes."

I smiled and poked his arm. "Is work still dead boring?"

He blinked. "Actually, no. I made a friend there, so the hours feel shorter."

"That's awesome. What's his name?"

"Her name is Isla."

Her. A new friend. "Isla. She sounds pretty. I mean, that's a pretty name."

He saw through me. "Don't be jealous; she's just a friend. You have friends who are guys."

Not guy friends with pretty names like Isla who make work hours feel shorter. "I'm not jealous," I lied. "We should go on a date."

Adam frowned. "I want to, but I'm kind of tight on money right now."

"I'll pay."

"I'm tight on time too with my shifts."

"What about next week?"

"I can't plan anything until my work schedule is released."

The negative feelings infiltrated my chest again, placing weight on my lungs. "I understand."

A WEEK PASSED, and I didn't see Adam. A sense of dread settled within me, powered by doubt, jealousy, and loss of confidence stemming from both our inability to see each other often, his inability to say "I love you" back, and my inability to impress Mr. Sedaris. Uncertainty made itself at home in my heart. Chilling it, slowing it, as if preparing my heart for a frozen, sleepy hibernation.

"Evie, you need to talk to him about how you're feeling," Sarah told me after watching me stare at my phone for ten minutes, waiting for a message, a call, or a smoke signal. "I don't like how sad you've been looking lately."

My phone buzzed with a message.

<u>Adam</u>: *Baby, it feels like I haven't seen you in forever. I miss you. I miss your laugh, your quirky sense of humor, and kissing you. Hell, I'd give anything just to be holding your hand right now. Please tell me you're free tomorrow.*

<u>Me</u>: *I am.*

<u>Adam</u>: *My place.*

My heart warmed, thawing and rejecting the negativity swarming my feelings.

"We're fine," I said to Sarah.

MY LEGS STRETCHED and managed a split in the air before I fell and landed on my feet. My hands went up in the air as I spun my body, fast, faster, and faster still. The world and classroom around me faded, and all I felt connecting me to it all was a string. A single, thin string tied to someone who got further away each day. The string thinned every hour of not seeing him.

My body tumbled down, aching with sadness. I bottled it up quickly, not letting anything show as I bent. Standing, I finished with a reach toward the ceiling and a foot pointed at the floor.

Soft clapping sounded around the room but none of it came from Mr. Sedaris. He had watched my solo practice for the winter showcase, the most important of my dances, and he remained expressionless. Worse than disappointed. Expected.

"Miss Turner, I have warned you, time and time again. You must let your emotion show. Express with each movement a story, a feeling—*anything*. You continue to show no growth. The winter showcase is still a month away, but I will not tolerate less than what I ask for, do you understand? My class is about letting everything out. Eighty percent of the grade will be your final solo performance on stage. Work toward that, or you will fail modern dance."

DINNER WITH ADAM started off nice. Romantic. He cooked pasta and chicken for us, and he even lit a candle on the dining table. Code for: *I want to get laid tonight.* I needed it too. We ate fast and talked a bit, but it was clear where the night was headed. It was also clear that both of us yearned to begin.

We moved over to the couch to "watch a movie." He hummed his normal tune, playing with pieces of my hair. Five minutes into the trailers, he leaned in and captured my lips with his. The kiss started slow and built into something neither of us could have expected.

Hands everywhere. Fingers in hair. Nails scratching down his back. His palm over the side of my breast. Moans. Groans. Animalistic growls.

Then, we were in his bedroom. Clothes on the floor. Skin against skin. He rose over me, supporting himself on one arm as his hand trailed down my body to between my legs. I gasped at his touch and felt the familiar heat wrack me, suffocate me.

"So wet." He flexed his fingers inside me, finding my hidden spot and teasing me there.

An orgasm tore through me as surprising and welcome as a birthday party thrown a day in advance.

A condom package ripped open. He aligned our bodies. And he was inside me.

His thrusts were fast and erratic at first. Like we had

lost our usual rhythm and had to rediscover it. He said, "Look at me, Evie."

I met his eyes. I didn't know why, but mine filled with tears. Everything I'd bottled up was coming out, unable to be shut down. "I love you, Adam."

He moaned and quickened the pace of his hips slapping against mine. He pounded into me, his movements as fierce and uncontrollable as the emotions flooding through me.

"I love you," I said again.

He shut his eyes, breaking our eye contact. Breaking something else too, something deep inside my chest as he did not respond.

Stars dotted my vision as my body spasmed in unison with his.

"*Evie*," he moaned my name like I was his. Like I was the one. Like he loved me.

I tried once more to mend the crack I felt emerging in my chest. I just needed to hear it once. Once. "I love you," I whispered.

He kissed my lips.

The crack in my heart released a cool feeling, which slipped into my veins, like liquid poison.

25
LOVE WILL FIND A WAY...UNLESS IT DOESN'T

*W*inter

ANOTHER WEEK PASSED before I had the courage to bring it up to him. "Why won't you say 'I love you?' Do you not love me?" I asked him.

Adam avoided my gaze and pulled away from where he cuddled me on his couch. Snowball Scarface jumped up and took my cuddle space away from me. Bitch. "I don't want to talk about this," he said.

"Well, I do want to talk about this."

Ding, ding.

The champion, Eve Turner, is yet again challenged by up and comer Adam Pierce. In the ring, Adam dodges her with an "I have work in an hour; I don't want to fight." She hits him with an "It doesn't have to be a fight. Just answer my question." He bobs and weaves and lands a "What do you want me to say, Evie?"

She falls into the ropes but bounces back into the ring.

"Do you not love me?" I asked. "Or do you still not believe in love?"

My question made him flinch away from me. It took half a second for him to wipe away his hurt expression and shoot back. "This isn't fair," he said. "Just because you say you love me, I have to love you back right away?"

My confidence took a major hit. "No, but I want to know if it's because you can't."

The sound of his angry intake of air echoed in my ears as we stood in silence. He answered through clenched teeth, "I am not so emotionally damaged that I can't love someone."

Backtrack. Backtrack, backtrack. "I—That's not what I'm saying."

"Isn't it? You think since I won't say I love you that I'm not capable of love?" He stood from the couch and moved in front of his bedroom door, keeping his back to me. "I think you should go. We're just going to fight more if you stay."

"Better to fight than not see each other again for a week because of busy schedules." I hugged myself and stared at the carpet. "We're in a relationship. I know you need to work, but being with someone means making time for her."

"Being with someone also means understanding

that it's not all about you. I have to work, Evie. I need the money. My parents aren't paying my way through college like someone I know."

Low blow. Yes, my parents paid for my education. Did that make me less of an adult in his eyes? More like a "kid" he was "babysitting?" Hurt feelings from past summers rose within me. Even though I had said I'd moved on from them, I hadn't.

A chink in my heart stung like a paper cut spritzed with cold lemon juice. "What's going on isn't okay, and you shouldn't be making me feel guilty for feeling this way," I said. "We hardly see each other anymore. Every time I think of you, I just think about you not saying 'I love you,' and working more and more. This coldness is setting up inside me, and I'm worried about where our relationship is going. I can't deal with all this...sadness and anxiety anymore. I need to focus on my classes." *I'm about to fail dance. I've never failed anything. I've never felt so...inadequate.* Even my boyfriend didn't love me.

His frozen chuckle made the hair on my arms stand. "You need to focus on your classes; yet, when I need to spend time working for money, I'm selfish for not giving you enough attention."

"It's not about attention."

"Isn't it?" he asked. "Did you never think maybe the reason I won't say I love you back is because I don't love you? No, you jump to the conclusion that I'm incapable of love."

Tears prickled my vision, stinging one-fourth as

much as the two more cracks that chiseled themselves into my hardening heart. "Is it me then?" My voice came out higher and louder than I expected. Like I hung on the edge of an emotional cliff, pleading with him to give me a hand up. To save me. But his hands were in his pockets as I clung on for dear life. "Am I that unlovable?"

"Evie, no. No." His hands were in his hair, pulling again with frustration. "Why do three words have to be so important to you?"

"Because they're all I've ever wanted to hear!" I yelled at him. Every emotion broke through me, flooding the atmosphere of his apartment. "You watched your parents fight every day, but I watched mine kiss and go on dates and surprise each other with heartfelt gifts. I may not be a child of divorce—but, newsflash, having two parents so obviously in love with each other just showed me what I was missing. Every day, feeling lonely. I have read romance, watched movies, and *waited* for someone—anyone—to tell me he loved me. To tell me he wants to be with me and hold me and keep me and be there for me. Every summer, I thought you might love me. Even after you hurt me, even after I vowed not to go near you, *every* summer was about you. Do you know how dumb and weak that makes me feel?"

"It's your pride then?" he asked. "That's why you need to hear it? Not because you want to hear it from *me*, but just because you want to hear it?"

Tears soaked my face and blurred my vision of him. At least, blurry Adam was a little bit easier to look at. "I can't handle being the person in the relationship who is clearly the one more in love. I have given everything to you, *years* to you because you made me feel more than I ever thought possible."

"You're the one who didn't want to be in a relationship with me to begin with Evie. You didn't want to be vulnerable. Now, you're pressuring me."

"All I am asking for is for you to say three words. Eight letters. Say it, Adam."

The pain on his face echoed the pain in my chest.

"Say it."

His mouth opened and closed and opened and closed, as my hopes rose and fell and rose and fell. In the end, I was left numb.

Days passed in a blur of…

Sedaris: Not good enough.

Adam: Evie, I have work tonight, but I need to see you.

Sarah: You need to cut him loose, Evie. He's dragging you down.

Sedaris: Do you not have emotions, Miss Turner? Because that is the only excuse for the way you dance.

Adam: I'm sorry about the fight. Come over. We'll talk about it.

Sarah: If you see him, you two will either hurt each other worse, or have sex and avoid your problems.

Sedaris: Are you sure you are meant to be a dance major?

A couple of weeks before final exams and the winter showcase, I sat in my room, clutching my head. The funny thing about pushing the bad things out is that when one slipped in, they all did. Sobs possessed me. My body fell into my pillows, overwhelmed by it all.

I clutched onto the one stuffed animal I had brought with me to school. A pink turtle that Adam found in a store and bought me when he could not win the one at the amusement park.

An hour into my cry fest, my phone buzzed with a text from Adam.

<u>Adam</u>: *Baby, I'm coming over. I miss you.*

But I didn't want him to miss me. I wanted him to love me.

After his knock, I opened the door and let him inside. My splotchy, red face made it obvious that I had been crying.

Adam sucked in a harsh breath, appearing as tortured as I felt on the inside. "Baby, look at you…" He clutched at his chest, fisting his shirt over his heart. "I'm making you feel like this?"

What could I say?

His voice cracked as he asked, "Do I really make you feel unlovable?"

I pressed my lips together.

Adam's head dropped along with my hope. He took a moment before saying, "Maybe we should end this before it gets worse. Before I do something worse…"

"You want to break up with me?" I asked. Rage. Like a vengeful ghost possessing me. Powerful, overwhelming rage. "Classic relationship phobic Adam Pierce. Running away. I should've known."

"Evie."

"You would really rather break up than tell me you love me?"

"I can't keep hurting you. It's the one thing I promised to never do."

I could barely look at him. He was ending it. Just like I knew he would. He would always pull away. Always. "Maybe you were right before," I said. "You are broken."

He staggered back and inhaled sharply, but not as sharp as my words. He looked as if I had just ripped his still-beating heart out.

"Maybe we were just meant to be a summer romance." I walked back over to my door, opening it so he would leave. I made it to the doorknob but could not move any farther because of his gentle grip on my wrist.

His chest shook with each agonized breath as he stared at his hand.

"Adam?"

It took a moment, but he let me go with a gut-wrenching sadness in his eyes.

He let me go.

A DAY? Four days? A week? Who knew? Time was crazy like that. Passing without permission. A part of me wondered what number of "*Screw him*" Sarah had reached. I went to classes. I did homework. I ate some—few—meals. I deleted all of Adam's voicemails and text messages before allowing myself to listen or read his excuses. I couldn't let him in. If I let him in even a little, everything hurt. It was safer to be numb. He chose to break up with me instead of saying he loved me.

Everything hurt. Breathing. Blinking. Acting like there weren't shattered bits of my heart stuck in my lungs and ribs, scratching and slicing with each step or breath I took. Like shrapnel.

One of the days, Adam knocked on my door. Lucky for me, Sarah ripped him a new one through the wooden barrier, so I didn't have to see his face.

November was long gone. The first week of December disappeared. Then, it was time for finals.

My sadness melted into anger. Into spite. At him and myself. How could I let a boy break me like this? I had thought broken hearts were exaggerated in movies and books.

It felt like he died, like he had killed off the person I knew and loved and trusted. It felt like part of me had died too.

26
THERE ARE OTHER FISH IN THE SEA...
THERE'S ALSO TRASH IN THE SEA

"Hoes before bros."

"Uteruses before duderuses."

"Ovaries before brovaries."

"Chicks before dicks."

"Another shot," Sarah instructed the bartender. She showed him our fake IDs that told him we were one year older, lived in Ohio, and were legal to drink. "Make that two shots."

When she told me to drink, I drank. When she told me to not think about Adam, I didn't think about Adam.

When the vodka kicked in, he was all I could think about.

"You know what? Eff him," I said.

Sarah gave me a small smile. "Honey, if you want to sound like a badass ex, you need to learn how to say 'fuck.'"

"And he tried to make me feel guilty about how I was feeling. Like honesty and communication aren't important." I tipped back another shot, despite Sarah's protests. "He's an asshole."

Sarah's eyes widened as she slow-clapped at my words. "Oh my God, Evie, you just cussed."

"He's an...effing asshole."

She smiled and rubbed my back. "Baby steps."

I slapped the bar, getting the cute bartender's attention. "A guy broke my heart a few...weeks? Was it weeks ago?"

Sarah nodded, still rubbing my back. "It's been a while."

"Sorry about that," the bartender said.

"He doesn't know what he's missing," I told him. "I'm a dancer." My words slurred as I leaned closer to him. "I can put my leg, up, up, behind my head."

He turned to Sarah. "No more drinks for your friend."

"That's fair."

I threw my hands up in the air. Sarah pulled them back down. "You know what?" I asked. "Why am I so hung up on one guy? *I'm* the dancer who can put her foot behind her head."

"You're really clinging to that one detail, aren't you?"

My barstool wobbled as I stepped down and surveyed the bar. There were wooden tables everywhere with peanut shells and condensation rings from past drinks. The music was a low beat with inaudible lyrics. Most people had left, as it was around one in the morning, but a few guys caught my eye. Especially one.

Black hair like Adam's but green eyes to make him different.

Sarah shook her head at me, reading my thoughts and disagreeing with them. "I don't think a rebound is the right thing for you right now."

I left Sarah, despite her protests, and approached the Adam look-alike as he stood to leave his table. I bumped into him before he made it to the bathroom door. "Bonjourno."

The guy smiled and raised an eyebrow, amused. "Were you trying to say Bonjour?"

Leaning my weight against the bathroom door was not smart because that opened it and led to me stumbling. "I said hello in French."

"Wow, you are quite drunk, aren't you?"

"Not too drunk." I tried to wink, but it could have appeared as some hard blinking.

"Not too drunk for what?"

An image of Adam popped into my mind. It hurt. I didn't want to hurt anymore.

I grabbed his head and kissed him. My lips pressed against his. No sparks. It was just lips against lips. He deepened the kiss, and there was still no electricity. It was just saliva mixing with saliva.

His hand cupped the back of my head, and I kissed him harder, faster. He thought my yearning was for him. He made a noise in his throat and leaned me against the wall, pressing against me. And it was wrong. It was wrong. It was all wrong.

"I'm sorry." I tore myself away from him and ran to the exit.

I thought feeling desired would help me. It did not. I thought kissing someone else might cause the same sparks. It did not. Getting over Adam was like trying to trade my most prized sentimental possession for some cold, plastic, or metal appliance.

Still drunk, I walked home in the cold. The wind bit my pores and nibbled at the tip of my nose. It sliced through my thick winter jacket and cut into me. Stabbed me. The pain made me feel less numb.

I closed my eyes and embraced it, opening my arms. "Do it," I whispered to the wind. The wind stilled, needing more clarification. "Finish the job."

It picked up again and rustled all the tree leaves above me. Considering it was December, only a few leaves still clung to tree limbs. Leaves died and fell every year, but each year they still hung on like it would be their last.

"You're going to fall," I warned the leaves. A couple of people on the sidewalk looked at me like I was crazy for talking to trees and speed-walked away from me. "You always fall. But you grow back, so it'll be okay. You'll be okay." My eyes watered, half due to the bitter cold. I worried my tears might freeze on my face and cause frostbite or hypothermia or some other cold issue. If Adam were here, he could have told me all the possible symptoms. There had to be a "When Winter Strikes" documentary on that stuff.

The wind blew harder at me this time as I passed the campus library, causing me to wobble on my already unstable feet. Alcohol and balance did not mix.

"Finish me!" I yelled at the wind, my speech still slurred.

"Evie?" His voice came from close behind me and stabbed me harsher than any cold gust of wind ever could.

I turned and tipped my nonexistent hat to him. "Mr. Pierce."

His eyes blazed. Angry. Sexy. Hurtful. Bad. "Are you drunk?"

"*Are you drunk?*" I mimicked him then dropped the act. "You bet I am."

He caught me when I stumbled and held me close. "Ridiculous," he grumbled and wrapped an arm around my waist.

I slapped at his hand as it pressed against my stomach, but he did not let go. He dragged me in the direction of my dorm building. "What are you doing?" I asked.

"Where's Sarah?" He ignored my question and spoke in a gruff tone. "She just left you to walk home alone?"

"I may have run off," I admitted. "And I don't need a caretaker."

He smirked and rolled his eyes. His beautiful and alluring and upsetting eyes. "You do realize I'm supporting all of your weight right now?"

The wind blew harder at us, and I almost fell and took Adam with me. "Not now, wind," I told it.

"You're not even wearing gloves," he growled. "You know how cold it is today? Plus, alcohol makes you more susceptible to hypothermia."

I laughed. This was my Adam. Too bad he was not mine anymore.

We made it a bit closer to my dorm, but my feet scraped along the ground, slowing us down. With the distance prolonged by my slow steps and awkward silence, he became impatient. "Fuck this," he said and picked me up. He cradled me against his chest and walked me two more blocks to the entrance of my building.

As he carried me, our faces got closer, and I analyzed his expression. "You look angry."

"I am angry."

I stared at him some more as he walked us inside. He brought me into the elevator. "Are you angry at me?" I asked.

"I am so fucking angry at you, I can barely look at you," he replied.

My eyes widened. I blinked several times. He was angry with me? I was supposed to be the angry one. "Why? *You* broke up with me."

"*Why?*" His blue flame eyes locked onto mine. "First

off, I didn't break up with you. I said, *maybe* we should break up because clearly being with me was causing you pain, and you proceeded to call me broken. Then, you blocked my number. You blocked me on all your social media. I knocked on your door eleven times, and you wouldn't answer."

"I didn't want to hear from you."

He scoffed and set me down in front of my door when the elevator opened on my floor. "I got that, but we were in a relationship, Evie. You block a psychotic ex or a stranger. You don't block me, after everything we've been through. We had things to talk through. We needed to cool down. Breaking up wasn't what I—" He stopped himself from saying something. "You avoided me like a coward. It was immature."

My jaw dropped open. He had never talked to me this way before. It was harsh and...honest. "I—I am not a coward." I tried to unlock my door, but my hand shook too much to get the key in the lock.

He took it from me and opened it. "You say you want love, but you don't. You want something easy. Some fairytale. Love is painful and hard sometimes."

"What would you know about love?" I shot back. "You can't even say it."

He let out a deep sigh as he walked into my room with me and glanced at my unmade bed. He then went to my dresser and riffled through the stuff on the top.

"Don't walk home drunk again." He grabbed something from my dresser and set it on the small table beside my bed. Aspirin. For my morning hangover?

"Worried for me?" I questioned.

He stared at me. His anger merged with sadness. "Of course."

"Careful, I might start thinking you care about me."

His fists clenched. Sadness gone. Welcome back, anger. "*Of course*, I fucking care about you. If I didn't, I would have just said it." If he didn't care, he would have said he didn't care? Or if he didn't care, he would have said *I love you*? And what did that mean for me? For us? Nothing, because we were done. Broken up. Broken.

"Evie," he continued, softer now. "If there was ever a girl I could love, it'd be you." Hope inflated my chest only to be popped like a balloon. "But those words don't mean the same thing to me."

"What do they mean to you?"

He closed his eyes. "When I was younger and I found out about my mom cheating, I waited for her to tell him and be honest. But instead, she ended each night saying 'I love you.'" He turned back to look at me. "To me, those words are only said when someone is trying to manipulate the other person. They are said when they're the only thing left holding a relationship together. They...doom people."

No wonder he did not want to say the words.

"It's not that I'm unlovable?" I asked softly.

"Baby, you're so lovable. I'm just broken. You were right."

"You're not broken." My words slurred, but he got the gist of it. "I need to accept you as you are. I needed to stop pushing you." I rolled over on my mattress so that I faced him. "Do you think soul mates exist?"

He stared at me for a while, blinked, then said, "I don't know."

"Do you think there's only one person out there for each person?"

He placed a hand on my cheek. "I don't know."

"If there is just one person for everyone. Do you think you've met your person yet?"

I was so drunk and exhausted that I nearly passed out before he whispered, "Yes."

He was about to leave when I said, "My winter showcase performance is next week."

His hand hovered over the doorknob. "Yeah?"

"Yeah."

More silence.

"Are you inviting me?"

Something in my chest tightened. "I don't know." My drunken thoughts were not very coherent. "I just wanted you to know."

"Okay."

"Okay."

He left.

MORE DAYS PASSED until it was my last night at Genia

University for the fall semester. The night of the winter showcase for my modern dance class. My performance decided whether or not I failed the class. I waited backstage, gripping onto the sheer fabric I was supposed to use as a prop. It was hot pink and reminded me of my stuffed animal turtle. I had hidden the turtle in my bottom drawer so I didn't have to look at him each day.

"You're on next," a tech person in all black whispered to me as I held my breath.

The clapping for my classmate's solo before me went on for a minute. She left the stage, and the lights dimmed to a cool blue. I walked onto the X and dared a look at the crowd. A familiar face stared at me from the front row. Adam. Adam was here. My chest squeezed. My throat clamped. Knots tied and jerked around in my stomach.

My music started, light and airy, but I no longer felt light and airy.

My hand, gripping the sheer pink fabric, lifted and placed the small, squared sheet over my head, covering my eyes. Through it, I could not see Adam's face. That helped.

My arms stretched up into the air, slow and graceful. But I was not feeling slow and graceful.

In my head, the music changed. What once sounded light, sounded heavy. It settled inside me, and my body took over.

I dropped to my knees, fast and hard. Pain shot up my leg, but it was nothing compared to the aching in my heart. I leapt and fell back down in a split. Not graceful. It hurt. My jumps were fierce, and my spins were tight. With every move I made, my heart felt lighter in my chest. The shattered pieces cut into me less than before. I threw my emotion out onto the stage.

I danced my heart out.

Every time I had waited in the back seat of my mother's car, wondering which version of Adam I would meet that new summer. Every time I had opened up, then closed, then opened again. My heart broken, mended, and incinerated. Every time he kissed me, and the world fell away, and there was no doubt that nothing would ever feel as good again. Every time I saw his walls go up and pretended not to have seen it. Wanted not to have seen it. Every time I fooled myself that we were meant to be.

As the music gained speed, my motions did the same.

At some point, my pink cloth fell from over my face, and I realized I cried as I danced. Tears streamed hot and wet down my cheeks. I did not spare time to wipe them. They felt like badges, war scars.

Adam still sat in the front row, watching me.

It was over. A finale. Curtains falling on a stage. An end. But how, after everything, how could it end? How could we never talk to each other, laugh, or touch? *Why can't a first love be a forever love?*

After jagged, harsh movements, I calmed. The music slowed back down. My body sank to the floor, reaching out one last time, before curling up, into itself. An armadillo with her armor.

Once I stood backstage, Mr. Sedaris found me and hugged me like he hadn't hated me all semester long. "That, Miss Turner, was modern dance."

Modern dance felt good.

LETTERS TO ADAM

Dear Adam,

    I'm never going to send this letter, but Penny said it might help to write it. Like I'm releasing my feelings. Here it goes:

    My parents keep asking me what happened between us. I don't know what to tell them.

    I miss you so much. We used to text all the time; call once a day. Every time I sit in silence, I think I hear my cell phone vibrate with a message from you. Every time I look at my phone, I think about how I blocked your number and I want to unblock it.

    I can't stop thinking about how mad you were at me. Like I did something wrong. Maybe I did do something wrong. You wanted to break up to save me from pain, but that hurt way worse.

    I miss how we used to laugh and kiss and touch. I miss how when I felt down, you held me. It's crazy how much I miss being held. I lay in bed and imagine ghosts wrapping their arms around me. And ghosts terrify me. That's how lonely I feel.

I'm not mad anymore. I don't feel spiteful or vengeful like the movies say I should feel. I just miss you.

Last night was New Year's Eve and I had no one to kiss. I didn't want to feel lonelier at the stroke of midnight so I went to bed at ten o'clock.

Dear Adam,

First day back at school for the spring semester. I almost walked to your apartment building out of habit. I'm trying to change that habit.

Dear Adam,

You know what's not fun? Being single on Valentine's Day. The red roses and chocolate-covered cherries I'm not receiving make me bitter. I know before I said I'm not feeling vengeful. That's not totally true.

I did, however, receive two Valentine's Day cards. One, as you know, was from you. The "I'm sorry" doesn't help. The "I miss you. We need to talk. Unblock my number" helps even less. Nice creativity, slipping the card under my door, so I had no choice but to pick it up and read it and feel worse than a typical heartbroken girl on Valentine's Day. Very kind of you.

Who was the other heart-shaped card from, you ask? A guy in my women's history class. His name is Peter, and he cares about women's oppression. Isn't that sexy? He's

Letters to Adam

so sexy. I dream about kissing him. I want to rip his clothes off and—

I'm lying. I don't know why I am, because I'm not even sending this letter to you, so I'm lying to myself.

I did not even know Peter existed before he handed me that card after class. He is cute, I'll say that. He has dimples, and he blushed when he introduced himself. He called me pretty. It reminded me of when you told that amusement park worker that he was wrong because I'm "fucking beautiful." I still tingle when I think of that.

I tingle when I think of you a lot. After the initial feeling of cold sadness at the thought of you, warmth seeps in and I think about the times when we were so good together.

Dear Adam,

I'm worried about the summer. Those two weeks when I know I'll have no choice but to be near you. I'm worried you'll say something to break down the wall I spent this time apart trying to build. If you tell me you love me, I'm worried my wall will come tumbling down. If you don't tell me you love me, I'm worried the other pieces of my heart will shatter with no possible repair.

Poetic, how we started with a summer.

And this summer feels like it will finally be the end.

27

A BLEEDING HEART ATTRACTS SHARKS

The Next Summer

"I, um, sorry... Did you want to—"

"If you wanted to—"

I started again, avoiding eye contact as much as possible. "It doesn't matter to me."

"Whatever you want." Adam motioned to the spot of sand where we had both tried to lay down our towels, beside James.

There was no avoiding Adam when it came to "family beach day," the day when Maryam and my mother made hanging out together as two families mandatory.

"If you want to sit there, you should sit there," he

said. I met his eyes for a second then glanced back down after seeing a reflection of pain in them.

I took a step back and offered the space to him again. "He's your brother, you should get to sit next to him."

James grinned, loving the attention. "I'm popular."

"For God's sake, one of you just sit down," my mother, ever the calm wallflower, announced. My dad reached over and took her hand as if telepathically trying to tell her not to get involved. *Thanks, Dad,* I shot back with my telepathic powers, but the message did not go through.

"I still can't believe you two broke up." Maryam settled into her beach chair while Adam spread his towel on the left side of James. I spread my towel on the right side of him. "What happened? Adam wouldn't tell me."

"Evie wouldn't tell us either. I want to know," my mother won the least-able-to-read-her-daughter's-expression award.

"You two were so good together. I mean, 'Adam and Eve?' Adorable."

"I'm sure they have their reasons," my father said. "They don't need to tell us."

I hoped if I gave them a little, they would be satisfied and move on to a different, less painful subject. "Sometimes things just don't work out."

"Psh," Maryam waved away my statement. "That's

the typical response. I want dirt. What did Adam do to break your heart?"

"Why do you assume *he* broke it off?" Mom turned to Maryam, with an edge in her voice. "Eve is capable of ending a relationship."

Adam and I stared at each other above James's head as our mothers gossiped and fantasized about our love lives.

"I bet he was pushing her for something more... physical, and that's why they—"

"Mom," I shouted.

Everyone went quiet. I looked down at my feet and dug them deep into the sand the way I wanted to do with the rest of my body. *Hello, thank you for this job interview. Why do I want to be a sand crab? Well, I'm trying to escape one of the most awkward moments of my life, and the ability to sneak below ground is appealing. As you can see, I have many sand crab references.*

"We both got our hearts broken," Adam told them, and they accepted it and moved on.

I laid back on my towel and closed my eyes, trying to drown them out and not focus on Adam's words. *We both got our hearts broken.* He wasn't wrong.

My phone buzzed next to me, and I opened my eyes to look at it.

Unknown Number: *Sorry about my mom.*

I blinked a couple of times then glanced over at Adam, who stared at his phone. How had his text gotten through? I had blocked his number.

Unknown Number: *If you're wondering how my texts are coming through, it's cause three months ago, I had to get a new phone and a new phone number. Not because I creepily did some tech thing and overrode your block.*

Me: *If you knew you wouldn't be blocked, why didn't you text me before now?*

Unknown Number: *You needed space.*

I took a deep breath. I had needed space.

Me: *Thank you.*

Adam: *I needed space too.*

What did that mean? Had he moved on? After a minute of looking at his message and not knowing how to respond, I put my phone down and stood. "I'm going swimming. Want to come, James?"

"Nah, I gotta work on my tan."

Ah, ten-year-olds.

"I'm going on a walk," Adam said and took off down the beach.

I soaked my feet in the water before moving deeper into it. By the time the water was level to my chest, I could see Adam walking back toward our families. Through my sunglasses, he would not be able to tell I watched him.

He took a couple of steps toward where they sat, then he stopped and turned to see me in the water. I played it cool and swam around a bit. Quick glances in his direction showed him walking toward me.

Don't. Please.

He headed straight for me. He ran to the water,

screaming, "Evie!" The lifeguard's whistle went off and a couple of other people shrieked. When I looked back over at him, I found that he had dove into the water and now swam toward me with a frantic expression.

I turned to see what all the fuss was about and saw a dark gray fin cutting through the water. Fear froze me. I stopped breathing.

Adam's arms circled my waist and began pulling me to the shore. I tried to help him, but my limbs had locked into place as I stared at the fin only a couple of feet away from us. Shark. Shark. The scary *Jaws* music of *dundun-dundun-dundundundun* played in my head.

Adam yanked me through the water until the waves crashed at the back of our knees and knocked us down into the sand. He helped me back up and did not stop moving me until even our feet were out of the water.

"Oh my God," I cried and clung to his slick chest. "I could have died. You could have died." I slapped at him, still catching my breath. "Why did you rush in after me?"

He pressed his forehead to mine. "How can you ask me that?"

"Because...we're not even together."

"Just because we're not together doesn't mean I don't—" He cut himself off. My mind filled in all the possible heart-pounding blanks.

Option number one: "Just because we're not together doesn't mean I don't *want you alive and not eaten by a shark*." Option number two: "Just because we're not together doesn't mean I don't *care about you.*" Option number three: "Just because we're not together doesn't mean I don't *love you.*"

"What were you going to say?" I asked.

The lifeguard's loud whistle sounded again, and Adam and I both tore our gazes off each other long enough to see that the "shark" was gone. We also saw that there had never been a shark. The lifeguard pulled a teenager in a gray wetsuit with an artificial shark fin attached to his back out of the water and cursed at him.

"It wasn't real." My lungs opened up again, and I sucked in a steady breath. I looked back up to see Adam staring down at me. The intensity in his eyes caused my heart rate to go right back to frantic. His hands still clutched my upper arms, as if he was afraid to let go. "It wasn't real," I repeated.

"I thought I would…" Adam trailed off. He held me closer and shook a bit with what I assumed was relief. He bent down. For a second, I worried his lips were headed for mine, but he kissed my forehead. My stomach unknotted itself. A single kiss on the forehead, and every one of my muscles unclenched and relaxed.

He nodded at me and staggered away.

"It wasn't real," I said again. But what he had done, the way he had jumped in the water—that was real.

※ ※ ※

AFTER THE SHARK SCARE, I stuck to the pool when it

came to swimming. For the next two days, in fact, I stayed by the pool. I sat back in one of the lounging chairs and read a steamy novel with an apple on the cover—a professor and student romance—and pretended like my thoughts and heart were not a tangled mess over Adam and his: "Just because we're not together doesn't mean I don't..." *Don't what, Adam? Love me?*

Today, the Pierce family joined me at the pool. They sat in a different area, giving me my space, but I could still see Adam swim in the deep end with James. Staring at Adam just made me think of him more. If he had said he loved me, what would I have done? Forgiven him for everything and kissed him? Would hearing him say those three words now fix everything or was it all too broken to be put back together?

"Evie, do you mind if I put Adam's towel and bag over here?" Maryam asked me after walking over to my lounging chair in the corner. She pointed at the empty seat next to me. "There's not enough room over there, and I thought you two would be fine sitting next to each other."

No. Not fine. "Um." I glanced at where her and James's stuff was, on the other side of the pool. There were four empty seats around them. "Are you sure there isn't room next to your chairs for Adam?"

She pushed her sunglasses on her nose and smiled. "I'm sure."

Maryam-the-matchmaker threw Adam's towel down

on the chair next to mine and walked away, back over to where her belongings sat.

"Wow," I said to myself and put my book down. I could run. I could pack my stuff up and leave before Adam was forced to sit next to me. But I didn't want to. I wanted to be near him, hear his voice. I pulled out my phone and tried to distract myself. I opened my social media and scrolled down, liking the pictures of friends and friends of friends. My finger hovered over the search button, and I looked up to make sure Adam was still swimming and distracted.

I searched Adam's name, unblocked him, and clicked on his profile. The first few recent pictures were of him and James reuniting and hanging out for the summer. The smile on my lips was inevitable.

Falling into the post vortex, I scrolled to older photos. He did not post much, but I found one immediately after our breakup. A picture of two cups of coffee. One black—the way he liked it—and one with cream—the way I liked it. It was three days after we had broken up and the caption was "*I forgot.*" He forgot not to make my coffee too? He forgot I would not show up at his door searching for a kiss and some caffeine? He forgot not to tell me he loved me?

Eventually, I was all the way into his pictures from a year ago. I stumbled across one of me and the pink turtle he had bought me after not being able to win the one at the amusement park. In the photo, I snuggled the stuffed animal and gazed up at the person photographing me with absolute adoration. His caption read, "*The two cutest things in the world.*"

Before I knew what had happened, I had clicked "like" on the old picture. A ding sounded beside me. Adam's phone was in the bag Maryam sat next to me. Adam's phone got the notification that I had just liked his one-year-old picture.

Adam's phone was going to kill me.

If he saw that notification, he would know I had been scrolling through all his photos, cyber-stalking him. Oh, God. My thoughts were a loop of *shoot, shoot, shoot, shoot.*

I looked over at Adam, who still swam around with James several feet in front of me. His muscular back was to me as I dug my hand into his bag and fished out his phone. *Just delete the notification. Everything will be fine if you just delete it. He cannot know you still care. It would just make things worse.* I hid his phone in front of my book; to the outside world, it would just appear that I was reading.

I tapped on the screen. It requested a password. Password. Shoot. At least it didn't need a thumbprint or a face ID. Another reminder of how old-fashioned Adam was. What would Adam have as a password? From the lock picture, it had four letters. Maybe something from *The Godfather*. I typed 'Cats,' and it buzzed. Incorrect. I typed 'Mobs,' and it buzzed. Wrong. I had one more try before it would lock me out for half an hour. *Come on, Evie.* Four letters. Four.

I typed "Evie," and the lock faded. His home screen appeared. *Don't think about how your name is his password. He probably forgot to reset it.* Didn't he say he got a new phone? *Shhh.* I deleted the notification and threw his phone back in his bag before anyone saw me.

A minute later, Adam pulled himself up the ladder and out of the pool. Water trailed down his body, down his happy trail of hair leading under his swim trunks. Droplets of water clung to him and licked him everywhere I had once licked him. Adam began walking toward his mother who pointed him toward me. He turned and saw his stuff beside me.

He was a foot away when he shook his hair out and some of the water splattered onto my warm thighs. Instead of wiping the water away, I left it there. It felt like a piece of him I was allowed to keep.

"Sorry," Adam said, understanding what his mother had done in an attempt to get us to talk to each other. Still, he laid on the towel beside me and stretched under the sun. Water pooled in his belly button. I wanted to dunk my tongue in and swish it around. *Stop being gross, Evie. Your obsession with the boy is venturing into obscene.* No one found belly buttons sexy. So, why did his make me want to kiss him? Ridiculous.

"The sun is hot today," he commented, crossing his arms behind his head, which made the extra lickable muscles bulge.

"Mmmm," I agreed. Hot. I picked my book back up,

using it as a physical and emotional wall. He took both down.

"What's your book about?" He teased me. "More porn?"

My jaw dropped, and he chuckled. "It's not porn. And it's about a professor."

"Hmm, is that why you like being called a good girl, Miss Turner?"

A boiling heat wracked me. Until I saw he meant it as a joke. Lighthearted teasing. Still, his pupils dilated when they connected with mine.

"You don't have to sit next to me because your mom put your stuff here."

"I know," he said and leaned back. "I like being around you. I've missed this."

"Me too." *Note: when swallowing pride, keep a glass of water nearby, in case it chokes you halfway down your throat.* "I shouldn't have blocked you and handled everything so immaturely. It's just—it hurt to see you."

He sat up, facing me, and placed his feet on the side of my chair, close to my left hip. "It doesn't anymore?"

Not as much as not seeing him. "No."

"What does that mean?"

I let out a breath. "I was thinking maybe we could try being friends. I can't—I can't imagine going another year without seeing and talking to you again. You were such a big part of my life and...I've felt empty without you."

"I miss you too." His face crumpled with sadness

that mimicked my own. "I fucking hate how things ended with us. I hate that—I didn't mean to... I guess it doesn't matter now." I wished it didn't. "I know we can't go back to how things were, but I can't stay away from you either," he said. "It hurts too much."

"Friends, then?"

"Do you think we can be just friends?"

One second. Two seconds. Three seconds passed. "I think we can try."

Still, a small voice whispered to me, "*Liar.*"

ADAM'S HEAD moved between my legs while my own fell back on my pillow at the sensation. Need, unadulterated need, ran through me. The tension below my stomach swirled and rose.

Fingers in his hair. His tongue flicked against me right where I burned for him. My moans filled the room.

"Please," I begged him to push me over the edge.

"I like it when you beg, Evie." His mouth left where I throbbed for him as he moved over me, aligning us. And I needed it so bad. I missed this. I missed him.

"Please, Adam."

"Fuck." He groaned and plunged into me. "You feel so good. Nothing is better than the way you feel."

I wrapped my legs around his waist, pushing my feet into his back to make him thrust harder, faster. My nails raked down his back as he speared in and out of me.

"*I love you, Evie.*"

I shot up in bed, jumping out of my dream. A glance down at my lap informed me that my pesky hands had found their way between my legs during the night. My breathing evened as I laid back and closed my eyes.

Steamy dreams of Adam had plagued me a month or two after our breakup. The worst part of them was when he would apologize or tell me he loved me. Waking up was a cruel reminder. Subconscious Eve was evil.

I glanced at my phone and saw a notification. Adam had liked a photo of me from seven months ago. Had he somehow seen that I had liked an old photo of his or had he fallen victim to the social media vortex as well?

A week ago, I would have sworn Adam Pierce and I could never be friends, but I did not feel that way anymore. Seeing him was still bittersweet, but the sweetness won out each time.

28

PLAY WITH FIRE AND YOU MAY BE CREMATED

My jaw hit the tiled restaurant floor when I saw Adam's father at the table with the rest of the Pierces. Adam's expression was solemn but it lightened when he saw me. His back straightened, his shoulders dropping their tension. Like seeing me was enough to change every bit of his sour mood.

"Henry..." My mother trailed off. Did Mom know the reason behind the Pierce's divorce? "We didn't know you were coming to dinner."

"The timeshare is as much mine as it is Maryam's," Mr. Pierce responded.

Adam's major issues stemmed from his father, from the pressure his father put on him and how his parents handled their separation. For how tough Adam acted, he was very sensitive to the people around him. From the icy atmosphere at the table, I understood where he had gotten it from when we were younger. A sliver of me worried his father's presence would send Adam back to his old, walled-off self, but instead of looking anywhere but at me, his eyes were glued to mine. His hand went to my knee under the table.

It felt like he was using me as a lifeline. It felt good.

"So..." My mother started again but did not continue.

We all sat in silence.

"You look beautiful, as always," Adam whispered to me.

"You too. I mean, masculine and beautiful. Handsome."

"Are you two together now?" Mr. Pierce asked Adam and me.

In actuality, I did not know what to say. We were friends. We weren't together, but we were always...more. "Umm."

"I'd like to know too," my mom added.

Adam waved the waiter over. "We're ready to order."

I rushed to look over the menu, caught between chicken strips and a burger. "I need more time."

Adam looked at me with a powerful expression, but I had left my analysis of what-each-of-his-faces-meant at home. He said, "I don't." He didn't need more time. For what?

"I'll take the lobster," Mr. Pierce said.

Anger settled in my stomach like barb wire. He ordered lobster while his son worked every night in college to pay for tuition. Jerk. *Jerkjerkjerk.*

"Wow," my father commented on Mr. Pierce's diet. "Celebrating anything special tonight?"

"I'd say so. We sold the timeshare."

"What?" I asked before Adam's, "You *WHAT*?"

"I came down to enjoy it for one last summer." Mr. Pierce picked up his folded napkin in front of him and placed it on his lap. "Maryam and I decided it was not worth it to keep paying fees on it."

"You sold it?" Something inside me crumbled. Maybe my heart. Maybe my appetite. "It's gone?"

Mr. Pierce nodded. "We found a buyer several weeks ago. We got a good deal for it. Maybe next summer, we'll go somewhere hotter."

"We?" Adam questioned. Mr. Pierce ignored him.

"A timeshare was never right for me," Mr. Pierce said. "You get bored of going to the same place again and again."

My parents glanced at each other. I screamed internally at the thought of them selling it as well. It was like my childhood home for two weeks every year. "What about all the memories?" I asked.

"We'll make new ones," he answered.

Adam again inquired, "We?"

"Well, then…" My mother unfroze and stepped back into the conversation. "We should try to make this the best summer yet."

"Since it will be the last one," Maryam said.

We sat there in more silence.

Adam's hand slipped off my knee.

Timeshare Boyfriend

EACH DAY FILLED me with a sense of doom. Deep down, I knew I would still see Adam in school, but school had only a year left. We weren't officially back together. He still didn't love me. This, losing the annual timeshare, could be the end of us. For years, I thought we were endless. Timeless. Even if I failed some of my college classes, we would eventually graduate. And get jobs. And move. And we would not have a place to come back to every year.

Each day, I hung out with Adam and James, but Adam grew quieter and more pensive. Sad. Scared. Each day meant one less day we had left to spend with each other. Still, there was a newfound determination in his eyes that I had not seen before. Though he was quiet, he spoke through his actions. He held doors open for me, washed the sand out of my flip-flops, and had a towel ready for me whenever I got out of the pool. He bought me ice cream and gave me a standing ovation at karaoke.

There was something deeper at work. When he handed me a frozen treat, it felt like he was trying to say, "*I'm sorry.*" When he bought me a cherry necklace I had my eye on in a shop, it felt like he was trying to say, "*I don't want to lose you.*" When he looked at me, it felt like he was trying to say, "*I love you.*" But he did not say anything.

The urge to scream at him won out at the mid-week

mark as we walked along the beach at night. "Just tell me what you're thinking," I begged.

"What do you want me to say?"

Anything. "That you're as terrified as me right now. That you can't sleep because each hour of sleeping is an hour wasted of not being around each other."

"I am terrified."

"You don't seem it," I said. "You've been pulling away from me more and more. You were the one who wanted to break up. Maybe deep down, you want this. Maybe it would be easier for you if we never saw each other again," I spewed poison faster than my body could make it. I just needed him to break the wall he had put up and tell me he didn't want that for us. That he saw a future for us. Because I did.

"I don't want that."

"Then, what do you want?" *Do you want me?*

He took my hand and stood there.

"Say something, damn it," I yelled and kicked sand, which the wind blew right back onto my legs. "Don't just give up."

He paused then bent to pick up two seashells. He put one in my hand and turned toward the water.

"What are you doing?"

"We're going to make a wish," Adam said.

It was the first time in my life that I had no interest in a wish. I just wanted him to act as scared as I was. "Would you just talk to me?"

Instead, he closed his eyes and threw the shell into the waves.

Everything built up until one night before bed. He texted me after my parents had gone to sleep.
Adam: *Let me in.*
And I did.

Maybe it was the fear or the urgency or the need to feel that he was mine at least once more before it ended forever, but I let him in. The truth was, I would always let him in.

Without a single word, he stalked inside the unit, leading me to my bedroom and closing the door behind him. He remained silent as he curled a piece of my dark hair around his finger. His other hand reached up and cupped my cheek. His touch left a trail of heat, unable to ignore, as his thumb stroked the edge of my lips. A fool would have leaned into the caress. I was a fool.

My tongue came out and licked my lips, succeeding in also licking his thumb.

I kissed him. Slow and hard and full of meaning. This was different from our usual kiss. It held pain and regret and...hope. Yearning. Want.

His lips collided with mine, and our bodies spoke and screamed and whispered all that hurt too much to say.

"Please," I said.

He pressed me up against the light blue wall. Our tongues clashed with the kiss. Our hands stripped off our clothes.

My fruity pajama pants dropped to the floor.

He picked me up and threw me on the bed, crawling over me. His eyes scanned over my bare body. "So fucking beautiful."

I grabbed his head and kissed him with everything I had.

Naked. Fondling and wanting and needing more. More. His fingers moved between my legs; my hand wrapped around him. We moaned into each other's mouths. He ripped a condom wrapper with his teeth and rolled it on.

He sank inside me, thrusting again and again.

I yelled his name, muffled by his hand over my mouth, and saw stars. It had been so long. Too long. Being with him felt right.

"Don't give up on me again," he said, a pained expression on his face.

"Harder, Adam," I said.

His hips lost their rhythm. They became erratic. But I still needed more. I reached a hand down and helped myself out.

"Yes." Adam watched my rubbing fingers and closed his eyes. "Faster, baby. Fuck, I can *feel* you squeezing me."

"Tell me something has changed, Adam," I said, my voice cracking from pleasure and heavy emotion.

He pulled up my legs and changed the angle, hitting the spot I dreamed about. "Evie!"

I came.

"I can't lose you, Evie. I can't lose this." His words slurred as he pounded into me. "You feel so fucking good."

"Tell me it'll be me in the end. That it's always been me."

"Evie," he whispered my name and stared so deep into my eyes, I swore he could see my soul. And my soul was fracturing.

"Three words, oh—" I broke off when my back arched off the mattress. "Eight letters."

"I need you." He gave me a different three words and eight letters. "I need you."

"More, Adam." I moaned and moved my hips up to meet his thrusts. "Give me more."

We hit the point of no return. Language became babbling. Moans became guttural, uncontrollable sounds. My core throbbed around him.

I came again and so did he.

Thirty minutes later, we were back at it. An hour after that, we still couldn't keep our hands off each other. Then, we fell asleep.

29

ACTIONS SPEAK LOUDER THAN WORDS...UNLESS YOU HAVE A MEGAPHONE

*A*dam slipped through my fingers faster than the hot tub bubbles I cupped in my hands. Even though we had sex, nothing had changed. Would anything ever change? He didn't want to hurt me. He *wanted* to love me. It was obvious.

Maybe he did love me. Maybe he just couldn't say it.

As the last few days of the timeshare slipped away, he was around less and less, fading from me. I would not let him fade from me. I loved him.

I loved him.

I sat, watching my favorite movie, and paused it. At every turn, Wesley fought for Buttercup's love. She had lost hope in him. She had thought her love had died years ago. He told her that death could never stop true love. Later, Wesley beat death for her again. She did nothing for him back, other than almost killing herself at the end with a knife that looked more like a letter opener. Ouch.

I would not be a Buttercup. Or a Juliet.

I was not going to let him slip away.

I would fight for Adam.

My body shot up from the couch, and I ran to leave the unit.

My father laughed at my abrupt fast pace and asked, "Where are you going?"

"Going to go win a princess," I shouted back.

When I knocked on the Pierce's unit, no one answered, so I called his cell phone. "Where are you right now?"

"I'm kind of busy—"

"You're on vacation. Where are you right now?"

His tone was surprised, most likely from the seriousness in my own. "I'm on the first level, near the pool entrance."

I took one look at the elevator and thought, "*Not romantic enough.*" The stairway was narrow and lit with flickering lights. It smelled like bananas and sunscreen, but I welcomed the odd scent into my lungs as my knees and thighs burned. I sprinted down the stairs for four levels. I then took the elevator down the last two.

When I found him, he stood in front of what looked like a maintenance closet. Was he busy getting extra towels? Oh well.

"Adam Pierce, I love you," I announced, using my

diaphragm to project the sound nice and loud, and hoping my feelings might finally penetrate him.

His eyes widened; he glanced around. No one was near us so maybe he was checking for any possible exits. After all, a girl profusely sweating with red cheeks and her hair in a messy bun proclaiming her love would alarm anyone.

"You don't have to say it back," I told him.

"Evie..."

"I'm serious. You don't have to say it, Adam. They're just words." I could have laughed at the realization. I had wanted to end things just because he couldn't say a few sounds, a few syllables in an order I wanted? "In the end, words mean nothing. Actions are what matter. Every text you send me with the sole purpose of making me smile. Every second you spend listening to me talk about everything and nothing." Adam loved me; he just couldn't say it. As someone who loved him, I realized I did not need to hear it. "I've loved you for ten years. At times, I tried not to, but I did anyway. We're messy, but I have never felt more alive than when I'm with you. Like that scene in *The Wizard of Oz* when everything changes from black and white to color."

"Did you reference a movie that isn't *The Princess Bride*?"

"And I'm about to do it again." I took two steps closer to him, eliminating the distance between us. My arms went around his neck as I pulled him to me. "Let me make you an offer you can't refuse," I quoted *The*

Godfather in a bad Italian accent. His eyes lit up. "Be with me, completely as you are, no pressure but that we exist together. We will always be honest and real and anytime we see a wall come up, we will throw a love grenade at it."

He chuckled at "love grenade" and shook his head. "The things you say." He held me tighter.

"I love you, Adam," I said, and my whole world lost its weight. Everything that had weighed me down was lifted.

His arms enclosed around me before he pulled back. "I want to show you something." His hand dipped into his pocket. *I'd love to be shown that, please and thank you.* Instead, he pulled out a small key. He stuck it into the maintenance closet lock and opened the door.

Pausing, I asked, "Um, are we breaking in to steal towels and toilet paper?"

"Shhh." He pulled me into the small dark room and turned the light on. Half the walls were painted light green, the other half yellow, as if the decorator could not decide on which color was worse. There were no towels or toilet paper. The room was empty except for a single painting of the beach and a wooden chair that looked ready to break.

"What are we doing in here?" I was down for a quickie but not in such a sad-looking room.

"It's ours."

"What?"

"I bought it for two weeks every summer. It's not

really a room—" He blushed. "—but we could put a bed there and there's a bathroom right through there." He gestured around the small space. "Now that I bought it, they said they'd paint the walls."

"You can't afford this."

"Actually, I can," he said. "Timeshares aren't as expensive as you think, and this room was cheaper than probably any other ones that exist. I spent the last couple of days pooling my earnings together and signing the contract."

"This...is ours?"

"I know it looks rough. There's no window—"

"We'll get a painting of a window."

"And there's no kitchen—"

"We don't need food to survive."

He laughed then released a shocked sound when I threw my arms around him and wrapped my legs around his waist.

"I love it," I cried. "I love you. It's perfect."

"You're perfect."

And together, we were perfect.

~~~

HE SENT me a text on the last day of our timeshare.

Adam: *Where are you right now?*

Me: *In the living room. Eating some sour gummy worms. Why?*

Timeshare Boyfriend

"ERIEBRUVNER." The loud, muffled sound came from the beach outside through the sliding glass door.

I stood and opened it.

Seven floors below me was Adam holding a megaphone on the beach. Behind him, written in massive letters in the sand, was "*As You Wish.*"

"EVIE TURNER," he said into the megaphone.

I flailed my arms around, shouting. "Shh! Other people will hear you!"

"YOU ARE THE MOST BEAUTIFUL GIRL IN THE WORLD TO ME."

My arms came down as my heart melted in my chest. "Go on."

"IT MEANS SO MUCH THAT YOU ACCEPT ME AS I AM, AND I WANT YOU TO KNOW I DO THE SAME. ONE THING I KNOW ABOUT YOU, IS THAT YOU LOVE BIG ROMANTIC GESTURES. SO, HERE IT GOES …" He moved and picked up a boom box, holding it above his head as he aligned the megaphone with the speaker. Out poured a tune so familiar that I lost the ability to move before recognizing exactly what I knew it from. It was the song Adam always hummed to me and I never knew what it was. I recognized it now that I heard the lyrics. The song he had always hummed to me when he held me or it was quiet, even back when all we had were those short summers together, was Tony Romeo's "*I think I love you.*"

He loved me. This whole time, he loved me. Before

we had even become a couple, he hummed that song to me and I wondered what it was.

My legs ached as I ran for the steps and leaped down seven flights of stairs, this time skipping the elevator entirely. All I could think was: *Adam*.

I ran out to the beach where he stood still holding up the boom box.

My legs turned to jelly beneath me. "Song. Playing." I struggled to catch my breath from having run down so many stairs. I was a dancer, but cardio sucked. "You always hummed it to me. '*I think I love you.*' It was that song the whole time. Even when we were just friends, you hummed it to me."

He dropped the boom box into the sand and cupped my face. "You have never in this lifetime ever been 'just' a friend to me, Evie Turner."

Oxygen? Please fill my lungs. "What am I to you?"

Our lips pressed together into a gentle, yearning kiss. It sparked a heat and connection I'd forgotten was possible to feel.

"You are the girl I have been in love with all of my fucking life."

30

THE HEART THAT LOVES IS ALWAYS YOUNG

The Next Summer, Seven Years Later

"I'm half-sad my parents didn't come to the timeshare this year, half-happy that we have the unit to ourselves," I said to Adam as I wheeled in our suitcases. "I'll finally get to sleep in the master bedroom. Mwahaha." I tried a maniacal laugh. I failed.

He turned around to face me. "What did I say about the evil laugh thing?"

"That it's quirky and adorable?" I pushed up on my toes and smacked his lips with a light kiss. "I agree."

"It'll be nice to relax." He set the bags down and threw himself on the couch. "I can't wait to read a book on the beach and go to bed before midnight."

We had both been working long hours so this vacation

meant a lot to us. It felt like freedom and a romantic getaway wrapped up into one. Few people can say they visit the place where they fell in love two weeks every year.

"We're old people," I realized after his comment. "Reading books, going to bed early. Oh my God."

"You're twenty-seven, you're not old."

"Are we getting stale? Tell the truth."

He stood and grabbed my hands in his. "Us? No way." He bent down and kissed me. "We get better with age. Like wine...or trees."

"I like trees."

"See?" He chuckled and kissed me again. A small peck. A *boring* peck? "We're fine."

"Your first instinct to us having the unit to ourselves was to read books and go to sleep at nine o'clock. It should have been to have crazy sex all over the apartment, or buy tequila and take shots. We're one birthday away from investing in real estate."

He chuckled and pulled me to him. "I didn't know you wanted crazy sex all over the apartment."

"It's like you don't even know who I am anymore."

His right eyebrow rose. "You want me to touch you right now?"

"Babe, I'm so horny that if you licked one of my nipples, I'd probably come."

He closed his eyes and groaned. "That was so fucking graphic, and I loved it." He pulled me to him and unzipped the back of my dress. "And I love you."

"Did...did you handcuff me to the bed?" Adam asked, incredulous, after waking up to his wrists chained to the headboard.

"All we've been doing is reading on the beach and going to shows." I climbed over him and pulled down his boxers. "We're boring."

"We're not boring—" He cut off when I squeezed his erection in my hand and stroked him up and down. "Fuck, baby, that feels so good."

"This morning, we're going to be wild." I flicked my tongue over the tip. His moan was a double espresso to my sex drive.

His chest rose up and down as his breathing became shallow at my mouth on him. "At least unshackle me so I can touch you too."

"The handcuffs make it wild."

He yanked on them and hissed. "Are these real metal? How did you get these?"

"A magician never reveals her secrets."

"You're not a magician." He groaned as I increased the pace of my hand on him. "Fuck, but what you're doing feels like magic." His hips bucked up, off the mattress. "Shit, babe, I'm close. Stop." I squeezed harder. "Oh, God. Stop, I want to be inside you."

I released him and granted his request because I needed him too. So freaking bad. After crawling up his body, I kissed him and aligned us. He pushed his hips up and impaled me. "Adam!"

"Perfect. You are fucking perfection to me." He struggled against the handcuffs. "Baby, please let me out of these. I need to touch you."

"Here, touch me." I leaned over until my nipple hung above his mouth. "*Yes.*" Pleasure. Heat. Tingles. Everything built up between my legs. I rode him, but I still needed more. One of my hands trailed down and rubbed the spot calling out for any kind of friction.

"Are you touching yourself right now?" Adam glanced down at my fingers working in circles between my thighs, and he let his head fall back on the pillow. The bucking of his hips accelerated, his cock twitching inside of me. "That's so fucking hot."

We came together, our mouths dropping at the utter power behind our spasms and pleasure. "Geezus."

"You were right. I like wild us." Adam grinned, catching his breath. "Can you get me out of these handcuffs now?"

I stroked his damp hair out of his face. "I'm going to be honest with you, I have no idea where the key is."

※※※

EVERY MOMENT with him was magic. We tried kayaking and snorkeling, and we still went places we had gone to together our entire lives. We made new memories even better than the last. My favorite place of all? The old arcade shop on the pier.

"Close your eyes," he instructed me.

I snickered and elbowed him. "We're in public, don't get kinky now."

"I'm not getting kinky." He laughed. "Besides, you're the kinky one in our relationship."

I closed my eyes per his instructions. "Fine, what now?"

"Now, I'm going to win you something from this claw machine. It's supposed to be romantic. Stop asking so many questions."

"How is it romantic if I can't choose what you win me?" His quarter slid into the old machine, and the whirls and dings sounded as it came to life. "What if you choose something horrible? Like an ugly stuffed animal?"

"This machine doesn't have any stuffed animals."

"See? And what if I wanted a stuffed animal? You've already lost."

His grin was audible as he *shh*-ed me. "I need to concentrate."

I rolled my eyes behind the lids. "You know how to win at claw machines with your hands tied behind your back."

He laughed again, and I smiled at the sound. "What would that look like? Me using my mouth on the controls?"

A teasing moan escaped me. "We all know how

talented you are with your mouth." Just last night, he had—

"Now look who's getting kinky in public."

"Guilty." I reached out, my eyes still closed, and touched his back. My hands lowered down, down, down...

"Hey!" He brushed my hands away from his butt. "This is supposed to be a romantic moment, not a sexy one."

"I enjoy a mix of both." The sound of *ding, ding, ding* and him moving away from me told me Adam won something from the claw machine. "Can I open my eyes now?"

"Yes."

In front of me, Adam kneeled on one knee, holding out a sparkling ruby ring.

"That's real," I said, staring at it, shocked.

"It is." He took my left hand and looked up at me. "Evangeline Turner, will you—"

"Stop." My right hand covered my chest. "I think I'm having a heart attack."

"You're twenty-seven."

"Age is but a number."

He smiled at me and waited as I caught my breath. I then gestured for him to continue. "Evie, from the moment I saw those red cherry Popsicle-covered lips of yours, I wanted to kiss you. We were just kids, but I knew what I felt was more than a crush or young love. You understand me, accept my flaws, make me laugh...

and I love you so much it hurts. Like being with you causes my heart to grow in my chest each day and my ribs have to stretch to make room."

"Sounds uncomfortable."

"I want to spend the rest of my life with you. I want to buy you Maraschino cherries and watch *The Princess Bride* with you every Valentine's Day. I want to sit in the front row of all of your shows and listen to your laugh on repeat. I want to marry you. Will you marry me?"

My chest flooded with emotion. Every moment leading to this beautiful one. Still, I couldn't help myself. "No diamond?"

"I thought you'd want a ruby more."

"You were so freaking right." I tackled him to the ground and kissed him like he was a pool of water in a desert, and gosh was he delicious.

He broke the kiss to groan painfully. "Babe, your knee is on my stomach."

"Deal with it." I yanked his head back to mine, our lips crashing together, sparks flying through me. "I'm your wife."

"Fiancée."

"Boy, shut up and kiss me."

Ten Summers Later

. . .

"How old is your daughter?" the woman asked me as we sat by the beach in our sand chairs. I watched my beautiful daughter, Eden Pierce, play in the water with the woman's son.

"She's eight."

The woman's jaw dropped, then she grinned like I had told her she won the lottery. "Our son is seven!"

"Cute." I rejoiced a bit as well. "They can be time-share friends."

"Maybe even more than friends." She moved her chair closer to mine. "Look at the way she's smiling at him."

I laughed, thinking back to Adam and I being pushed together by our parents when we were kids. "They do make a cute couple."

"Who does?" Adam appeared behind me with two cherry snow cones. My daughter inherited my obsession.

"Eden and..." I turned to the woman.

"Arden," she said.

"They're going to fall in love," I told him, taking my cherry snow cone from him.

"The hell they are." Adam frowned at his little girl splashing the boy with saltwater. "Eden," he yelled and got her attention. "I've got your snow cone."

I snickered. "You can't tempt her away from boys with sugar forever."

Eden ran over to us and took the treat from him.

So the woman would not hear him, Adam leaned down and whispered, "Stay away from that boy."

She pouted, looking just like Adam. "Why?"

"Because you're too young for boys."

"Why?" Eden and I asked in unison.

"Because they are only interested in one thing."

"What?" Eden and I continued to tease him.

Adam grumbled under his breath and sat in the chair next to me. "Go play in the ocean." He waved her off. "But stay close." Once she was out of hearing range, he growled into my ear, "Stop trying to play matchmaker with our eight-year-old daughter."

"I have no idea what you mean."

He rolled his eyes, his lips curling at the edges. "You're trouble, Evie Pierce."

I grinned and turned back to Arden's mother. "We were thinking of taking Eden to miniature golf tomorrow, would Arden like to come along?"

Adam growled again.

"That'd be great."

We watched the two of them play for close to an hour. At one point, Arden handed her a seashell.

"Aw, he seems like a sweet boy."

Adam narrowed his eyes on him. "Sweet boys are dangerous."

"What about bad boys?"

He glanced at me. "Dangerous too."

I held his hand and squeezed it. "Some girls like bad boys because they can turn out sweet."

His lips stretched into a sexy smile. "Some girls?"

"I know of one."

THE END

Don't want to miss another M. K. Hale romcom?

Join her newsletter:

http://www.mkhale.com/contact.html

Follow her on Instagram, Facebook, & Twitter: @mkhaleauthor

Join her Facebook Fan Group for Exclusives:

"M. K. Hale's Hotties"

If you enjoyed the story, I would LOVE if you would be willing to leave a review or help get the word out about this romcom to others who might enjoy it! Thank you for reading!

ACKNOWLEDGEMENTS

I spent the entire summer of 2018 with writer's block. I tried to write a fourth novel and kept getting stuck early on in different story ideas. As a student at the time, I only had three summer months to focus on writing a novel each year. By the last week of July, I felt like a failure. I was full of doubt. Then, I went with my parents to stay at our annual Myrtle Beach timeshare. I relaxed for one day before I saw a young boy and girl meeting and playing at the pool and thought to myself, they could stay friends each summer. Thus, TIMESHARE BOYFRIEND was born. I wrote the first draft of 82,000 words in two weeks and two days. If you ever have writer's block or doubt, know something is coming. Something will always come.

I want to thank Summer, Rachael, Sammi, and Atousa, my original beta readers for this story.

Thank you to Leisa Rayven, one of my favorite

authors who took a chance at reading a book from a stranger and offering essential feedback. (Readers, if you haven't read BAD ROMEO before, do so now!)

I want to thank my literary agent Stacey Graham for believing in this story even though the time jumps made the age ranges harder to sell to a traditional publisher.

Thank you to my parents who champion me to everyone they know—even though my books contain sex scenes. It's appreciated! Thank you to my aunts for believing in me and my uncle who always asks, "What's new with your book?" I cherish being able to respond, "Which one?"

Thank you to my mom—my best friend—who has spent countless hours listening to me talk about characters and plots while we walk around the neighborhood, and she pretends to not be bored.

Thank you to God/Fate/Life for all he has given me.

Finally, THANK YOU, READERS! YOU ARE THE REASON FOR MY EXISTENCE. I hope you enjoyed Adam and Evie's story. If you did, I would LOVE if you would be willing to leave a review or help get the word out about this story to others who might enjoy it!

I'm forgetting to thank somebody; I just know it. So, this is for you! Insert name here:

_____

ABOUT THE AUTHOR

M. K. Hale writes romance novels starring dirty-talking heroes and the witty women who leave them tongue-tied. She specializes in romantic comedies and has dabbled in comedy for years, including standup, improv, and sketch comedy. She believes laughter is the best medicine, except for, you know, actual medicine.

She obtained her English degree from the University of Maryland and spends her free time reading as many romance novels as humanly possible. "Hating Him" was her first new adult romantic comedy.

Follow her on social media: @mkhaleauthor
    Facebook Fan Group: "M. K. Hale's Hotties"
    Join her newsletter:
    http://www.mkhale.com/contact.html

MORE BY M. K. HALE

HATING HIM: A Steamy New Adult Sports Romantic Comedy

Accidentally seducing the wrong guy has never been so right.

Mandy has a plan to move on from her cheating ex by seducing her best friend's brother. Instead, she mistakenly seduces a stranger with a body from an erotic fairy tale. For Mandy, an art major who only paints in black and white, Brandon adds a dangerous splash of color to her life.

Brandon Gage is used to getting what he wants, so he won't give up his pursuit of her despite her telling him she's been in love with his roommate Jake since high school. After a sports injury, he becomes her patient at the health clinic where she works and hatches his own plan to make Mandy forget about Jake and fall for him.

He soon learns that pretending to date her only makes him want her more. Who will be the winner in "Operation Mandy"?

MORE BY M. K. HALE

DISOBEYING HIM: A Steamy New Adult Opposites Attract Romance

He craves control. She craves chaos. The only thing they might crave more is each other...

Nate

Allie Parser is driving me crazy on purpose and waiting for the moment I snap.

To say we are fire and ice would be misleading. We are mint

toothpaste followed by a big gulp of orange juice. Pulp included.

I want to strangle her, and she wants to straddle me.

She says I need to stop living life by rules.

She doesn't want to know what I'll do to her if I break mine.

Allie

Nate Reddington, heir to his daddy's fortune and my RA, is cold, closed off, and a little obsessed with control (hello, pair of handcuffs under his bed. How are you?). But I can fix him.

He is used to women on their knees for him, but I'm more likely to kneecap him than obey.

As a psychology student, it is basically my job to "My Fair Lady" him and turn this icy man into a warm human being.

Maybe "warm" is the wrong word. Because Nate Reddington, red-faced and about to crack?

Scorching hot.

A FREE STEAMY HALLOWEEN NOVELLA BY M. K. HALE

COSTUME MISCONDUCT

Costume Misconduct

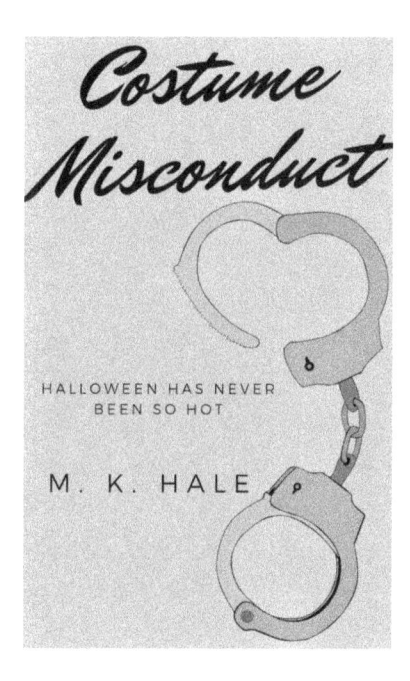

HALLOWEEN HAS NEVER BEEN SO HOT

M. K. HALE

Some like it cop.

Tara Callihan's plan to save money this Halloween by wearing her father's old cop uniform unravels when she gets mistaken for a real police officer while breaking into her friend's ex's apartment. She could have come clean, but instead she rolls with the lie because the chemistry between her and the officer who caught her is enough to make the cold October night feel hot.

He wants her help to catch the culprit? He has already

caught her. She just hopes he won't throw her back in the water once he finds out she is not a real cop and has been lying to him the whole night.

Halloween has never been so hot and so hilarious in this steamy, contemporary rom-com novella.

CPSIA information can be obtained
at www.ICGtesting.com
Printed in the USA
LVHW030237080722
722993LV00001B/48

9 798986 140209